The Ideal Woman

D1411724

The Ideal Woman

Roy Espiritu

THE IDEAL WOMAN

iUniverse books may be ordered through booksellers or by contacting:

iUniverse LLC
1663 Liberty Drive
Bloomington, IN 47403
www.iuniverse.com
1-800-Authors (1-800-288-4677)

ISBN: 978-1-4917-3046-1 (sc)
ISBN: 978-1-4917-3048-5 (hc)
ISBN: 978-1-4917-3047-8 (e)

Library of Congress Control Number: 2014906190

Printed in the United States of America.

iUniverse rev. date: 06/20/2014

To the three gems in my life—Jonathan,
Jacqueline, and Justin—and the pearl who
made them possible, my wife, Alicia

PROLOGUE

"Amber Pearl Gomez O'Neil. That is my full name. Gomez is from my mother's maiden name. O'Neil, of course, from my father. In my mother's culture, the mother's maiden name lives on. It becomes the child's middle name. Thus, it is possible to trace a relative from the maternal side by finding out if you have a common middle name."

"Interesting," I said.

Pearl, or Pearly, as people close to her called her, was a handsome woman. She spoke animatedly, gesturing with her hands. I couldn't help but notice them. They were tiny but well tapered. Though it is said one can gauge somebody's real age by looking at his or her hands, her hands belied her age, just like her face.

"And where did you learn to cook?"

"My mother."

"Is that common?"

She paused. It took her a while to answer. She appeared embarrassed, like it was a private matter. She lowered her gaze. "It probably is common for most. For me, it is more a passion. I enjoy cooking. I love to cook. So with my mother," she finally answered.

"Is it possible your grandma passed on the skill to your mother, who passed it on to you? It was a tradition, wasn't it?" Actually, I wished she would answer yes, like there was something fascinating and exciting about women passing on culinary skill from mother to daughter to granddaughter down through generations without a break.

"My grandma cooked. I wouldn't say she was passionate about cooking, though. Not like my mother. My mother cooks because she loves to, not because she has to."

I smiled. "You have a live-in cook."

She looked straight at me. "My grandma had. My mother grew up with a live-in cook."

My comment was meant to be a joke. Her answer surprised me.

"Well, you see . . . my mother comes from a very prominent family. It is not uncommon for a rich family to have live-in help. A lot of times, that includes a live-in cook."

"Cool."

She flashed a smile. She looked younger when she did. "You can say that."

I turned off the tape. We had been talking nearly uninterrupted for a good three to four hours. "Let's call it a day."

"Yes. Let's—" She stood up and towered over my short stature.

I felt jealous. She laughed and covered her mouth, embarrassed by her reaction. My cheeks tingled.

Is that how Oriental women respond to their own faux pas? I wondered.

The next day, we met at her restaurant, Salakot. The place wouldn't open until noon, so we had plenty of time. Or so I thought.

Pearl was dressed in a simple, pale, short-sleeved blouse paired with dark pants and black stilettos. It was a complete departure from her demure demeanor yesterday. She had pulled her hair tight at the back with a simple hair band. Her posture was perfect. She motioned me to take a seat. A help passed by, carrying a basket of fresh produce. She hurried to catch him.

She disappeared into the kitchen. I could hear she was talking to him in her mother's native tongue. She had told me she was bilingual. Again, I felt a pang of jealousy. I only spoke English.

"Where were we?" Coming back from the kitchen, she pulled a chair and sat across from me.

"We were talking about your family's live-in help."

"That's not what I mean." She placed an expensive leather bag on top of the table and spread out some more family pictures, mostly black and white except for the more recent ones.

I picked up one in color. It was a younger Pearl. She wore a full-length gown and a tiara. A crowd was behind her. They were holding candles, the women wore veils or covered their hair with handkerchiefs, and some were reciting the rosary while some were holding sparklers.

"I was a *sagala* at a Santa Cruzan. I was one of the Reyna Elenas. Was I a looker or what?" She laughed lustily.

I did not see any modesty in her, not like yesterday. "You have to tell me what this Santa Cruzan is all about."

"Definitely." She described in detail the pageantry that was Santa Cruzan. She rummaged through the stack of pictures to show more about this May festivity.

She was a fascinating study while she talked, intense and involved. I was enthralled looking at her while she motioned with her hands as much as perusing those pictures.

I gathered some more black-and-white pictures of a handsome woman with a white man. At various times, a young child was with them. As they matured, the young girl grew up to be a young woman, Pearl.

"My family: Mom, Dad, and me."

"I can see your father was white."

"Is. He's still alive. So is my mom."

"She looks Caucasian."

"She is a half-breed. Like me."

I pulled out some more pictures I had seen before. It was an image of an Oriental man and woman. "These are your maternal grandparents. I remember you telling me that."

"Yes, That's Tatay and Nanay. It means father and mother. That's how I learned to call them."

"Neither looks Caucasian."

"No, they aren't."

I furrowed my eyebrows.

"No family is perfect. You heard that saying. They say, if you look one or two generations back, there will always be a skeleton or two hiding in the closet, a hooker, or a swindler maybe. A murderer, perhaps."

She looked past me, like I was not even there. Pearl spoke like it was gospel with no embarrassment or apology in her tone. She excused herself and disappeared in the kitchen. The clang of pans was heard, along with the continued chopping and rush of water from the faucet. Again, her commanding voice was heard.

And why should she be embarrassed? I thought to myself.

When she came back, I pulled some more pictures, also in black and white. I singled out those of an Oriental male, square-jawed and well-built, sporting a crew cut. Confidence oozed in that aristocratic look. He was handsome in a manly way. At times, he was with a group of buddies. At times, he was in a formal native attire, *barong tagalog*. I recognized him wearing his graduation gown with two petite, well-dressed women on his sides. There was a picture of him with Pearl's grandpa, the one she called Tatay, each proudly holding fighting roosters in their arms.

"That's P.J.." A softness was in her voice. Pearl cast her head down, hiding her face.

I noticed her rapid breathing. She raised her head and looked me in the eyes. I saw sadness in those eyes. But it didn't last long.

She smiled at me to bring me back to her previous mood. "P.J.," she said to herself. Her smile widened. She reached for my recorder and turned it off. "You seemed more interested in my family."

I turned the tape on again.

"Let me remind you. You are writing about a successful cook, an owner of a popular ethnic restaurant, a businesswoman, and a host of her own culinary TV show."

"I remember. I am. Do you realize your life would be a better read? Have you thought about that?"

"Stop. I allowed you to interview me to write a success story about a restaurateur, a TV personality," she said emphatically.

"Amber Pearl O'Neil's story transcends more than her being a cook, a restaurateur, a TV personality," I said, countering.

"You forgot to add Gomez. Don't forget the Gomez. My mother's maiden name."

"I am sorry."

"You are forgiven."

*   *   *

The last time I saw Pearl was at a well-appointed restaurant in a five-star hotel. We'd had several sessions up to then. It had been six months of one-on-one interviews. She was a meticulous person. She read my draft, pointed out "mistakes" and misquotes, and crossed out several paragraphs of what I thought was very well-written prose. I intentionally did not bring any pen or paper, nor my tape recorder. I was planning on rehashing and asking her permission about the other project I had been toiling about all along.

She arrived a few minutes late. She immediately recognized me in the crowd before I could raise my hand. The hostess accompanied her to my seat. A few heads turned around, recognizing her. But even without face recognition, Pearl could still make heads turn. She walked with grace and assuredness. I suspected she enjoyed the attention.

She ordered a mixed drink. She said she was not hungry. I felt embarrassed I had ordered a full dinner.

"Well?" She rested her head on a hand.

I swear any full-blooded male would be tempted to offer marriage to her that moment. And she was probably old enough to be my mother. My wedding ring brought me down to earth.

"Where's your tape? No pen. No notepad. I'm impressed."

"That was intentional." I wiped my mouth and grabbed my glass of water. "I am really serious about writing your story." I kneaded my hands. I was not nervous, but I was anxious she would say no.

She remained quiet. I grabbed the chance to pitch my other project. I reiterated how her cooking adventure and successful TV show paled in comparison with her life story.

"And you are using my real name. My parents. P.J.. I could sue you."

"That's why I am asking your permission."

"I can say yes. Later change my mind. Then sue you."

"I trust you. You can trust Oriental girls."

"Don't forget." She waved a hand to stress a point. "I'm not a full-blooded Oriental girl. My father is white." She smiled a curt smile.

I didn't know how to take it. *Sarcasm? Self-deprecating statement perhaps.*

"That's what makes you an interesting read."

"Convince me."

"I've been trying. Look, now you act like a typical American woman. Sure. Confident."

"And Oriental woman?"

"Complex. Contradictory. Fascinating. Admirable."

"Those are hasty generalizations. You have to do better than that to convince me." She sipped on her drink. "You are a writer. You disappoint me."

"Oriental women can make us agree to something and make it appear it was our idea in the first place."

"What do you see in me?"

"At times, you are like your mother. Soft, vulnerable, and yet underneath—"

"Unpredictable?" She finished my sentence. "An enigma? Unfathomable?"

I was inspired. "And yet strong. Look at your grandmother, Tinay. Look at P.J.'s grandmother. They are strong women."

Pearl smiled a pensive, mysterious grin. "Perfect. Perfect women."

"Like the title of my book."

She nearly nailed the title. It was close.

"What is the title of your book?"

I had to grab my glass of water. Shaking, I opened a leather case resting at my foot. I took out a manuscript and placed it on the side of the table facing Pearl. I could not control the shaking of my hands. Again, I was not nervous. I just wanted her to say yes. Otherwise, I had a lot of explaining to my publisher. I shelved the other book without their knowledge. And with this alternate book, I still had a lot to explain.

I saw the gradual change in her face. She looked at the title and then ran her fingers on it. She whispered the title to herself. She grabbed the manuscript and scanned a few pages with an eyebrow arching at times. Without saying a word, she pushed the manuscript toward me.

"This is your own copy," I said.

She remained quiet, finished her drink, and stood up to her full height. She took my breath away. Pearl turned to leave.

I was disappointed. "Aren't you interested in reading my book?"

"Mail it."

*   *   *

I didn't hear from Pearl until exactly two months had passed. She sent me an e-mail. The note was very brief.

To: Roy Espiritu
Topic: personal
Yes.
Amber Pearl Gomez O'Neil

I sent her a thank-you card. A week later, I received a certified package from her. It was her own diary. She attached a note. It was also very brief.

Please destroy after reading.

I lied to Pearl. I did not have the courage to confess. Without her permission, I met her mother, Aurora, on several occasions. Aurora gave me personal recollections. She was extremely helpful in filling in the blanks in Pearl's story.

During those clandestine interviews, Pearl's dad, Red, would occasionally be present. He was very observant, like Pearl. He would listen to his wife while he sat by her side. On some of those interviews, he would smile at his wife's comment and shake his head. A dagger look from Aurora almost always halted his smile. He would grab his wife's hand, which Aurora would pry away, but he would not let go. Aurora would finally lower her eyes and smile sheepishly at her husband. The mannerism reminded me of their daughter.

Aurora was alone the last time I talked to her.

She handed me a rectangular tin can. "It's yours. It would help you."

She signaled me to open it. Inside were clippings of the Santa Cruzan where Pearl was a Reyna Elena. I was expecting it would be clippings of her daughter. It wasn't.

"Those are pictures of the other Reyna Elena, Rosario Rosales. She was the same age as my Pearly. As you can see, she became very popular. She was a good actress."

"That's her when she won the best actress." Aurora sided close to me, pointed at a picture of the woman holding a trophy. "I saw the film. She deserved it."

"You must be a fan."

"I wasn't. I started collecting clippings about her, pictures, magazine articles after she committed suicide. I also saw the film where she won the award. I bought a tape. Well, I should say my Cousin Boy sent me a tape. She was very good in that film."

I knitted my brows. A newspaper clipping said she jumped from her hotel room.

"She was on a location shoot filming a story that they say could earn her another nomination for the FAMAS," Aurora said.

My brows remained knitted.

"Sorry, I forgot. That's the equivalent of the Oscar," Aurora said.

I continued browsing through the clippings. I perused some articles about the suicide. The movie she was making was a fictionalized account of the last few months of her life.

"You realized why I felt a certain kinship to her. Not just because she was my Pearl's age."

"I understand. Thank you so much. I will return them to you."

"No, keep them. Good luck on your book."

*   *   *

In respect to Pearl and her family, some names were changed, some minor characters were composite, and some were invented, a literary license for a better narrative. This is also to protect both the living and the dead.

This is Amber Pearl Gomez O'Neil's story.

CHAPTER 1

THE IDEAL WOMAN

Pearl bolted up, terrorized.

Her hands were choking her with their viselike grip. They woke her up. Her throat felt bone dry. She must have been squealing hard. It was the same dream. The bedside clock read two a.m.

Sweat drenched her thin frame and soaked her pajamas. She shivered. She nearly stumbled while stepping on the bedsheet. She fled to the bathroom. The cold water quenched her parched mouth. Satiated, she splashed water to her face. She saw fear in the eyes of the woman in the mirror—hers.

Pearl paced the room. It was not unlike the hundreds she had stayed at over different nights and different cities in the past. A closet with a half dozen or so wooden hangers with detachable body, a metal safe, an iron, and ironing board inside or down the hallway were standard features. A framed print guarded the head of each bed. There was a dresser at the foot of the bed with a TV on top. A separate table had complimentary hotel stationery and pen, occasionally with a phone directory or a hard cover with lists of amenities, glossy pictures of the hotel lobby, their restaurant, or the in-house gym. There was the requisite Gideon Bible in one of the bedside dressers.

This room was one of those she wound up staying for the night. She was on RON, or "remain overnight." This was when a flight attendant has to sleep over in a city toward the end of her flight. Some were "commuters." They flew to their home base rather than spend the night in a strange city. For those on RON, flight attendants usually shared hotel rooms. This time, though, Pearl was by herself.

Unlike other nights she was on RON, this was a night she would rather forget. It was the same day, that fateful August summer that it happened. It felt like yesterday. Like a wound, it continued to fester, the slightest rub causing it to gape, to bleed, and to smart. And unlike the sun, Pearl, at two past midnight, was already wide awake, unable to go back to sleep. Even the room she was staying in was on a twenty-four-hour vigil. Not a single light source was left undisturbed. With its drapes fully drawn, the room glowed like a lantern from a distance.

I should have called in sick, she thought.

Her naked feet left fresh marks on the carpeted floor. She navigated the TV's remote control. Irked, she threw it, creating a faint thud on the unmade bed. The gathered metallic rings of the tub curtain clanged as her feet touched the cold enamel. She closed the shower curtain with a violent tug.

Then hundreds, maybe thousands, of bullets of water sprayed Pearl's face. They dribbled down her neck, tingled her breasts, riddled her tummy, and peppered her legs. The cold liquid watered her soul, opened her lungs, and calmed the turmoil within her.

An hour later, her freshened body warmed the bed. The crisp white sheet rolled up to her neck. Pearl remained fully conscious even with her eyes wide shut.

Pearl, with her hazel eyes, light hair, and fair skin, all evoking of the West, was capped by her Midwest accent. Her soul, in contrast, exuded Oriental flavors and spices, *nipa* huts born from towering yet resilient bamboo trees, butterfly sleeves, powdery white beaches, colorful buntings aboard remodeled World War II jeep remnants, and replicas transporting brown-skinned natives along narrow busy streets.

Was it a paradox? Not if you know she was nourished by her mother's milk, slumbered with her mother's native lullaby, absorbed the exotic smell and palate, and learned her mother's tongue with relative fluency. She was indeed her mother's daughter.

As a young girl, her paternal grandparents, Oren and Martha O'Neil, would comment about her being "different" on their sporadic visits.

"Pearly, dear," Martha would whisper to her with the studied look of surprise, "what is it you're eating this time?"

Trained by her mother, she propped her cupped palms on Martha, brimming with sweets in multicolored cellophane wrap. "Want some, Grandma?"

There was a glimmer of surprise and reluctance as Martha and Oren exchanged glances.

"Grandpa?"

Oren, his mouth half full of the milky white sweet, spoke while powdery flecks flew from his mouth. "Whar are dtey?"

Pearl giggled with delight. "*Pulboron*, Grandpa."

The molded pastry from powdered milk, sugar, butter, and crunched *pinipig* grains crumbled in fine powdery dusts when eaten.

"*Pulboron*."

Imitating her mother, she begged Oren to whistle. Only her grandpa did not look amused at all, unlike her father.

"Please, Grandpa."

The O'Neils once more exchanged glances. Martha claimed the remaining half in Oren's palm to silence Pearl. She clutched her throat as she swallowed, dismissing Pearl's continued plea for a whistle with a wave of her hand.

"Hmmm, shweet . . ." Martha's muffled voice amused Pearl, who was five or six, to no end.

At age nine, when she understood more, she asked her father, Red O'Neil, mimicking Oren and Martha's query when her mother was not of hearing distance, "Why did you marry Mother?"

Red's face brightened up, but a pained look shortly eclipsed it. Only when she got older did she fully understand the meaning of that look.

"Your mother is from the island somewhere east," Martha and Oren O'Neil would tersely comment. They never seemed to remember or refused to remember her mother's birthplace or origin.

To an impressionable child, the island held a mystique only her mother could unravel.

"Where did you come from, Mother?"

That brought glitter to Aurora Gomez O'Neil's eyes. Aurora spun a globe in front of her, halting it to point to a group of islands south of Japan and north of Indonesia that faced the vast Pacific. It was a place dotted with seven-thousand-plus islands, more than half uninhabited, with lush tropical foliage where endless summers would welcome torrential rains brought by monsoon winds and angry typhoons ushered the rainy season. There was no snow and no falling leaves the color of gold, rust, or fire.

To Pearl's young mind, that was heaven. Her mother pointed at an asterisk in the middle of the northern island of Luzon, a place spelled M-A-N-I-L-A, the country's capital, where Aurora was born and spent her youth and where the natives had predominantly brown eyes, raven hair, and brown skin, and spoke Tagalog amidst dozens of tongues.

Coexisting with the locals were transplanted, naturalized, or second-generation Chinese in their own tightly knit community, each major city with its featured Chinatown. The natives eyed them with silent envy and suspicion if not with indifference. A few held studied tolerance. "Them" with their gilded and colorful temples and pagodas, hoarding among themselves, with perceived opulence and wealth.

They held the same sentiment toward turbaned males and women in *saris* whom they would refer to as Bombays, branding like a herd of cows any transplanted soul from India, Pakistan, Bangladesh, and the rest of the Middle East.

Aurora's parents, Tinay and Mario Gomez, fine specimens of the locals, had no traceable white blood running through their veins. Their daughter, Aurora, however, by quirk or jest of God, had brown hair and a narrow nose, unlike the natives. She was a head taller than women her age. She was a beautiful specimen of a Castilian woman with her smooth olive skin. Aurora was privileged by virtue of her looks, blessed by the gods, and exalted among the locals, the so-called mestizos and mestizas.

Thus, akin to being anointed with a whisk of a magical wand, Pearl learned she belonged to a "chosen few," according to her mother. She was the product of a union of a white blood, Red, and a nice native girl, Aurora. This was after pestering her mother insatiably about her funny accent and being bird-brained, according to Martha O'Neil, her paternal grandmother.

"I am a mestizo." Pearl's feet sprung repeatedly off the ground, and her hands, like cymbals, made noise together.

Aurora, looking amused, corrected her. "Mestiza, you are a mestiza. Mestizo is for boys."

Acquiring a new vocabulary, Pearl was extremely proud to tell her maternal grandmother, Tinay, who was visiting from the islands. "Nanay, I'm a mestiza."

Nanay meant "mother," but nobody bothered to correct Pearl, so she grew up calling Tinay Nanay, like Aurora did.

Tinay blinked repetitively, and her eyes watered.

Pearl was dumbfounded. *Isn't Nanay proud I am a mestiza?* she thought.

"Shhh . . ." Tinay held her fingers to Pearl's lips. "Be quiet."

Mario, Pearl's maternal grandfather, whom she called Tatay, which meant "father," pulled his wife away from Pearl. There was a short exchange of hushed and then raised voices. Even with Pearl's relatively fluent Tagalog, she was lost with the rapid staccato exchange of words above whisper between Tinay and Mario.

"She's just a child," said Mario, hushing his wife in a conciliatory tone.

"I can't help it, Mario." Tinay's voice was tremulous. "It brings painful memories."

"Stop being too emotional."

Triumphant she had an ally on her side, Pearl's confidence soared. "I'm a mestiza, Tatay."

"Yes, yes." A harried pace was in Mario's voice. "Enough. Can't you see you are upsetting your grandma?"

A cloud dawned on her innocent eyes, but not for long. *Nanay must be jealous. Well, I am a mestiza after all,* Pearl thought.

When she reached the age of twelve, Aurora, who used to jealously guard the kitchen, unlocked its door to her with its thousand and one secret recipes and senses beckoning.

"Pearl," Aurora said, "you're of ripe age now to learn skills you will need when you become a full-grown woman. You'll need these skills in life."

Pearl's first lesson was to cook the perfect rice—not too soft and not too dry. The ritual would begin by washing the uncooked rice in running water, stirring with one bare hand the milky water to remove the dirt and any remaining chaff, and repeating the process until the water was crystal clear and the grains of rice visible below.

"Rice should complement your food, enhancing the main course's taste and making it the main attraction. Improperly cooked rice could ruin even the most perfectly cooked main dish. Pedestrian cooking is the perfect avenue to drive someone away. Your future husband, in particular," her mother uttered. "Remember, the key to a man's heart is through his stomach."

Pearl learned to sojourn regularly with Aurora to Devon in Chinatown, riding the El at times from their home in Evanston, a Chicago suburb, shopping in their favorite Chinese grocery, and filling their tiny cart on cramped aisles with different kinds of noodles—*bijon*, *miswa*, *canton*, *luglog*, and *palabok*. The names seemed endless. There were herbs to bring out flavors—fresh ginger tubers, palm-sized onions, golden yellow fish sauce, red-orange *bagoong* shrimp paste, and dark brown *toyo* soy sauce. Her mother would remember things by memory alone. She would be the accessory brain to remind Aurora to buy powdered purple *ube* yam and restock the saffron rice seasoning, gravy mix for the *palabok* noodle, tamarind soup base, and chicken broth for *tinolang manok*, along with rice in twenty-five- or fifty-pound jute sacks from India, if available.

At fifteen, Pearl entered womanhood. She had her first period. It happened quickly, like a precise cut from a surgical wound, the warm blood anointing her. When she broke the news to Aurora, a flicker of worry dawned on her mother's face.

"You're a *dalaga* now, Amber Pearl. You're a young maiden now," her mother said while she stood naked in the bathtub. Aurora vigorously scrubbed her hair with *gugo*, a medicinal herbal root that promised to cure her newfound dandruff, a legacy of adolescent hormonal imbalance. "This *gugo* should do it," her mother said with utmost confidence, tipping the *tabo*, a water basin held by hand to rinse her hair.

Aurora ritually refilled the *tabo* from the faucet to finish washing her hair. Done, Aurora gazed at her daughter's wet nakedness with motherly pride and excitement in her eyes. Aurora soaped her back while she lathered up front. With the *tabo* full, her mother washed her with tepid water.

The noiseless flow blended with Aurora's gentle yet anxious voice. "Boys will start looking your way, Pearl. Be careful."

"Yes, Mother."

"They will always want *that* thing. Remember, they'll stop respecting you once you give in."

"Yes, Mother."

"A woman is like a delicate vase. You're priceless if untouched until finding its rightful owner. A broken one, even if fixed, is worthless."

Aurora paused to refill the *tabo*, as if giving Pearl time to digest what was said. Pearl remained quiet.

"The best gift you can offer your future husband is pureness of your body," said her mother.

Pearl thought of Brian, who blushed every time she caught him stealing furtive glances at her in school. He was cute with his freckled face, buttoned nose, and curly mane with reed-thin frame. *Could it be Brian?*

She quenched a smile, pretending to look pensive. Inexplicable warmth washed her body at the thought. If Brian were her destiny, they would have to wait until they were married.

"Are you listening to me?"

"Yes. Yes, Mother."

"Good!" Aurora's voice sounded stern. "Don't be like those girls. Girls from my place don't engage in those activities until they are married. And only with their husband. Boys can 'taste.' We are different." Aurora must have seen the perplexed look in Pearl's as she hastened to elaborate. "Boys can take advantage of you if you let them. Girls have a lot to lose, not them. Remember that."

Before she could utter, "Yes, Mother," Aurora covered her head with the towel and began to pat her hair dry. The ritual ended with her mother untangling her damp hair while she sat in front of the mirrored dresser, flattening the *suyod*, a double-edged, fine-toothed comb, against her scalp to gather loosened dry skin flakes. Not another word was spoken between them.

CHAPTER 2

A STRANGER AMONG US

"Dad, tell me how you met Mother." Amber Pearl relished the blush that reigned in her father's cheeks.

Red threw an amorous glance at his wife.

"Your father saw the most beautiful woman in his life." Aurora winked at her husband. "And he never let me out of his sight since."

In essence, that was true. It was also a lie. Red had never laid eyes on Aurora until after a year of knowing her. Yes, Red was smitten. But he knew more about Aurora's shoe size, the perfume she wore (Joy), her weakness for bags, the sound of her taped voice, her Catholic upbringing (the predominant faith in an Oriental country that surprised Red), her passion for blue, and the way she always looked forward to seeing the twenty-plus children in her kindergarten class on weekdays. These were facts he knew before he actually met her.

"Exotic Oriental girls looking for lifelong partners," read an ad Red's bored eyes laid on.

For a certain fee, Red O'Neil got a peek at hundreds of faces in black and white, in different poses of coyness, bewilderment, and anticipation. In fine prints were their vital statistics—the women's ages, weights, heights, and education. Good moral character was stamped on all of them, along with their dream of coming to America and marrying a white man. Included was Aurora's close-up.

Honorably discharged from the navy following an accident on board, with hormones still raging, unsure of what to do with the rest of his life, Red liked what he saw in the ads. He went to his barber and donned his starched uniform, which he ironed to perfection. The metal of his buckle gleaming and his shoes shimmering, he posed for a shoot in the navy outfit's full regalia with arms neatly tucked in his pants.

Aurora's image was the driving force for Red O'Neil to unlearn being left-handed, the Parker pen held stiff in his right hand with several tips bent from his laborious effort. In the end, he had to settle for a ball pen. The cursive words he wrote were so intense that the imprints were almost readable to the second and third blank pages. With his picture done and his letter of introduction fully edited, he mailed the letter to Aurora. It was the first of many.

Waiting for a reply seemed forever. Impatient, he wrote a second and then a third. Still without an answer, Red borrowed his parents' Underwood and labored to type words with his right fingers. *My cursive writing is the culprit. Why would anyone overseas bother with someone who can't write legibly?* he thought.

Aurora finally replied after his sixth attempt. It was not Red's typewritten report that broke the spell. It was to please the instigator, the one who stole Aurora's picture and sent it to the recruiting agency without her permission, Cousin Boy. Aurora's letter read:

Dear Mr. O'Neil,

> *I am impressed by your perseverance. Though I don't know you at all, you seem to be a nice person. Before you get the wrong impression, my picture and short biography was sent by my Cousin Boy without my knowledge or permission, of course. I am sure he meant well. But please erase any thoughts in your mind that I am cheap and of loose character.*

Sincerely yours,
Aurora Veneracion Gomez

"What attracted you to Dad, Mother?" Pearl asked, caressing the end of the bony knob and taut flesh of Red's forearm with its missing hand.

"His smile," Aurora voiced without hesitation.

In reality, Red's picture with both arms tucked in his pockets intrigued her more than anything.

Amidst the luggage and boxes of different sizes and shapes parading for identification at the luggage claim, Aurora first met Red. She actually did not see him coming. Aurora recalled the presence of a warm body pressing beside her, startling her. A towering man, smiling widely, was gazing down at her. He looked exactly as Aurora had seen him in black and white, only this time he was in living color.

Their eyes said everything their mouth withheld.

"Size eight." Red gazed at the familiar black pump Aurora wore.

Aurora groped for words. "It's very comfortable, especially for traveling."

It was an unorthodox first gift. Aurora saw bewilderment in her mother's face at the sight of the black pump shoes from her overseas admirer. Shoes, socks, and slippers all meant the same. Her mother, Tinay, was certain the relationship would not last. They were all meant for walking, for running away. Everyone knew that, or so her mother thought.

"Are you frightened?" Red propped his left arm for Aurora to see on top of the round wicker table.

They were in the sunroom, supposedly away from the prying eyes of the O'Neil clan, to give them ample time to rest and get comfortable with each other. There was no need to. They felt perfectly at ease the very first time they met face-to-face . . . even with Red's handicap staring back at her.

Before Aurora could answer Red, the French door swung open as a shrill voice dominated the tiny room.

"This must be the Aurora I've heard so much about." It was Aunt Millie.

Aunt Millie sprang toward them. Her hair-netted bun sashayed with her constant motion. Blonde ringlets adorned her forehead. She extended her gloved hand to Aurora. A narrow, mustachioed man in a long-sleeved white shirt, butterfly tie, and pressed linen white pants in suspenders followed close.

"Don't bother, Aurora." Aunt Millie motioned Aurora to remain seated. "So you're a teacher? Those children must be a handful . . . That's why I didn't have any." Aunt Millie pointed a vacant chair to the thin man, ignoring his flabbergasted look with her last comment. "Larry,"— Aunt Millie glared a split second at her husband with a frozen smile on her face—"why don't you sit beside Red? I'll sit here." Aunt Millie pulled a wicker chair beside Aurora. "You should have seen the change in Red. I kept telling my brother how his son has changed since he got serious with his pen pal from the Far East. And may I say I was expecting a short, black hair, dark-eyed, exotic-looking woman. You don't look Oriental to me at all. Are you a mix breed?"

Aurora blushed. A wry smile crossed her face. Red squeezed Aurora's hand to ease her discomfort at his aunt's prying question. She returned Red's strong grip to draw strength.

Aunt Millie paused to catch her breath, undeterred. "All his life, Red wanted to be in the navy. It shocked the family to learn of his accident. Oren has not updated me yet what happened with your case against the navy. I'll ask Martha. And how did he tell you?" Aunt Millie rested a hand on Aurora's. "I must tell you how proud I am the way Red carried himself, just like an O'Neil. Isn't it, Larry?"

Uncle Larry's lips opened, though no words came out.

"My goodness, I forgot. This is Larry." Aunt Millie paused. "Or should I say Uncle Larry?" A girlish laugh followed.

No, Red had never told Aurora about the accident. Red was loading her luggage in the car when she caught a glimpse of knobby white flesh for the very first time. Before she could confirm her curiosity, Red had tucked his left arm in his pocket and it remained hidden throughout the trip home to the O'Neils.

That evening, the tone of Aurora's mother on the phone was desperate. "Isn't it kind of a rush? You hardly know the man, Aurora. Plus, he's foreign." Tinay emphasized the last word.

"I love him, Nanay. I know him well." Aurora was nearly tempted to point out that, at twenty-four, she was an adult. It would, of course, be disrespectful, so she kept it to herself. "He's different from the others I've met, Nanay. He respects me. His family seems nice." Aurora recalled the very formal and reserved way Martha and Oren O'Neil greeted her.

Well, some people take a while to warm up. She smiled to herself at the thought of Aunt Millie.

"I don't know, Auring." Her mother addressed her by her pet name. "Marriage is not like cooked rice you could spit out when you're singed. Remember that saying."

Aurora remained quiet.

"You are a señorita here, Auring. Here you have your own driver to bring you anywhere. Your own *yaya*, Candida. God bless her soul. To this day, she remains loyal to the family, taking care of you all these years since you were a baby. You even have a maid to carry your books in school or shade you from the sun. Here, you don't have to worry about expense. You can buy anything you want without regards to money. Auring, I don't want to sound materialistic. You know I am not, but please put sense in your head. Don't throw away what you have here. You don't even know how to wash dishes, much less cook." Tinay was emphatic. "Imagine my daughter's hands becoming rough and calloused. *Santa Maria.*"

Aurora elected to remain mum. She could see her mother making the sign of the cross, raising her arms in despair, and sighing. *I could learn to cook.*

She enjoyed watching the family's live-in cook, Juling, make dishes. Juling was from Pampanga, a province with refutation for their women's culinary skills and talent. Juling's *bibingka*, *ginatan*, and *suman* sweets were to die for.

"And what will my *amigas*, my friends, say? It's embarrassing, Auring. It's *nakakahiya*. It's a shame."

Aurora heard her father's voice next on the phone. "Put that man on the phone, Aurora." Her father bellowed.

"Yes, Tatay." Aurora motioned Red, who was listening nearby, to come. "*Opo*," she added hastily as a sign of respect to her father before giving the phone to Red.

A flushed Red greeted Aurora when he joined her after more than an hour of overseas call with Tinay and Mario Gomez.

"And . . ." The ring of anticipation and nervousness was evident in Aurora's voice.

Red smiled triumphantly at her, squeezing her hand and vanishing all her qualms.

"Perfect timing, son." Oren's eyes narrowed at the sight of Red walking toward him and his wife. "Just perfect." Oren pulled the empty chair beside him, flopping its cushion to signal Red to join them.

The lit globe above the round wicker table cast a jaundiced tint to Martha's and Oren's leathery skin, aging them more. Two huge weeping willows, mature silver maples, and a crab apple tree outside surrounded the screened sunroom. The crackling chorus of their leaves from occasional gusts of summer wind were silent witnesses, jurors, and rumormongers; in contrast to the carnival atmosphere a few hours before.

"We're just talking about you." A modest smile crossed Martha's lips. It emphasized the furrows in her face from years under the sun as a farmer's wife.

"Yeah?" The angry veins in Red's arms seemed to pop up as he grabbed the propped chair to sit on.

What was it that made my parents stay up late and sit in the sun porch that gets chilly at night, even during summer? By seven, they were usually in bed.

"Remember your Grandma Ethel from my side of the family?" Oren asked. "A handsome woman, no nonsense, raised a half-dozen kids . . ."

"Of course he remembers." A hint of annoyance was in Martha's tone. "Your Uncle Pete, his wife, their children . . . your cousins. Your Aunt Matilda, bless her departed soul. My only regret was that her husband didn't even wait a few months . . ." She sighed but immediately got her bearing. "But everyone married well. Married the right people."

"The man was lonely," Oren said, defending. "It's hard for a man to sleep in a cold bed at night."

"Is that all I'm good to you?" Martha's pitch rose.

"Listen before you croak. You were the mother of my children. Still are. Help you raised them the way they should. Spend every single night with you."

Red met his father's eyes. They were icy blue, deep, and unfathomable. He then looked at his mother's. Like his father's, they were cold.

"I raised my children well," Martha said. "I thought I did." She ran her gnarled fingers on top of each other. "Your two sisters both married right. And what happened with Mona? You and her would have made me a proud grandma—blonde and blue eyes."

"Yeah?" Red recalled Mona's heaving naked body, alabaster white without blemish, surrendering to him with abandon. Then there was the sight of Mona whining, demanding, untrusting. Red's carotid pulses quickened.

"What happened?" Oren asked again.

"I don't think we're right for each other."

"Then look around," Oren said, bellowing. "Jesus, there's a bunch of women in town, unattached, waiting to be . . ." Oren took a deep breath. "To be hitched. Good Irish stock, like your grandma. Swiss or French would be just fine. Even a Polack would be a lot better. Martha and I would even settle for Fiona, that Italian girl on the south side of town."

Red stood up. "You know who I want."

"Why?" Oren said.

"Why her?" Martha asked, seconding her husband.

"Why not?" Red's ear began to sting.

"She's not one of us," Martha and Oren uttered in unison.

The stinging spread from Red's ears to his face. That was how he earned the moniker Red. He would blush bright red at the slightest provocation, pleasant or otherwise. He gnashed his teeth.

"We're putting some sense in your head," Oren said.

"Think, Red," Martha said, pleading. "The children—"

"They will be your flesh and blood," Red said, pointing out.

"And what will people say? How will they be treated? Aren't you afraid?" Martha stood up to her full height. "The looks. The whispers. I could just imagine."

"You're absolutely right. I should be afraid. Afraid of you, my parents . . . your prejudices and your ignorance. Aurora and I are getting married. You are invited. Whether you show up or not is up to you."

"Don't turn your back on us, young man. We're not done yet."

The French door shut closed.

*   *   *

The tiny, embroidered clusters of jasmine and *sampaguita* flowers were jewels adorning the bodice, sleeves, and train of Aurora's wedding gown. The dress was of *jusi*, a silky material from strands of banana fibers. A dozen *bordaderas* labored for months to embroider them, painstakingly using *callado*, a century-old method of embroidery producing stunning results.

The held breaths of the bridesmaids were palpable in the room. Basking in their admiration, Aurora pirouetted in front of the floor-length mirror. It was a Pitoy Moreno original, a very good family friend back home. Pitoy, as he was fondly called, was considered the premier couturier of the time. Without previous fittings, the gown felt perfect. Of course, it was unthinkable to try on a bridal gown until the wedding day, less back luck were to happen.

Tinay herself resplendent in her blue butterfly-sleeved *terno* similarly executed by Pitoy Moreno, locked gaze with Aurora in the mirror as she entered the room. Light bulbs flashed, cameras clicked, and giggles broke out while pictures were taken, first of mother and daughter and then the rest of the entourage. Soon, the rustle of satin and silk faded, leaving the two women alone.

Martha and Oren O'Neil elected to stay in the public area of their modest house, entertaining their clan.

"Reminds me of my wedding, Auring." Tinay's voice quivered slightly while she straightened Aurora's headdress anchored by a family heirloom, a diamond tiara. A drop threatened each corner of Tinay's eyes. "You look very happy." Tinay paused. "Not that I wasn't. Of course, I was happy," Tinay said to convince herself, it seemed, more than anyone else.

"I am, Nanay." Aurora reached out and patted Tinay's hand on her shoulder. "Red's a good man."

Tinay ignored Aurora's comment and tightened her grip on Aurora's shoulders. "I have a surprise for you." Tinay swiveled the stool Aurora sat on, producing an exquisitely beaded rosary for Aurora to admire. "The pope personally blessed it."

"Ang ganda." Aurora gasped in admiration. "Beautiful." Aurora circled a few strands on her wrist. Its beads shimmered and captured the colors of the rainbow while light played on its surface. She clutched the crucifix in her palm.

"It's Father Francisco's gift for your wedding."

The image of the frocked priest, patrician, rotund with the palest brown eyes imaginable that always sparkled at the sight of Aurora, danced in her head. Father Francisco was an ubiquitous fixture to all important events in the Gomez clan. Father Francisco, aside from Mario, was the other man who saw her grow from a toddler to a young woman, the one person Aurora would share secrets she wouldn't even tell her parents. He was her own private father confessor. He was the one instrument prodding Tinay and Mario to allow their only daughter to travel abroad, alone, to meet Red in person.

"How is he doing?" Aurora asked.

"They have upgraded his condition. The latest I've heard, he is out of ICU."

"He should quit smoking."

And wine should be confined to celebrating the mass, Aurora thought.

"Look what he's missing, Nanay. My wedding would have been perfect if he were here."

Aurora recalled growing up, seeing the priest loosen up, becoming amorous toward young women, and bantering with them, noisy and unsteady, uninhibited as spirits conquered him. There were quite a few silent glances and nervous laughter among the Gomez family, friends, and guests. Most looked the other way. Tinay would signal Aurora to get him and lead him to a quiet place, away from the crowd.

And she would. Like a miracle, leading with her hand, he would be transformed instantaneously, meek like a lamb, smiling bashfully, while somebody would ferret out the wine glass away from him.

Mario, her father, would remain a silent witness, though never leaving Father Francisco's sight. Mario's expression remained a blank canvas during these encounters. His demeanor was unflinching like a cold statue, seeing yet unseeing.

Through the years, Aurora would occasionally hear pointed comments, not limited among some guests but even among the extended Gomez clan—the numerous first- and second-degree aunts, uncles, cousins, grandparents, nieces, nephews, and in-laws. These perpetrators vanished in different directions as she drew near.

"She's the only one he listens to."

"I told you so."

"It's true."

"Quiet." The first coconspirator cautioned everyone. "She's coming this way."

Aurora tightened her grip on the rosary. "Look what he's missing," she said again.

Tinay nodded. "Make sure you send him some wedding pictures."

A torrent of emotion overcame Tinay. Her shoulders shook violently.

"Nanay, please." Warm liquid wetted Aurora's hand.

She debated. *Were the tears for me, Father Francisco, or my wedding? Were they tears of joy or despair?* Regardless, old folks consider it *malas*, bad luck, to shed tears in a wedding. It could portend an unhappy marriage. She wiped her hands dry.

"A mother is entitled to this." Tinay dabbed her cheeks with a laced silk handkerchief. "You'll understand this when it is your turn to marry off one of your daughters."

"Nanay . . ." The comment somewhat eased Aurora's fear. She reached for her mother's hand.

"And remember, we want plenty of grandchildren. At least a half dozen. You heard the old saying, grandchildren are the *tubo*, the profit. Your father and I want lots of profit, lots of *tubo*." Standing tall, Tinay turned to leave, the wisp of her expensive perfume trailing her.

As the mother of the bride and accustomed to tradition, Tinay was involved in all the details of the wedding. If she had her way—and she never tired of reminding Aurora—a wedding back home would be just perfect. The Gomez family would definitely agree. First, she knew exactly the perfect venue, the Santuario de San Jose in San Antonio Village, the nuptial sight of the crème de la crème of Metro Manila's high society. Though new hotels had sprouted along Dewey Boulevard, Tinay still considered the main ballroom in Manila Hotel the premier site for wedding receptions in the sixties. Pilita Corrales, the inimitable chanteuse known as far south as Australia and far north as Hong Kong, could provide the perfect entertainment. Rafael, Pilita's manager and brother, certainly would not turn down her request, well, given sufficient notice.

Tinay rattled off prominent families and important people they were friends with to Aurora's deaf ears—the Zobel-Ayalas; the Sorianos; the Puyats; current president Garcia and his lovely wife Inday; John Hickerman, the US ambassador to the Philippines; Ambassador Jose Romulo and his wife (who she was positive they would take time off from his busy post from Washington, DC, to attend); the mayors of Pasay and Caloocan cities; the Vera-Perez movie magnates; the Nepomucenos; the Sigeon-Reynas; the Lopezes; and the very charming Ferdinand Marcos (who may be running for a senatorial seat in the near future) and his beautiful wife Imelda. And the list went on and on.

Tinay imagined truckloads of fresh flowers—roses, lilies, carnations, and orchids from Baguio city, the Philippine summer capital—to decorate the pews and the altar.

The bubble burst when Aurora said no to all of these. It was a slap to tradition, too, to learn that in America the bride's family pays for the wedding. Money, of course, was not the issue, but they would be the laughingstock in Manila when people heard this, especially with her exclusive clique in the mahjong sessions.

And who was this "white ghost" who claimed their only child, a lowly assembly-line factory worker, an ex-navy man, a left-hand amputee whose only saving grace was light skin, blond hair, nasal twang, and eyes the color of sky?

In vindication, the wedding entourage bore Tinay's seal and blessing. It had the requisite bridesmaids, flower girl, and ring bearer. It also had the added requisite pairs of candle, veil and cord sponsors, and the half-dozen pairs of wedding sponsors, the so-called *ninongs* and *ninangs*. Tinay would have opted for a full dozen sponsors. And the coin bearer was a young boy carrying *arias*, minted gold coins to signify prosperity for the wedded couple. Tinay basked at the surprised look of Red's clan who were not accustomed to the traditional Filipino wedding.

At the country club, Tinay did not waste time. As soon as the newlyweds sashayed on the dance floor, Tinay pinned paper money on Aurora's wedding dress, a tradition in the Ilocos province where she hailed from, confident the Gomezes would beat the O'Neils with money raised while Aurora and Red danced to a live band.

A wave of Tinay's hand and sweeping glance were all that was needed before the whole force of Aurora's clan, including those not from the Ilocos region and unfamiliar with this tradition, stood up one by one and joined the revelry with crisp paper bills to tuck, pin, or slip on the bride's gown and the groom's finery.

The soprano pitch of Aunt Millie's voice rivaled the band. "Gosh, am I really seeing what I'm seeing?" She yanked Uncle Larry to the dance floor and signaled him to follow suit by tapping the wallet in his pants. "We can't let them bamboozle us. Where's the money?"

Not satisfied, Aunt Millie began to ogle every table, imploring every single O'Neil kin, friend, or any friendly white face to contribute for the O'Neils. "Show 'em the spirit, guys!" Her shrill voice once more competed with the live music. "C'mon, guys. Show 'em the money."

CHAPTER 3

No Ordinary Baby

Aurora's miscarriage spread like wildfire among the Gomezes in Metro Manila.

"Aurora and Red's blood must be incompatible." An aunt gasped.

"Her husband is *Kanu* (American). He probably didn't give in to her cravings."

"Americans don't believe in that," an uncle uttered. "Plus, how would he know?"

"That's what I kept pointing out," said a female relative. "Look what happened."

"I am sure, had the baby lived, it would have been beautiful. A white blood mixed with Filipino always produce beautiful babies," said one with a ring of regret.

"Wait a second. Aurora is beautiful by any standard," said one, boasting.

"Didn't the Bachelors' Club choose her one of Manila's ten most beautiful six years ago?"

"It was five," said one. "They only choose five."

"Aurora does not look Filipino at all," a relative whispered in conspiratorial tone, gathering accomplices along the way. "She looks more like a mestiza."

"She is," said another, conniving with the previous speaker. "Didn't you hear the rumor?"

"I'm sure Tinay and Mario are devastated," one cousin said, feeling sorry.

"Mario? You should hear how Father Francisco reacted to the news. Heard he cancelled masses that day," said a gossip, igniting fire to smoke, "feigning illness."

"Let us not talk about that," said one, admonishing. "Show your respect to Father Francisco."

"She probably did lots of heavy lifting." It was, indeed, the most probable cause of the miscarriage, assumed another.

"I can never live in America. Can you imagine not having a *yaya* to care for your baby. Not to mention your *labandera* (washerwoman), your cook, your *hardinero* (gardener), the live-in help," said one, lamenting. "Visit the States, maybe."

"That's why she had the miscarriage," another said, secure of the validity of her assumption. "Imagine being three months pregnant and doing all the housework. Especially Aurora. She was a señorita here."

"Why didn't Tinay and Mario send for Candida? Wasn't she Aurora's *yaya*?" another asked. "She could help for sure."

"You know how people in America are. They keep things pretty much to themselves. They probably didn't want Tinay and Mario to hear about their own daughter's pregnancy," said one.

"Nonsense. It's our right to know. Red would have received an earful from me if I were Tinay. His name's Red, correct? And what kind of a name is that? They do give weird nicknames," an in-law said.

"Boy must be feeling guilty. He pushed Aurora to marry Red, didn't he? D'you think Red can provide for his family? I heard they are not really considered well off in the States." This one offered another inside scoop, on condition of anonymity.

"Hear this. Tinay and Mario spent for their daughter's wedding. Everything."

"Is that so? I couldn't show my face in mahjong session if I were Tinay. Poor Mario." A deep sigh followed this one comment.

"Of course Red could provide for his family," another said in defense of Red. "It's not hard to find a job in America."

"Lucky him. Bless his soul. Being an amputee, he'd be jobless here," said one.

"And they'd nickname him *putol* (chopped off)."

"*Sinabi mo* (you said it)," said another.

There was a chorus of laughter.

"Tinay and Mario won't let that happen," said another in a serious tone.

"That's for sure. Didn't they buy a house for them? Was it Forbes Park or San Antonio Village? The house alone is worth a fortune, designed no less by Locsin. Hear the architect, Leandro Locsin. *De kampanilya* (the best), of course. Just to convince Aurora and Red to settle here," said another.

Tinay kept a tight upper lip through all the news, half-truths, and innuendoes that sifted her way. One thing was certain. She wouldn't let this happen again. Aurora would have a healthy baby next time. *Itaga mo sa bato* (carve it in stone), as they say back home.

They did buy a house for Aurora and her husband. The house they bought for Aurora and her husband was in America, not Metro Manila. Actually, it cost them twice as much, considering at that time the Philippine peso was equivalent to fifty US cents. Nevertheless, the house was in a prime location in Evanston, a Chicago suburb, a four-bedroom colonial paid for in cash by Mario and Tinay Gomez, she was proud to say. And no, Leandro Locsin was not the architect.

They expected unending gratitude from Aurora and her husband. Tinay assumed they would have a permanent room in the house to stay when they would come to visit or, if they wished, stay for good. Mario and she would not be a nuisance. They did not need to depend on Aurora and her husband for anything.

Aurora should know. And everything would be "just fine." Yet Tinay could still not reconcile that Red was married to her *bugtong na anak* (precious only child) or even addressing him. Doing so would mean he was *pamilya* (family), a member of the Gomez clan, which was hard to swallow. Red had yet to prove worthy of the family name. She would have settled for one of Aurora's numerous suitors—several scion of prominent Manila families, a few doctors, or several lawyers—all professionals, all thoroughbred Filipino.

Mario and Tinay did stay for most of Aurora's next pregnancy. It was hard for them to get used to the four seasons, winter in particular. Tinay could very well remember come Christmas that their Manila abode had been decorated with fake snowflakes to simulate the white Christmas they could only dream about in the Philippines.

She had mailed and received Christmas cards with pristine sceneries of snow. Popular holiday songs like "White Christmas" and "Frosty the Snowman" were playing on the airwaves, all of them beautiful folly. What were her friends, relatives, and business associates thinking? They had never seen snow turned into muddy, slippery slush, layers of cumbersome clothing to ward off the cold, the shivers, the numb fingers and toes, and mist from their mouths in spite of the crackling fireplace and turned-up thermostat to the amused grin of Aurora's husband. Whether her Mario would get used to this did not really matter. That was his problem. Plus, how would Tinay know? Men were different.

Aurora's second pregnancy was eventful, to say the least, with morning sickness requiring hospitalizations for dehydration, unseen mood swings, and unusual craving for *makopa*, a bell-shaped, pinkish red fruit with inner whitish pulp. Tinay implored the help of their *katiwala* (trusted help), Pepe, on their vast farm property and rice granaries. Pepe ingeniously hid a dozen or so *makopa* in a sealed can to pass strict inspection by American custom officials.

Proud of her achievement, Tinay displayed the freshly washed *makopa* in a crystal bowl for Aurora to relish. "Auring, look what we got you." Tinay was ecstatic. "You can really depend on Pepe." Providing a pregnant woman's craving was one way to assure a full-term pregnancy. "Look."

Aurora pouted and crinkled her hose. With a dismissive look, she waved an arm away. "I don't like them anymore."

Just like that. Tinay was reminiscent, though not as painful as the house and lot refused by Aurora and her freeloading husband. She could still clearly recall her daughter's very words like it happened yesterday.

"We can't accept the offer, Nanay, Tatay." Aurora's head bowed in shame, an ingrate to their generosity. Her voice was barely audible. "Red won't."

Tinay was speechless. Mario gripped his wife's hands. It was unimaginable.

"You refused," Tinay was finally able to say, "the house? Why?"

Because your husband said so. That imbecile.

"*Opo*," Aurora whispered. It sounded like thunder to Tinay. Aurora kept her head down with her fingers crossed. She evaded Tinay's and Mario's eyes. The tightening of Mario's jaw and nervous reach for tobacco did not escape Tinay's. As he nervously lit the cigar Tinay's disdain for Red intensified.

Mario promised to quit smoking. Look what he is doing. It's all Red's fault.

She playfully slapped Mario's cheek to get his mind off his disappointment. "You know, everyone knows you are a very good lawyer, except . . ."

"What . . . ?

"You'd be the perfect one if you just quit smoking. And you'd smell nicer."

Mario pulled her toward him. Tinay buried her face to his chest.

Red was downsized from his job. This time, Tinay smelled victory on their side. With Aurora's precarious pregnancy, they had a strong argument to convince them to move to the four-bedroom house. If needed, Tinay was willing to plead their case to Red. She could not imagine the newly built colonial house with green shutters standing like a white elephant, its curtains flapping aimlessly on its windows.

Tinay was ecstatic when Aurora and Red finally moved in with them to the new house. It seemed things were still working in her favor. Now, she had to focus her attention on her daughter and the coming baby.

"What is your husband doing?" Tinay's eyes widened, hissing. She was visibly annoyed, pointing her finger at Red who was in shorts and dirty shirt with a gallon of paint, a ladder, a bucket of water, some rugs, and a paintbrush.

"We're converting this into a nursery," Red said. "It's next to our bedroom, convenient for Aurora."

Tinay ignored Red. "Tell your husband he can't do that. Not again after your miscarriage. It's *malo*, just plain bad luck to prepare and buy stuff for the baby early in pregnancy. You don't want another miscarriage."

"Nanay . . ." Aurora's tone was diplomatic. She threw a worried glance at Red.

Red's face was livid.

"Exactly, this is your mother. So do as I say. Tell him."

Red laid down the paint and brush, walked out, and came back with a large white cloth to protect the wooden floor. He started to wash the walls of the room.

"Is he deaf? Hasn't he learned his lesson?"

"Please, Nanay . . ."

Red dropped the bucket, threw the washcloth, and dragged his feet on the way out.

"Did you see how he treats your mother? Did you see? That ingrate."

Aurora remained quiet. She burst into tears.

"Now he is making my daughter cry. *Santa Maria, ipag-adya mo po kaming makasalanan sa salot*. Mother of God, protect us sinners from pestilence."

Aurora turned her back to Tinay and rushed toward their bedroom.

"Good. Tell your husband how lucky he is that he has a roof over his head and his family doesn't have to worry where the next meal would be. He should be grateful."

The following weeks were a study in quiet demeanor among Red, Tinay, Mario, and Aurora. Everyone was avoiding running into each other. Everyone was tiptoeing, staying in his or her own territory.

Husband and wife were talking in conspiratorial tones to each other. Red would be gone most of the morning, presumably looking for a job.

The smell of chicken and biscuit permeated the air.

"Nanay, Red is here." Aurora, ripe with her baby, was peering inside her parents' room and smiling from ear to ear. "He got a job."

Tinay's one eyebrow arched, pulling herself straight and pretending not to hear.

"Nanay . . ." Red called Tinay, showing his face. "I bought us lunch. Let's eat. Where's Tatay?"

Tinay responded with a wry smile, avoiding Red's eyes. Without uttering a word, she motioned the couple to leave her alone. She showed up with Mario in tow. She signaled Mario to take a seat at the breakfast table. The four of them shared lunch. Mario talked animatedly with his daughter and son-in-law while Tinay remained quiet.

Things seemed to have settled down until Aunt Millie gave a baby shower a couple months before Aurora's expected delivery. Tinay visibly showed her displeasure.

Haven't the O'Neils learned their lesson? Baby clothes, receiving blankets, diapers, and, worst, a crib is courting disaster. These are last-minute items to prepare, lest something awful happens again to this baby.

In spite of Tinay's unending diatribe and verbal complaint about Red and his relatives' ignorance, Pearl was delivered on her very expected date of arrival, a healthy eight-pound wiggling, tiny human being who constantly cried, a good sign she would grow up with a beautiful voice, Tinay announced back home. She recalled hearing menfolk in the rural areas even climb coconut trees with their wives' *inunan* (afterbirth) tied way up high to ensure a lovely voice that could hit high notes. The higher the *inunan* could be brought up, the better. Tinay did not waste time to call *Ka* Lucia, her favorite cousin who had immigrated to Canada.

"And who does the baby look like?" *Ka* Lucia eagerly shared the news to Fe, her significant other who was listening. "Aurora just had a baby. It's a girl."

A dog could be heard barking from a distance. "I don't know yet. I'll ask."

"*Ay, ay, naku,*" Tinay interjected. "She reminds me of Auring when she was a baby herself with long lashes, big eyes, and tiny nose. And the baby's fingers, you should see how long they are. Typical Gomez, no doubt."

"*Mana sa lola,*" *Ka* Lucia said. "She took after her grandma, who else?"

"And what does Aurora's in-laws, your *balae,* say?"

"What do you expect? They claim the baby is an O'Neil. I say no except for her white skin."

And blue eyes, which is not bad. Who would imagine I would have a grandchild with blue eyes. Not in my dreams. Santa Maria, I hope the color does not change, as I've heard in some cases.

"Tinay." The continued barking broke Tinay's thought. "Fe wants to know the baby's name."

"You don't believe me, do you? Come over and see the baby yourself. They haven't decided on the name yet."

"We will visit. Don't worry."

"When?"

An impish laugh was heard, joined by Fe's contagious guffaw.

"Empty promises. You always do that. You two . . ." Tinay's voice trailed.

"Fe's new in her job, if you didn't know. I have to make arrangements with my work."

"Always busy. Busy making money." Tinay pointed out. "That's all you two think about."

"Look who's talking. We have to work." *Ka* Lucia paused. "You don't." She followed with a hearty laugh.

"Enough. This is your first granddaughter-in-cousin. Mind you, when I die, you will visit me for sure."

"*Santa Maria,* don't say that. It's bad luck."

"I tell you."

"Cousin, we will visit. We'll plan on it." There was momentary silence. The barking stopped. "I really have to go. She's signaling me. The food is getting cold. And Fe says *kumusta* to everyone."

"I'll let you go then. Call me back."

"We will. And *kumusta* to Mario, Aurora, and her husband. What's his name again?"

"I'll let everyone know." Tinay ignored the question. She was in a good mood, and there was no reason to spoil it.

Tinay elected to stay home when it was time to pick up Aurora and the baby. That gave her time to prepare for the baby's arrival. A day prior, she had prewashed the baby's clothes and stacked them neatly. The feeding bottles had been sterilized, though she hoped Aurora would breastfeed. The crib was all set, decorated with toy carousel and rattle even this early. On the side, she made some rice cake and fried plantain banana with jackfruit wrapped in *lumpia* wrappers for guests, something out of the ordinary. She had not seen anyone not like her rice cake. She wished she had some fresh coconut juice with its meat for refreshment. She had to settle for soda and a choice of either hot tea or coffee.

Martha and Oren came to visit. They brought some balloons and a streamer. Red's two siblings and their spouses were there, along with Aunt Millie and Larry. Tinay had hoped that Red's aunt would not show up. She had not forgotten and forgiven for how Aunt Millie planned the baby shower. It was good nothing happened. Plus, the woman was loud and constantly calling attention to herself.

Ah, her poor husband, Tinay thought.

Oren took pictures and surprised himself exchanging pleasantries with his son's in-laws and actually warming up to them, even with their thick and funny accent. He even dared to sample the rice cake and the fried banana with jackfruit with his stark palate.

And before anyone could refuse, Tinay handed cut pieces of the glutinous rice cake to everyone else.

"Don't be shy, *balae*. I know you like it." Tinay ignored Oren's wince as she placed another piece of rice cake on his plate.

"He has lactose intolerance," Martha said.

"It's glutinous rice with coconut," Tinay said reassuringly.

"And you, *balaeng* Martha?" Tinay placed an extra helping of the dessert on Martha's plate without waiting for an answer.

"I'm okay. Please, I still have a lot," Martha said.

"You eat like a bird. That's an extra small piece I gave you. Don't say you can't finish it, or I'll never talk to you for the rest of my life."

Soon everyone had their fill of Tinay's dessert, leaving no room for the apple pie that Aunt Millie had brought.

Martha cradled the baby. Oren had to content himself with cuddling close to his wife. They sure took notice of the baby's fair skin, light hair, and bluish eyes. Of course, the eye color could change, but it was unlikely to be the color of Aurora's, they thought.

"What's *balae*?" he whispered.

"Don't ask me." Martha saw the baby holding tight Oren's finger. She tilted her head, making sure her husband noticed the baby's tapered, long fingers, unmistakably O'Neils.

"Came up with a name yet?" Oren queried for everyone to hear while nodding his head to Martha's astute observation. Yes, their granddaughter had long, tapered fingers, typical of the O'Neils.

"Millie would be nice." The owner of the name bellowed.

There was a clearing of the throat.

The rest ignored the comment.

Her name is Millie. That's right. Tinay smiled at the woman who caught her observant eyes. She couldn't help but notice the rail-thin husband standing beside the woman like a ghost, immaculately dressed with starched shirt, linen pants, and bow tie, hardly saying a word to Aunt Millie's constant chatter.

What a spineless clod. Tinay smiled her widest grin at Larry when their eyes crossed path. "You're so . . . neat."

"Or you could . . ." Aunt Millie glared back at Tinay as she talked. "Name the baby after their grandmas. Martha and . . ." Aunt Millie continued to look at Tinay without batting an eye.

"Tinay." Mario placed an arm on Tinay's shoulder and rubbed it lightly to ease the mounting tension he could sense between the two women.

"Tinay?" Aunt Millie's penciled eyebrows arched.

"Kristina." Tinay continued to glare at Aunt Millie. "My full name is Kristina. With a *K*."

"With a *K*. That's better." Aunt Millie's eyebrows settled down. "Martha . . . Kristina . . . Martha . . . Whatever, definitely a lot better than . . . What did you say your nickname was again?"

But Tinay had already turned her back to Aunt Millie to claim the baby from Martha.

"Tinay," Mario said. Again, an amused smile threatened to escape from his lips.

Inexplicable contentment dawned on Tinay as she got her turn to cradle the baby. For that brief moment, everyone seemed inconsequential. She and the baby were all that mattered in a universe all their own. She smiled from ear to ear at Red as their eyes met. Contrary to how she had always felt, she felt a tender spot for Aurora's husband at that moment.

"Everyone." Oren motioned the crowd to get ready for a group picture.

"Mario," Tinay bellowed as everyone began to crowd around her for the shoot. "You take the picture, Mario. Come over here, *balaeng* Oren. Mario will do the honor. Mario, don't let our guest do that. *Nakakahiya.* It's embarrassing. C'mon, *balaeng* Oren, *balaeng* Martha. Join us."

Everyone had a big smile on their faces as Mario took the picture, ignoring and shedding any differences. For one brief moment, they were color-blind, not speaking or hearing any evil word, for among them was no ordinary baby.

CHAPTER 4

A GATHERING STORM

The airport's public address system blared its last call for Aurora's flight. "Final boarding call for Pan Am flight 375 to Manila at gate 10."

"Your dad, Amber Pearl," Aurora spoke in grave whispers. "Take care of him."

Pearl cradled and squeezed her mother's hand to warm and ease the flow of blood. Her mother rarely called her Amber Pearl except to make a point crystal clear.

"I need to go home," Aurora said. "Nobody knows how much longer Nanay will be with us, you do understand. Remember what I told you."

Aurora released Pearl's grip and gazed at her husband. *How is Red going to survive?* Red was totally dependent on her for everything—cooking, housekeeping, and budgeting.

Red smiled at her. His wink failed to hide his sad smile. Aurora would miss that lopsided grin. Red pulled her tight to his chest. He planted a warm kiss to her lips before letting go. Aurora blushed, flustered at the unexpected public display of affection. Married for a good many years, she could still not shake the false modesty she was accustomed to. In public, an embrace between spouses was acceptable. But locking lips in public was totally unacceptable. Such public display of affection. She could just imagine her parents—Tinay and Mario—squirming uncomfortably, gazing the other way if they were present.

Aurora turned her back to Red, rushing toward the gate and avoiding eye contact with him, embarrassed. She was suspicious the crowd was observing her every move, and who wouldn't?

She waved a hand, stage whispered to Pearl, and stole a look at her daughter. "Take care of your dad . . . Yourself too."

Pearl continued to wave an arm, holding and digging Red's hand with the other until the plane was just a speck in the sky.

Father and daughter retraced their steps back to the parking lot. The heavy sounds of their footsteps echoed on the pavement, disturbing some snowflakes as they reached the open section of the large parking space. They kept to themselves.

Red dangled the car keys in front of Pearl when they reached the car. He expected Pearl's face to light up. Pearl had recently passed her driver's test.

"Yes?" Red wiggled the key.

Pearl reached for the passenger's front door.

Father and daughter remained silent on the way home, buried in their own thoughts. The only sound was the windshield wipers clearing the light snow that had started again. By the time they were on the highway, the snow was heavy, slowing their trip home.

Pearl could still hear her mother's voice.

"Dad wants his rice cooked just right. Not too soft. Not too dry." Aurora had pointed out earlier.

"*Pansit* noodles should be served hot. With plenty of *sahog*— ingredients. That's the secret to its taste. Lots of *sahog*." It was another reminder from Aurora.

"Your dad wants his fried *lumpia* roll with salt and vinegar."

Like an obedient daughter, she listened and made mental notes to everything said.

The following days stretched into weeks. They blended undistinguished from one another. They were punctuated by cold nights, the soft landing of snowflakes on the rooftops, and the eaves of their colonial house decorated with icicles that reflected a dozen suns.

Aurora's overseas calls never faltered, coming every few days if not more frequent. The tone and timbre of Aurora's call would be somber one moment and ecstatic another time. Nanay's condition was like the weather.

"Nanay has a dry cough," Aurora said. "Chest x-ray showed nothing according to the doctor. She was started on antibiotics since her white count and immune system are down."

"*Pag-asa*, ray of hope," Aurora said, gushing one time. "Nanay gained weight and hasn't been throwing up her food."

"Nanay lost everything she's gained." It was Aurora talking another time. "She's been vomiting constantly from her chemotherapy."

Red listened to all of these. He didn't complain or display any irritation until the "short stay" exceeded the third month.

"Your dad's with her," Red spoke, his words measured and said as calm as he could.

"You mean Tatay and Nanay," Aurora whispered, disappointed Red did not address them as she saw fit.

"Yes, your mother." Red clenched his jaw. He could feel his cheeks burning. "Nanay . . . Nanay is not alone. Tatay's with her."

"Nanay needs me." Aurora's voice trembled. She could not believe her visit would be an issue.

"I need you too."

"Nanay could die anytime. My conscience will bother me to no end if I abandon her now."

"Nobody's abandoning her. I told you that she can come here and receive the best treatment available now."

"Nanay wouldn't hear of it."

"I'm sorry then, but your place is here with me—now."

"A daughter's obligation is with her mother in times like this. She is the only mother I have. My family needs me. That is expected from me. Can't you understand?"

"I am your family, your husband Red and your daughter Pearl."

Aurora clenched her throat. Pearl could hear them. "Amber Pearl, get off the phone." Her voice continued to shake.

"Pearl could listen for all she wants."

Pearl got off the phone. She could hear the rapid palpitation in her chest. It rivaled the loud argument of her parents for nearly an hour.

There were more phone calls the following weeks. They were mostly private calls. Pearl was asked to hang up as soon as Aurora and Red got connected. She couldn't hear her parents, but there was no mistaking Red's agitated voice, and not infrequently, his angry tone reverberated through their bedroom wall.

Lately, she could clearly hear Red at the top of his voice, no longer caring that Pearl could hear him loud and clear. Most calls were at night. Pearl barely slept those nights. She tossed in her bed, routinely getting up for ice-cold water to quench her dry mouth.

Pearl immersed herself in school to get her mind off the first storm in her young life. Otherwise, her free time was spent in the kitchen perfecting her mother's recipes, imagining that by doing so her father would be in a better mood.

After all, didn't Mother say the key to a man's heart is through the stomach?

One weekend, she rushed early to the kitchen after a sleepless night to enliven her dad's mood. Aurora's kitchen was eclectic. There were rows upon rows of *atsara* (grated unripe papaya with green and red peppers and cucumbers soaked in vinegar), hung strips of salted milkfish and swordfish, jars of preserved fish and shrimp sauce, preserved fruits and sweets with purple yam, *mongo*, caramelized coconut meat, sweetened preserved chickpeas and *langka* for making *halu-halu*, a plastic bag of *chicharon* pig rinds, preserved *tapa* meat, endless stacks of canned baby corn, jackfruit, chestnuts, quail eggs, and bags of different noodles of varied texture, color, and thickness. To an untrained eye and palate, Aurora's kitchen evoked a thousand and one senses that Pearl was beginning to explore.

Pearl lined up things she would need. While the ox tail boiled to soften inside the pressure cooker, she gathered the mortar and pestle to grind freshly roasted peanuts. She rinsed a couple eggplants and sliced them into healthy cubes. She washed and separated the leaves of green leafy *bok choy* cabbage and rinsed green string beans with cold running water. She had watched Aurora cook *kare-kare* before, though this would be her first time to do it alone.

Done, Pearl set the table for two. She placed the steaming jasmine rice and *kare-kare* at the table and generous amounts of shrimp *bagoong* sauce in a tiny saucer for herself and her dad for seasoning.

The door leading to the garage opened. It was Red in his work clothes, oily and dirty. His blond hair was unruly from a previous restless night.

"Hi, Dad. I thought you were still in bed."

"Been up since six." Red's voice was light, not a trace of last night's dark mood with Aurora's overseas call. "The car needs some tuning." His eyes rested on the table.

"Your favorite, Dad."

Everything seemed perfect so far.

"So you've been up early yourself." Red chuckled and nodded his head. "Why don't you go ahead, Pearl. Dad will need to freshen up quick."

Pearl's chest heaved with pride. Though this was her first try at *kare-kare*, she was confident it tasted just like her mother's. She had followed everything Aurora had hammered into her head to the letter.

Dad should be done freshening up soon.

He was usually quick to freshen up. And just perfect, *kare-kare* was best served piping hot. It took her dad a while, though. Red reeked of cologne. His ironed plaid shirt was neatly tucked into his jeans with his curly hair combed sleek when he joined her. Pearl felt disappointed. The steamy rice was already lukewarm rather than hot. The fat from *kare-kare* was beginning to settle and solidify.

"It's fine, Pearl." Red stopped Pearl in her tracks when she stood up to warm the food. He quickly filled his plate with a tiny piece of meat and small serving of rice. He didn't season it with shrimp sauce as he used to. He didn't even bother to sit. He returned his daughter's long, inquisitive gaze. "Don't mind me. Keep eating."

"I am, Dad. You're the one who must be hungry."

Red sported his signature lopsided smile, a deep reddening of his cheeks like a child caught in a lie. Regaining composure, he finished his plate, eating voraciously. His plate was empty in no time. The trace of his mischievous smile lingered.

Encouraged by Red's apparent gusto, Pearl pushed the bowl of *kare-kare* toward her dad. She laughed.

"That was good, Pearl." Red pushed the dish away from him, patting his tummy. "Excellent."

Pearl stopped laughing. Her father didn't like her cooking after all. The frustration that crossed her face faded fast. Her mother had always pointed out never to show defeat easily, but to subtly ask what needs to be improved.

"Was it too watery, Dad? Perhaps a few more drops of fish sauce? Does it need more *achute* for color? Too bland perhaps?"

But Red had already put on his spring jacket, raring to leave. "It's perfect, Pearl. I've got to go."

"It's the weekend, Dad."

"I'm meeting somebody." His voice was impatient. "Don't wait for me."

He took big strides toward the door to the garage. He hesitated briefly and turned around to wink at his daughter. He gave her another quick smile. "Pearl, it's as good as Aurora's."

Father's conciliatory gesture, Pearl thought. Her dad always had a healthy appetite. Always. If her *kare-kare* was really that good, he would have eaten more.

Missing a chance to borrow the car for the weekend added to her disappointment. It rained most of the day. She called some friends to come over. Nobody could make it. Bored, she turned on the radio.

"On continuing development, President Carter announced today . . ."

She flipped to her music station. It was playing one of The Carpenters' latest hits, "A Kind of Hush." She lip-synched to the music.

"I'm going down south to Louisiana tonight.

Well, I'll just close my eyes. And everything's all right.

And though I'm really far away, I'll make my getaway.

And no one really know that's I've been gone.

One more time for the good times that far outweigh the bad.

One more time for the good times when love was all we had."

When she got tired of listening and lip-synching, she turned on the TV. She was hoping it was Wednesday so she could watch her favorite angel, Farrah Fawcett of *Charlie's Angels*.

She must have fallen asleep. Darkness covered her room. Somebody had turned off the TV. The bedside clock's long hand pointed at ten past nine. Her dad must be home.

Noises were coming from her parents' bedroom. Her dad must be talking to her mother. There was no shouting. There were no raised voices. In fact, her dad was laughing animatedly.

When the clock pointed at ten with no sign of her dad coming out of the bedroom, she left her room. Her stomach growled from hunger pangs. Her parents had one unwritten rule. She was not to bother them if the bedroom door were closed. She broke the rule. It took her a few minutes to get used to the darkness but only seconds to hear the sounds of the unhooked phone dangling from her dad's hands competing with his loud snore. She placed the unhooked phone back.

Pearl ate dinner alone, heating the still generous amount of leftover *kare-kare* and some rice. It was nearly midnight when she woke up to the phone's incessant ringing.

It was Aurora. "Have you been on the phone for hours?" She sounded annoyed.

"No, Mother."

Who was with Dad on the phone?

"Where's your dad?"

"I'll wake him up. How's Nanay?"

"Same." Her mother sounded tired. This time, Aurora waived the usual ritual of talking to her first. "Get your dad. And hurry up, Amber Pearl."

Pearl tiptoed going to her parents' bedroom. She wanted to imagine this was not happening. She wished that her mother would hang up when her dad picked up the phone. She wished that it was all a dream.

Cold water doused her, and she realized that she was already standing beside her parents' bed. Her dad was sleeping soundly. She could picture Red's irritated gaze and snarl upon being awakened.

And he was indeed in a sour mood when Pearl woke him up. He growled with displeasure from being disturbed from his sleep. Rancid breath mixed with alcohol permeated the air.

"It's Mother."

Red nodded and waved her away. It was not long before his voice reverberated from the room. Her parents were quarreling, no doubt about it. She reached for the pillow and buried her head to drown the angry voices.

What happened to my quiet and gentle dad? When is Mother coming home? Why can't Nanay just die so things will be just like before?

She hastily made the sign of the cross to purge evil thoughts that crossed her mind, just like her mother would do.

Red began to come home late as a routine not long after. He began to spend animated hours on the phone with a mysterious person. Suspiciously, the line would get disconnected when Pearl answered his calls.

One unguarded moment, Pearl heard a woman's voice. "Red?" Realizing it was not him, the caller hung up. Pearl shut her eyes to vanish thoughts brewing in her mind.

Pearl, fearful of her discovery, would toil in the kitchen whenever time permitted. Whether it was a false hope the ritual could help patch things up between her parents, bury the truth in front of her, or take her mind somewhere else, she had no answer. Regardless, the kitchen, which used to be her mother's tiny kingdom, was hers now. It became the hubbub of her frenzied activity.

There would be the incessant sound of boiling water with chopping of freshly washed string beans, banana hearts cut crosswise, and cubed eggplants with a razor-sharp knife. Adept fingers painstakingly peeled paper-thin skin of still-warm roasted peanuts. She ran water to wash the rice grains she was preparing to complement the main dish. There was the muffled sound of the marble pestle crushing the just-peeled roasted peanuts she had chosen to thicken the sauce of powdered rice. She was perfecting her *kare-kare*.

Another time, she tried preparing *ukoy*, shrimp fritters that were also a favorite snack or starter by her father. At times, her dad would eat it with rice just like a main dish. She would start placing several whole shrimps in a pan with water to boil and then simmer until the shrimps were pink and tender.

She would discard the head and body shell, leaving the tails on. While the shrimps were cooling, she would prepare the dipping sauce with garlic clove, vinegar, salt to taste, and tiny fresh red chili. She would then sift the all-purpose flour and add baking powder and salt in a bowl. She would add beaten egg and cups of shrimp stock to make a batter with the consistency of thick cream. She would then add peeled and grated sweet potatoes to the batter, stirring in crushed garlic and drained bean sprouts. With ready heated oil in the frying pan, she would take a generous spoonful of the batter and drop it carefully in the frying pan to form a fritter about the size of large drop scone.

She would make several, and as soon as the fritters had set, she would top each one with the shrimp and a few chopped scallions. Then she'd deep-fry the shrimp fritters again until they were crisp and golden brown. She remembered they were best eaten fresh from the pan, first dipped in piquant sauce. A lot of times, she ended up enjoying them alone. Nevertheless, it was her own world where she orchestrated everything, a twelve-by-sixteen square foot of private domain, a space where she indeed reigned supreme. It was where earth met heaven, the closest she could be to paradise, even if only for a short period of time.

CHAPTER 5

KEEPING THE DEAD COMPANY

It seemed a frivolous task at the beginning, but not for long. After the introduction to the first dozen or so new faces, recalling names plus attached titles to denote their ranks or positions in the family hierarchy, it was a chore to Pearl. She planned to remember the faces with the names by taking note of an interesting facial feature, a distinct mannerism, a timbre of voice, a similarity to a famous person or a cartoon character, or even a peculiar smell.

Kuya meant the oldest son. *Ate* meant the oldest daughter. *Ditse* meant the second-oldest daughter. *Dikong* meant the second-oldest son and so on. These titles denoted respect. They were attached to a person's name. If it were obvious there was only one who held such a title in the family, the title could stand on its own. Or they could be used to address an older authority figure.

One's face blended with another after a dozen or so introductions. Everything then was a blur to Pearl.

"This is *Ate* Julita—Tatay's cousin who is married to Nanay's nephew, *Tito* Oscar."

"Meet *Tiyo* Pilo. *Tiyo* Pilo and Nanay are second-degree cousins. Their parents were distant cousins. Blessed their poor souls. He is really your grandfather-by-cousin. Address him as *Lolo* Pilo, which is more appropriate. *Lolo* means grandpa, if you didn't know."

"Don't you forget *Lola* Inez. She is the widow of Subas, who is Tatay's oldest paternal uncle."

"Pearl, this is Boy. *Tito* Boy. If your mother hasn't told you yet, he introduced your mom and dad."

"And this is Insiang, *Tiyo* Pilo's wife." Insiang offered her right hand to Pearl.

On cue, Pearl bowed while pressing the back of Insiang's hand to her forehead, a sign of respect. She learned to master this when she could barely walk, which pleased Nanay and Tatay, to wide-eyed disbelief and amusement of Oren and Martha.

"This is *Tiyo* Doming, Nanay's only brother."

"Remember *Ate* Julita? These are her children, Ruben and Rebecca."

With innocent and curious eyes of nine and ten, respectively, they gazed at Pearl.

"You should call Pearl *Ate* Pearl. She's older than both of you."

The two children nodded meekly.

The crowd kept growing and kept the room warm in spite of the central AC in full blast. The room's flush appointment was evident in its dark Philippine mahogany wall paneling, the dark leather upholstery of the chairs, oil paintings, and few choice antiques. It was a silent witness to the constant flow of people, where these introductions and family bonding were happening.

The private family quarter had a small kitchen with its marble countertops hidden by potluck goodies. There were endless trays of desserts—tropical fruit salad with pineapple chunks, *kaong* and shredded coconut meat, cubed sea gelatin and leeches, *leche plan*, fried *saba* banana in *lumpia* wrapper, *ginatan*, sweet purple *ube*, and hot foods in pots and platters, some simmering under tiny flames to keep them warm. A constant line was present to get food, some for second helpings. The young women, though, barely filled their plates, not even finishing what they had less they be labeled *gutom* or starving behind their backs.

On a cramped corner, the clicking of ivory slabs mingled with the burst of excitement and occasional laughter from the hastily set up mahjong table. There were occasional hurried shuffling of feet chasing toddlers who had ventured out of the roving eyes of their *yayas* or mothers. A small crowd of males gathered around a pair playing chess.

At the main chapel of the memorial home where Tinay's body lie in state, the silence was more evident. An unending queue passed by the casket. It had a glass top where mourners could view the body, visible from the waist. Except for her visibly thin face, Tinay looked beautiful and dignified even in death. Chairs were lined up beside the foot of the coffin, the nearest one occupied by Mario, visibly shaken and barely acknowledging a condoling handshake, a squeeze, or tap on his shoulder. There were a few times his eyes would light up, and he would respond animatedly to a familiar face.

Beside Mario was Aurora, in black, the color of mourning—black stockings on black pumps with a black veil covering most of her face. The men wore dark pants with white shirts with a black ribbon around one arm or a small one pinned in front of their shirts. A sea of black, deep blues, and grays pervaded the rest, contrasting with the yellows, pinks, oranges, reds, whites, purples from dozens of wreaths, and burning yellow incandescent candelabras guarding the coffin.

Among the row of chairs were two empty spots, the one vacated by Pearl and the other one intended for Red. He was present for a few days but had to return earlier to the States for pressing matters, an alibi met with quizzical eyebrows and a few snide remarks.

Interment wouldn't be until *Ka* Lucia, Nanay's favorite cousin from Canada, who couldn't come until the following week, arrived. Nanay specifically requested *Ka* Lucia's presence at her funeral, a dying person's request that should be heeded.

It would be a sacrilege to leave the deceased unattended during her remaining days on earth, lying in state the whole twenty-four hours as many days as the wake was. It was an excuse for wakes to have card games, *sungka*, mahjong, and the constant flow of food and endless gossiping to keep every living soul awake to keep the dead company.

Pearl, as everyone would imagine, did not find the respite she was looking for in the private quarter reserved for immediate family. Done with introductions, she took refuge on a chair with eyes shut until a pair of hands woke her up to ask if she needed anything.

"You must be starving." A friendly face who was recently introduced was peering down at her. Pearl could not recall her name. "You need to eat, *hija*."

"Need you ask?" A well-meaning voice seconded. "Here, give this to Pearl."

Then as one gave her a plate so she could eat, just as many hands were shoving food on her plate or offering drinks. Some looked eager to start a conversation with her, their so-called Stateside relative, a privilege to be associated with. A few threw shy glances at Pearl and kept a respectable distance.

Pearl's headache seemed to escalate. She stood up, leaving her plate untouched to the dismay of many.

"Poor soul," said one.

"Somebody save her food." Another pointed out. "She can eat it later."

As Pearl walked back to the main chapel to claim her seat, a tall, heavyset man in a priest's habit appeared.

"Father Francisco." Aurora wailed, rushing to meet him.

Heads uniformly turned in his direction. Aurora and Father Francisco embraced. They whispered to one another, finding solace in each other's words. Arms locked around each other's waist, they walked toward the coffin.

Aurora introduced her daughter to the priest. Father Francisco bent inquisitively. His face was as close as possible to Pearl who was sitting. His eyes burned with excitement. A pair of glasses teetered on his aquiline nose. Tiny lips quivered ever so slightly as his exquisitely tiny hands caressed Pearl's forehead, her hair, and then her forearm with awe and inexplicable adulation. His hand rested on hers.

"You are Pearl, Amber Pearl," Father Francisco said slowly, sounding disbelief and savoring the encounter. "Beautiful girl, like your mother, like Kristina." He always addressed Tinay by her full name. He paused to swallow. His eyes began to glaze. "Aurora, bring her along every time you visit. Please . . ."

Pearl remained quiet. She didn't know the priest, though she had heard his name a lot. There was a tug on her arm as Aurora pulled the priest away to ease the flow of crowd. Pearl's eyes followed the priest. She noticed his limp as Aurora helped steady his steps.

Mario's eyes narrowed for a brief moment at the sight of the priest. When Tinay was alive, he put up with appearances. He was polite, even cordial, to the priest. At this time, there was no reason for Mario to pretend. He crossed his arms to his chest, ignoring Father Francisco's handshake. An awkward silence followed. Pearl saw fire in her grandfather's eyes.

"Mario, Mario," the priest kept mumbling, shaking his head. His shoulders were hunched in defeat as he inched toward the casket, dragging a leg.

*   *   *

The sky burned while the funeral procession snaked on the narrow, winding road. Local businesses flanked the road on both sides. Several flower shops had samples of their trade spilling on the sidewalk. There were fresh flowers in tiered wooden stands, some potted and some soaked in giant pails and clear vases while display windows showed them in tall, woven rattan baskets. Some were shaped like a cross. There were round wreaths, harps, G-clefts, and open Bibles. There was a couple of card shops, a photo studio, and some clothing stores with colorful displays of bales of clothing materials. Their pungent preservatives contrasted with the aroma of fresh and not so fresh flowers from the nearby flower shops. There was a magazine stand with protective awnings for customers who were squeezed in rows of narrow *bangko* benches. The mostly juvenile customers were engrossed, reading the latest editions of comic magazines available to rent for a few cents. There were some *karinderya* food stalls, where everyone could savor hot viands like fish balls, *pansit* noodles, hot soups, rice porridge, pork blood with its meat, and desserts like rice cakes, chilled *kaong* with gelatin, *sapin-sapin*, *palitao* sprinkled with sugar and coconut, *halu-halu* with grated ice and a scoop of ice cream on top, and, for a few extra cents, a preserved cherry on top. There was fresh *buko* with its top sliced clean for a straw to savor its sweet coconut juice.

A lanky Chinese man was peddling *sago*, balancing metal cylinders on both ends with a bamboo pole on one shoulder. One metal cylinder was divided into compartments, the milky white gelatinous *sago* on one and golden syrupy liquid on the other for flavoring. The other metal cylinder contained the disposable bowls and utensils.

Some oglers on the sidewalk strained their necks to see the funeral procession that was purposely inching slowly to the plaintive tunes of the "Lord's Prayer," "I Believe," and "Ave Maria" alternately blaring in the air. Others went about their business, too busy to be bothered. Traffic halted to a standstill to allow the procession to pass through. Strangers' cars, buses, and colorful jeepneys slowed down to show respect to the deceased.

The clear sky began to turn gray as the hearse approached the cemetery. Gusts of wind blew the dried leaves from mango, towering acacia, guava trees, and delicate tamarind trees. The pine trees that dotted the landscape rained dried needles and cones. The tent's awning in front of the family plot fluttered fervently in the wind to signal a summer storm.

The casket was lowered from the hearse, placed under the tent, and opened for one final look at the deceased while a priest officiated the last rites. A few sobs broke the silence of the attentive crowd. When this was over, the coffin was finally sealed. Subdued sobbing gave way to wails and public display of despair among the women while the men stood stoic. Mario's lips were shut tight. Dark glasses hid the anguish in his eyes while he stood ramrod stiff.

On cue, small children related to the deceased were lined up along the sides of the coffin and lifted and then handed to waiting hands at opposite sides. Some say this was done to appease the dead and keep them from wandering the world of the living. Others say it was a sign of respect. A few of the children wailed in fear. Regardless, it was a tradition that was carried on.

Flowers and fistfuls of earth were thrown on the casket as the open earth gradually swallowed it. Suddenly, the sky poured. The deafening sound of rain drowned the sobbing. Dark umbrellas uniformly blossomed, sheltering the mourners, while some skittered like lost souls, reaching the sanctuary of their cars. But no one left. They waited patiently inside their cars while the rest braved the rain pounding on their umbrellas, huddling beside the pit under the tent until the gravediggers were done.

Only then did the parade of cars and limousines begin to inch out of the cemetery ground, gathering speed as they exited. The last one to leave carried Mario, Aurora, and Pearl.

The sky remained gray. Still shadows of angels, crosses, saints guarding tombstones, family mausoleums, and billowing silhouettes of trees shrouded the cemetery. In the adjacent Chinese cemetery, brightly colored minarets, pagodas, and dozens of ornate mausoleums as big as small cottages complete with private quarters were silent witnesses to their newest tenant.

Pearl wiped the moisture clouding her side window with a bare hand. Instinctively, she glanced back at Nanay's resting place. Lightning illumined the sky. The deafening thunder followed close. In that split second, Pearl saw the outline of a solitary figure under cover of a mango tree not far from the freshly covered grave.

Pearl shut her eyes. She was tired and imagining things. Her breathing soon relaxed. Her soft snore drowned the hum of the car's air-conditioning.

But Pearl was not imagining things. Indeed, under the cover of an umbrella, a grieving soul chose to remain hidden by the mango tree, long after the last of the mourners had left.

The man's face gazed blankly into space. Alone, there was no reason to hide sadness. But there were no tears in his eyes as his grief was too deep. His shoulders were bent, his posture stooped, his tiny lips were trembling, and his exquisite hands kneaded and clutched the handle of the umbrella.

It was Father Francisco.

CHAPTER 6

RITES OF COURTSHIP

The noise from the shutting of window curtains woke up Pearl. It was the *mayordoma*, Alma, the head of the Gomez household help. Her bones ached. She would have wanted to stay in bed and hibernate. Yesterday was the last day of Nanay's nine-day Novena prayer for the dead. It was a daily ritual of prayer for the souls of the dead who were undergoing purification in purgatory, that God may forgive all their sins and admit them into his kingdom forever.

"Leave them open, please."

The maid looked flustered. *Why would anyone want the sun to burn one's skin?* Everyone coveted alabaster skin like Pearl's.

"*Opo*," Alma answered as a sign of respect and obedience.

She opened the curtains and then cranked the windows to let in the morning sun. Finished with her task, she walked a few paces backward while slightly bowing her head before rushing toward the door, as if her presence were an intrusion.

"Wait."

Pearl reached for a fruit among the half-dozen or so golden yellow fruits in a bowl by her side table. It piqued her curiosity. She cradled the firm and smooth fruit. She hadn't seen anything that size.

"Mango?"

"Doña Esperanza's help brought them early this morning from their plantation. There's more in the kitchen, *Ate*. It's the best variety, *Kalabao*."

"There's more than one kind of mango?"

"*Opo.*" The maid was amused. She assumed everyone knew. "You want me to peel you one, *Ate?*"

In the kitchen, the pace was frenetic. Juling, the cook, was embarrassed that breakfast was not yet ready. The master's granddaughter could show up any minute, an unforgivable offense. Juling ran out of time preparing baked *pan de sal* and goat cheese snacks for her master's daughter, Aurora, who woke up early but did not want any heavy breakfast, and, of course, the master of the house, Mario, who requested *champorado* with fried *dilis* fish, omelet with *pan de leche* bread, and grated melon with creamy evaporated milk and sugar to taste plus black coffee.

The cook's eyes widened when her fear materialized. *Pearl.* She nervously cleared her throat. "Good morning, *Ate.*"

Pearl ambled lazily, wearing pajamas. "G'morning."

Juling shouted directions to her unseen help at the adjacent room in a dialect from central Luzon, which was alien to Pearl who spoke Tagalog. The cook's double chin and arms wiggled as she pointed her fingers to stress a point. Sweat adorned her forehead. She was livid and needed to vent.

With precision and rapid cadence, Juling diced fresh garlic cloves, sliced Chinese *chorizo*, cut some onions, and cubed some hams. Quickly, she scrambled several brown eggs, frying them in steaming hot oil. With ingredients for the fried rice ready, she scooped with *sandok* leftover cold rice on a platter. She sprinkled some cold water on it, breaking the chunks of rice in smaller pieces with her bare hands. There were crackles as Juling poured the rice in the hot oil left from frying scrambled eggs and then mixing back the rest of the ingredients to cook.

"My apologies, *Ate.*" The cook kept murmuring to Pearl, who did not mind the wait. "*Pasensiya na*, my extreme apology."

The smell of pork oil, onion, Chinese *chorizo*, ham, and garlic permeated the air. Juling wasted no time melting several cakes of cocoa the size of a silver dollar a half-inch thick with fresh *carabao* milk. She added some peanut butter, mixing the thick brown concoction with spiked wooden *batidor*, which she rolled briskly with her palms to thicken the melted chocolate in the bowl. She heated it in a deep pan until done before pouring them in a pitcher.

Pearl was oblivious to her surroundings. She held a ripe mango, pinched the fruit's pointed end, grasped the skin using her thumb and index finger, and worked her way peeling around the slippery skin, forming one continuous curl as the maid had taught her. The exposed fleshy fruit was succulent and smooth, unlike the kind she was used to, which was fibrous and not as near sweet.

"You like *manga, Ate?*" The cook commented while setting the breakfast table. "There's a lot more in the *kaing.*"

The cook pouted her lips toward a large coarsely woven basket lying at the *narra* floor of the immaculate kitchen. The *kaing* was out of place among the marble countertops and hardwood cabinetry with fancy trimmings. Pearl's eyes feasted on dozens of mangoes inside the woven basket.

Soon, Juling brought the fried rice in one hand, a saucer with vinegar and sea salt in the other, setting them on the table in front of Pearl. With lightning-rod stamina, her corpulent body disappeared, swallowed by a door to another room.

There was a quick exchange of staccato voices heard. She was obviously reprimanding someone. The room the cook went to was dark and dingy and smelled of burnt oil and strong food odor. Several pots and pans black with soot hung on the wall in contrast to the gleaming set in the main kitchen. A span of rectangular cement counter occupied the middle of the room. Water was constantly boiling on a cauldron with burning wood providing heat. Several native hens with their shiny brown feathers were cramped in a narrow egg-shaped cage with a top cover, awaiting their fate. A cutting board at one end of the counter had stringy *sitaw* beans waiting to be peeled, washed, and cut into smaller pieces. Morsels of *mongo* beans were soaking in a vessel of water. Stalks of cabbage lie waiting to be rinsed, boiled, or diced. Several fresh leaves of banana were on the table. A butchered pig hung by an iron peg to drain its blood. The floor of this cramped rectangular room was bare earth.

A juvenile male of fifteen who looked more like twelve was busy fanning red-hot charcoal with a heart-shaped *abaniko*, a woven fan to keep the fire roaring on a grill. Another young girl of ten who looked seven was insisting on handling him an *ihip*, a foot-long metal pipe to fan the flame. Adamant, the young lad kept shooing his younger help to leave him alone to his antics.

Food that could splatter, stain the marble countertops, or emit unusually strong odors were prepped and cooked in this tiny room. The head of the house and his family never even set their feet here. This was the "dirty kitchen."

"Stop bickering and hurry up, you two," Juling hollered. "*Ate* is waiting. Don't embarrass me more."

"*Opo, Manang*," the two help answered in unison.

When Juling came back, one hand held a steaming platter of huge beef sausages smelling of slightly burned caramelized brown sugar. The remaining hand held a dish of fried salted fish.

"*Batutay*!" Pearl exclaimed on seeing the sausages. "I love it."

"Yes, *Ate, batutay.*" The cook's voice rose an octave, proud she had made the right choice. She herself preferred the huge native beef sausage to other kinds.

"Nanay used to bring a lot when she visited," said Pearl. "I love it."

Juling nodded, satisfied and energized. With relish, she poured the thick cocoa drink in a mug. "Be careful, *Ate*. It's very hot." She then excused herself, once more disappearing in the "dirty kitchen."

Pearl feasted her eyes on her breakfast—steaming fried rice, huge golden brown *batutay* sausages, fried *daing* salted fish, vinegar and salt for dipping, and piping hot *tsokolate* to wash them down. She was enjoying her solitude until she noticed she wasn't really alone. Out of the corners of her eyes she could see tiny pairs of hands pulling down some slats of the window blinds. Two pairs of curious eyes ogled her.

The hands vanished when the angry voice of the laundrywoman, Inday, was heard. The *labandera's* voice got loud, distant, and then loud again as she chased in circles the owners of those two sets of eyes, her two young children whose excited and giggly laughs rivaled their mother's angry diatribe.

Inday, the *labandera*, was threatening them with *palu-palu*, a flat slab of wood she used in her trade to remove dirt and squeeze water from soiled clothes. She was using her *palu-palu* to shoo her children and leave Pearl alone. Inday was extremely embarrassed with her unruly children, a girl and a boy of five and six.

Her children took shelter in the adjacent building, the servants' quarters, squealing in shrill voices and enjoying their playful banter with their mother. Exasperated, Inday squatted down in her tiny wooden *bangko* stool to resume her chore, filling her *batya*, a flat, round, metal basin with raised scalloped edges with another batch of dirty clothes to rinse. The *labandera's* eyebrows were furrowed; her forehead was wrinkled from embarrassment. This was not the first.

Her first embarrassing moment happened when Aurora introduced her to Pearl. She was washing dirty clothes just like then. Suddenly, Pearl's eyes rounded, and Pearl's mouth made a high-pitched scream upon seeing the *batya*. It took some explaining to her that Pearl was not making fun of her trade. That would be losing her face. She took pride in her trade as a *labandera*, a washerwoman, no matter how lowly. To Pearl, the *batya* reminded her of a giant soda pop lid that was exactly what it looked like.

"*Santa Maria*, have mercy. Please teach my children some manners," Inday implored loud enough so Pearl could hear her. She'd had her share of embarrassing moments. That was enough.

* * *

The Virgin Mary's sculptured face had a serene look. Tapered fingers and palms were pressed together in perpetual prayer, perched on a boulder surrounded by cascading water. Fresh garlands of jasmine and *sampaguita* routinely replenished and adorned her opposing hands. Her head was bent, guarding the amoeba-shaped, man-made pool facing her. At ten in the morning, the sun began to show its scorching power, casting a warm, luminous sheen to the statue. An undulating wavy pattern of reflected shadow from the pool marked its surface.

Pearl's wet finger traced the length of the Madonna's nose. Its nose was thin. The eyes were deep-set, not unlike Pearl's. It was a likeness of a white woman, unlike the locals.

"Be careful, Pearly!" Aurora shouted. She was with Mario, cooling themselves under the thatched umbrella shade from *nipa* leaves in the shallow end of the pool. "Those rocks could be slippery."

There was a chilled pitcher of fresh *calamansi* juice on the circular table. Boiled *saba* bananas were stacked on a plate, a naturally sweet variety best served by simply boiling them in water and eaten while hot. Juling also prepared gelatinous *palitaw* sprinkled with grated coconut and granulated sugar.

Aurora remained in full mourning clothes. In contrast, Mario wore casual summer clothes with short pants. Unlike the women, he was not expected to wear black, the color of mourning, for a full year upon the demise of a family member.

"Pearl, have some *merienda*." Aurora waved to Pearl. "Have some snacks."

Pearl continued to ignore her mother. She jumped on the pool and threaded the lukewarm water.

"So . . ." Mario cleared his throat to divert Aurora's attention. "The decision was final then."

"*Opo*, Tatay. The divorce is final . . . Last week. Just before we flew here. I had to get Pearl out of school early this May."

"Pearly has an early and extended school vacation then." Mario lightened his voice, failing miserably. He puffed on his cigar. He coughed a long, dry cough. "I know. I know." He looked at Aurora. "I am cutting down on smoking." The cold, sweet, sour *calamansi* juice soothed Mario's parched throat. "Do you have any plans, Auring?" He held his cigar tightly between his index and thumb.

"Do I have any plans?" Aurora repeated to herself. She crinkled her nose.

"Take Pearly to Europe. Forget about the expense. Vacation is good for Pearly. It's a nice break for her." He puffed on his cigar. "After what happened."

"Yes, Tatay." Aurora stared blankly into space. "*Opo.*"

"It's good for you too, Auring. Two, three weeks, a month maybe. That should cool wagging tongues."

"I know what they say behind my back, *biyuda sa buhay*. A widow with a live husband."

"People will talk, Auring. Always."

"It was probably meant to happen, Tatay. As the old folks say, it's my destiny, my *kapalaran*."

"Red was a fool leaving you for that woman, that Mary. That's the woman's name, right? That good-for-nothing husband of yours. *Puñeta.*" Mario cursed in an audible whisper, "That invalid." He had never badmouthed Red until then.

"Mary, she's his wife now, Tatay." Aurora either did not hear or ignored Mario's scathing comment. "They got married right after the divorce was final. Yes. Her name is Mary."

"We don't have divorce here, Auring. You're still his wife. He's still your husband. You're just separated."

Aurora smiled with bitterness. Neither Red nor his family saw things their way. She imagined Oren and Martha referring to her as their ex-daughter-in law, somewhere from the Pacific, which was farthest from the truth.

Aurora imagined Red's older sister asking, "Is there anything to do if we visit your place, Aurora?" Or Red's younger one could ask, "Do you have running water and electricity?"

All those years she had been reticent and quiet to all those comments. She realized silence was probably taken as the truth. Aunt Millie crossed her mind. This time, bitterness faded from her smile.

She could see Aunt Millie bursting through the front door unannounced, her bathrobe flapping in the air and her breathing labored as the woman took giant steps to reach her at the top of the stair. Aunt Millie was alone.

Aurora expected a lanky man to appear behind the door.

"I heard the news, Aurora."

Aunt Millie was not wearing any makeup or painted eyebrows. Without them, she looked more human. "How are you?"

For the first time, Aurora did not hear continued chatter from the woman. She saw a faint trace of moustache and a few stubbles on the woman's chin. Aunt Millie was older than what she wanted to admit. A lot older.

Aunt Millie grabbed her hand, and it stayed there. "It must hurt. Don't talk if you don't want to. I know it must hurt."

Aunt Millie suddenly embraced her tightly. Her shoulders began to shake violently. Aunt Millie's bony hands caressed her back.

"I've been married to your Uncle Larry for so long that I take him for granted. I know, if something happens to him, I would be devastated. So I know how it must have felt."

The front door remained open, but there was no Uncle Larry coming in from the cold. His temporary absence felt odd. Aunt Millie always had her husband by her side.

"Uncle Larry?" Aunt Millie said, noticing her eyes riveted on the front door. "You can't rush the man. He has to make sure his toupee is set just right. I'll say you said hi." The woman began to dry Aurora's cheeks, patting them with a tissue.

"How is she handling it?" Mario's voice broke Aurora's reminiscing.

Mario was gazing at Pearl who was waving vigorously at them.

"She saw her dad before we flew home."

"That's good." Mario puffed his cigar. He inhaled and took some deep breaths to savor its aroma. "I can't believe it's almost a year now since Nanay died. In a week's time, Auring, you can again wear colors other than black."

"Yes, Tatay. I'll be done. I'll have my *babang luksa*, my end of mourning."

"Wouldn't it be nice? Worse time to wear black, summer."

"Stifling, Tatay."

"Have you started making phone calls yet, Auring?"

"*Opo*, Tatay." Aurora reminded herself to personally call on her *Tiyo* Doming, Nanay's only brother. He felt slighted being left out to a family affair and could still be holding a grudge. "Is there anything you want Juling to prepare for the *babang luksa* gathering?"

"That's a woman's job. You do that. Make sure you don't leave out anyone."

"I'll make sure the whole family is reminded of Nanay's first death anniversary." She should also place an order for *embotido* and *pansit luglog* for the occasion. She wondered if she should also have a whole roasted pig, *lechon*. She had already told Juling what to cook.

"I don't want the same thing happening, Auring."

"*Opo*, Tatay. I'll make sure." Aurora again made a mental note about *Tiyo* Doming.

"Reminds me. There's a good show at the Cultural Center. I got tickets for three tonight." Mario pulled the tickets from his wallet. "Nice way to end the evening and cool ourselves."

Aurora's eyebrows knitted. *Tatay in a concert, a ballet, or a musical?* She recalled Nanay elbowing Tatay as he started to snore in the middle of a show. He went to these events to please Nanay. He must have bought the tickets for similar reason.

Printed on the tickets was the musical *The King and I.*

"I heard it is good," Mario said. "And Anna will be played by . . ." He hesitated. "A Baby . . . Baby something."

"Baby Barredo. She's good. I have seen her."

At the Philippine Cultural Center's main theater, Aurora, Mario, and Pearl were seated in a coveted section. Pearl was all eyes and ears. Mario, in contrast, was caught yawning by the two women on several occasions.

During intermission, Pearl noted an elderly woman in expensive finery rushing toward them.

"Doña Esperanza," Mario said, gushing. "It's nice to see you. And thank you again. Thank you for the tickets. We are enjoying the show. Very much."

"Please drop the Doña. Don't we know each other? Doña is reserved for acquaintance. I kept looking your way, but you all seemed engrossed with the play. Didn't I tell you Baby Barredo is heavenly?" The woman kept eyeing Pearl. "My daughter Techie went to school with her."

Mario nodded. If she were looking their way, she must have seen him nodding his head, falling asleep. He wasn't following the play, much less listening to the music.

The woman approached and offered her cheek to Aurora. "Hi, *hija, kumusta?*"

"*Tita* Espe." Aurora returned the greeting, holding the woman's hands.

"Anna is really good." Pearl pointed out. "This Baby Barredo."

"Of course, but of course," Doña Esperanza uttered. "I couldn't agree more." Doña Esperanza kept looking at Pearl as if to size her up. Then her lips widened in a broad smile. She waved her hand, recognizing a familiar face. "That's Fe Panlilio, my jeweler. It seems everybody who's somebody is here tonight. And may I know who is this young lady?" She lingered her eyes on Amber Pearl.

"My daughter, Amber Pearl. We call her Pearl or Pearly. She's visiting."

"*Muy bella.* Beautiful girl. I saw her a while ago at Tinay's wake, but we've never been properly introduced. You've grown more beautiful than the last time I saw you, *hija.*" Doña Esperanza dabbed her cheek lightly on Pearl's. "Mario, keep an eye on her. She'll make a lot of men swoon." She looked at Aurora. "Auring, you've got yourself some stiff competition."

"Care for a drink, ladies?" Mario asked.

Mario got their drinks while the three women continued with their idle talk. Soon the lights dimmed a few times to signal it was time for the crowd to return to their seats.

The following morning, Pearl woke up to a basket of exotic fruits on the breakfast table delivered by Doña Esperanza's personal driver. Pearl was curious. First, there was the fresh mangoes, then the complimentary tickets to *The King and I*, and now this fruit basket.

"She's very generous, must be a very good family friend." Pearl's eyes feasted at the colorful fruits in front of them. She grabbed a yellow fruit shaped like an upside down cup holding its precious nut on top.

"That's cashew fruit. You can eat the fruit. Be careful, it stains." Aurora said. "Let Juling crack the shell of the nut. The shells are very caustic and stings."

"Must be the reason cashew nuts are expensive." Pearl said.

"We know Esperanza from way back," Mario answered with bemused smile. He grabbed a *makopa*, a pinkish-red bell-shaped fruit and placed it on Pearl's plate. "Your mom craved this when she was pregnant with you. I used to play golf with her husband when he was alive. They had two children. Pepito died when he was in his teens, a drowning accident. Techie, the daughter, is married to a scion of the Romualdez family, the political dynasty. Esperanza married into the Lopez family. Sugar barons. Owns thousands of hectare of land to sugar. I believe Techie has a son."

Mario paused to grab one *makopa* and took a bite. "Crunchy, isn't it? I haven't met the young man."

"You did, Tatay," Aurora said. "He was with Techie at Nanay's wake. Nice man. Law student. Ateneo, I heard."

"My alma mater." Mario chuckled with pride. "Hmmm."

Pearl busied herself examining the goodies. So far she liked what she had tasted. She eyed the torpedo-shaped green fruit called *balimbing*. She planned on tasting it when she was done with the *makopa*.

"Too bad *lansones* is out of season," Aurora said.

"I think *lansones* is in season around August or September," Mario said.

"What's that?"

"You'll like it, Pearly. It looks just like a cluster of grapes, except it's translucent pale yellow with thick skin," Mario explained.

"You eat it like grapes?"

"Not exactly. The skin is inedible. You peel each fruit. Inside, it's divided into sections like orange or grapefruit." Aurora explained.

"Really?"

"Each section has a seed though," Aurora said.

"Must be time-consuming to eat."

A maid interrupted their talk. "Phone call, *Manong.*" She handed the phone to Mario.

"Esperanza!" Mario exclaimed. "We were just talking about you." He paused. "Of course, and what's the occasion? Are you sure you don't want us to bring anything?" He nodded every once in a while. "I still know the way. We'll be there. I'll let them know. And thank you." He covered the receiver. "Pearl, it's Esperanza." But Pearl's mouth was full. "Pearl said thank you for the fruits. Yes, she's tasting them right now." Mario laughed. He gave the phone back to the maid.

"Esperanza is inviting us for an overnight stay at their beach house the following weekend. A get-together with her family and old friends. Good thing it doesn't fall on Nanay's anniversary. It's been a few years since we've been to their vacation home. Her husband's been dead a good many years. Come to think, she hasn't been in touch until lately. What could she be up to?" He threw a meaningful glance at Pearl.

Aurora did the same, though Pearl failed to notice.

"She's a widow, isn't she?" Pearl winked at her grandpa.

"*Puñeta.*" Mario laughed. "She's at least ten years my senior. Nanay would be turning in her grave."

"She looks young." Pearl teased.

"With some help," Mario said. "Lots of help."

"Tatay . . ." Aurora called her father's attention.

"All right." Mario motioned, zipping his lips. He stood up and disappeared from the room. The sound of his laughter faded. "Auring, you need to do some explaining to your daughter."

"What did he mean by that?"

"We don't think she is interested in Tatay. She's trying to get into our family's good graces. *Nanunuyo*, in other words," Aurora said nonchalantly, playfully rolling her eyes.

"I don't understand."

"She's courting the family. As I said, getting into the family's good graces. We call that *panunuyo*."

"Why would she do that?"

"Exactly what you need to know. It's not uncommon for a family matriarch or patriarch to eye somebody for his or her unmarried son, daughter, or grandchild. Any elderly family member can do the matching."

"Matchmaker." Pearl corrected. "She's eyeing me for . . ."

"Yes. And it involves the whole family, especially if they like you."

"Like a family courtship."

"Yes."

"And who is she matching me with?"

"You heard Techie has a son. I think she likes you for her *unikong apo*."

"What does that mean?"

"Her one and only precious grandson."

"I don't even know him."

"Not yet. You will."

"I get it. She is setting me up to meet her grandson at the beach house."

"Yes."

"And if I don't go?"

"If I were you, I would. As your father would say, go for the ride. You will love it. You will enjoy being the object of *panunuyo*."

Pearl looked at her mother. Aurora responded with an amused smile.

*   *   *

The beach house was a sprawling bungalow facing the open sea with its fine white sand. Cars were parked knee-deep. The revelry punctuated by laughter contrasted with the gentle touch of a cool sea breeze. Towering coconut trees guarded its periphery to keep unwelcome guests at bay. Its wide veranda faced the serene sea. Fresh banana leaves covered several rows of banquet tablets that occupied the center of the balcony. They were crowded with food served on wooden platters and trays and *palayok* potteries to keep them hot. There were fried tilapia, catfish, and stuffed milkfish in huge platters, side by side with pickled *atsara*, this time from preserved green mangoes in vinegar. Sliced ripe golden mangoes contrasting with unripe ones were displayed side by side on a round platter. Cooked *bagoong* shrimp sauce generously filled a deep *mangkok* container. The smell of female crabs harvested from private farms with their prized *aligue* eggs sifted in the air. There were golden *sugpo* shrimps and a steaming pot of mussel soup. A huge pot was laden with beef soup with generous cuts of meat and vegetables. Another pot had blood soup mixed with sliced pork. It sat side by side with another pot of chicken *tinola*. There were rows and rows of fried squid competing with barbecued pork and shrimp on bamboo skewers, plus a plate of pork and chicken *adobo*. The scattered *palayok* had *arroz caldo*, chicken *menudo*, *kare-kare*, *sinigang na baboy*, and *sinigang na hipon*. Wooden bowls were placed beside each *palayok* for filling one's portion.

Flown from Mindanao plantation for the occasion were freshly harvested pineapples. There was a pitcher of *sago* with its sweet brown syrup on a huge bowl. There was gelatinous rice with chunks of pork individually wrapped in pyramid-shaped *pandan* leaves. A flat, round wooden dish had purple yam sliced in square serving portions, each one with a granular mound of fried coconut drippings in the center. In addition, there were other sweets and desserts, such as *leche plan*, several varieties of suman, *palitaw* sprinkled with sugar and shredded coconut, *ginatang mais*, and *ginatang halu-halu*. The choices seemed endless.

Two costumed help wearing *patadyong* served refreshments from a miniature *nipa* hut. Bottled Coke, Pepsi, Royal Tru-Orange, Mirinda, 7UP, and San Miguel beer filled huge tubs. A table inside the *nipa* hut was studied with stacks of fresh coconuts, each one ready to be sliced open by a male servant, served with straw to savor its sweet, cold juice. For the daring and a homage to the southern roots of her late husband, Doña Esperanza had a male help wear an embroidered *barong tagalog* paired with dark pants. Roped on the man's shoulder was a long bamboo trunk that contained *tuba*, a potent wine from coconut tree.

A group of male servants wearing *camisa de chino* paired with tight, colorful, knee-high pants were busy with roasting *lechon* on a bamboo skewer over a charcoal pit in the open air. The pig's natural oil crackled as it dropped on the glowing pit. A servant religiously rubbed a clean cotton rug soaked with drippings to baste the pig's skin.

A group of young men and women wearing traditional costumes of *patadyong*, *baro at saya*, and *barong tagalog* were serenading guests with *banduria*, an indigenous string instrument. A pair of greeters presented *sampaguita* garlands to arriving guests. Colorful rows of triangular buntings hung between bamboo poles. The summer place was transformed into a venue for a town fiesta.

As guests mingled, their laughter punctuated the din and festive atmosphere. The men wore mostly short-sleeved colorful or embroidered polos with matching shorts. The women were adorned in *patadyong* (Filipino kimono) and *baro at saya* with *panuelo* (the *saya* skirt knee or mid knee in length in deference to the hot weather). Some women wore either *salakot* or straw hats to protect their skin from the cruel sun.

The latest hits from Sylvia La Torre, Yolanda Guevarra, Mabuhay Singers, and Ruben Tagalog occupied the air in keeping with the barrio fiesta motif. Of course, there was Pilita Corrales's own Tagalog record of *kundiman* ballads that was just released. The famous chanteuse, she was Doña Esperanza's personal favorite.

Some women brought *abaniko* fans to ward off the stifling heat. Others brought half-moon-shaped fans with painted sceneries or flowers. Some brought accordion-like Chinese paper fans that metamorphosed into perfect circles once opened. The younger maidens protected their delicate *kayumanging kaligatan* complexion by taking refuge under thatched umbrellas perched and randomly scattered in the surrounding property, shielding round, wooden tables with anchored *bangko* chairs. Quite a few swam the warm, crystal-clear, placid water while some chose to swim in the saltwater swimming pool. Not all women wore bathing suits. Afraid they may be revealing too much, they donned sleeved T-shirts over their underwear and shorts, shielding their bodies with their arms. Some children freely roamed to the consternation of their *yayas* and overprotective parents and grandparents.

"Lina, tell your children to behave. It's embarrassing to the hosts," an elderly male said, reminding his daughter.

"Petra, give my grandson a towel. He might catch a cold," a woman said to her maid.

Pearl, Mario, and Aurora all came in casual attire. They were never told to wear a costume. On their neck were *sampaguita* garlands from the greeters.

Doña Esperanza was smiling from ear to ear upon seeing Pearl. She wore a native dress like everyone else. "*Hija*, I'm so glad you made it. Auring . . . Mario . . . please, make yourselves comfortable." She pouted her lips, waving an arm dismissively about Mario's and Aurora's uneasiness with their attire. "You're both fine. I didn't want you to bother."

"Doña Esperanza, thank you for the invitation." Pearl dabbed her cheek to Doña Esperanza, who offered hers.

"Call me *Tita*, short for aunt."

"Yes, *Tita* Esperanza, what a lovely place you have."

"*Salamat*." Doña Esperanza expected that Pearl understood. She led her to the veranda and introduced Pearl to the guests.

Meanwhile, Mario and Aurora conveniently disappeared.

"There's so much food, *Tita* Esperanza."

"There's more coming, *hija*. I ordered some *pansit palabok* noodles and *bibingka* desserts. I know they are your favorite."

Pearl smiled. "Yes, they are." Her mother must have told Doña Esperanza.

"We have some Magnolia ice cream. There's mango, your favorite. Try their *durian*. You'll like it. They don't smell like the fresh fruit. There's *makapuno*, and you should try their *mangoosteen*."

"I will, *Tita* Esperanza." Pearl glanced toward the roasting pig at a distance. "Actually, I'm waiting for the roasted pig's skin."

"I'm impressed. You're right. It's the best part of *lechon*."

"Mother introduced me to Filipino food."

"I can see that. Look who's coming."

A slim woman in an elegant *patadyong* with *alampay* on one shoulder came smiling toward them. Her hair was pulled in a tight bun, and bejeweled *payneta* held them in place.

"My daughter, Techie."

After the brief introduction, Doña Esperanza cornered her daughter. Unintelligible whispers were momentarily heard.

"He's here somewhere," Techie responded.

The *rondalya* started playing to signal a new group of visitors had arrived.

Doña Esperanza excused herself. "*Hija*, please feel at home. Techie, take care of Pearl."

"Don't worry, Mama. I will."

Doña Esperanza disappeared to meet the new arrivals. Techie grabbed Pearl's hand and led her inside the main house, which was empty of visitors.

"It's noisy and hot outside." Techie motioned Pearl to sit on a cushioned rattan set. "It's a lot cooler here."

Pearl preferred the sun, the crowd, and the natural breeze to the air-conditioned quarters. Recalling Aurora's reminder it was rude to contradict the host, she nodded. She would speak her mind if she were with her friends.

"Is there anything you'd like?" Techie's smile never left her unlined face. She remained standing with her back pulled up straight. The aura of confidence was stamped all over her like anyone born with old money.

"Roasted pork skin."

Techie laughed. "You know your *lechon*. I think I know what else you'll like. I'll get you a drink too, *hija*. Fresh *buko* juice okay?" Techie turned toward the sliding door.

Left alone, Pearl could see the crowd through the sliding glass. The crowd continued to swell. She couldn't eye either Aurora or Mario.

The inside was bathed in the afterglow of the early-afternoon sun. Original Fernando Amorsolo and Carlos Francisco paintings adorned the varnished native *narra* mahogany wall paneling, which came alive from the sun's reflections. The pink marble floor from the island of Romblon cast a natural hue to the painted human figures. Wide sliding rectangular window frames on low windowsills filtered the light through tiny squared grids of luminous *capiz* shells.

Pearl was admiring an intricately curved three-paneled wooden screen with semiprecious stones and mother-of-pearl that she didn't notice somebody else had joined her.

"I see you like that."

Startled, Pearl turned her head toward the owner's voice. It was a young man, probably in his midtwenties. He was holding a plate-sized wicker basket lined with wax paper. It was loaded with food. He held a fresh *buko* in a tall glass in the other hand.

"Did you see the food? It's supposed to be an ordinary gathering," Pearl said. "Yes, this screen. It is gorgeous. I'm Pearl."

The man nodded with an amused smile on his face. His eyes turned into tiny slits. "I know who you are. I brought you some food."

Pearl accepted them. "Why, thank you." She noticed the air of confidence in him. He was quite tall for a Filipino. She had to gaze up to him. And she was not small.

"I'm P.J.. Techie's my mom."

"Hi." *He was the one.*

"My Grandma Espe keeps telling me about you. I don't remember seeing you at your grandma's funeral. She was right. How could I?"

"Espe?" She did not recall seeing him either.

"*Lola* Espe. Grandma Espe. Espe for Esperanza. You're not familiar with local nicknames."

"Not really."

"You'll learn." He grabbed back her food and drink and signaled her to sit. "Here." He laid the basket and glass of *buko* on the coffee table. "This way you're more comfortable." He sat opposite her.

"You're here on vacation?" P.J. rested his head on his hands and watched her eat. Pearl saw on him Doña Esperanza's eyes, inquisitive and intense.

"I've been here before."

"How do you like it here?" He smiled, "I know you have. Your grandma's wake, remember?"

"It's hot."

"I'm sure, to you in particular. It's cold here in December. Could get down to . . ." He paused. "I should remember. You use centigrade in the States. That would be in the sixties. Of course, we turn on the fireplace."

Pearl's amused smile did not escape P.J.. She, too, noticed his wide forehead, high cheekbones, pouty lips, ink black hair, and Oriental nose.

"It's warm to you. For us, it's cold."

"Yes, it's relative."

"You look young."

"I'll be a senior at St. Mary's High back home this fall."

"You are young. I go to Ateneo. Law. Two more years left."

There was pride in the timbre of his voice. P.J.'s eyes dimmed when Pearl did not register recognition. "It's a private school. Very expensive. And if you care to know, I am the captain of the school's basketball team." His eyes resumed its brilliance. "And may I ask what do you want to be?"

"I haven't thought about that. I'm not sure I want to go to college." She wrinkled her nose, annoyed.

P.J.'s one eyebrow arched, forming an inverted V. "A full-time housewife. A lawyer. Perfect. You have wide hips, perfect for bearing children."

"Excuse me?"

P.J. ignored her. He motioned her to keep eating. A rush of blood warmed Pearl's face. She could feel his penetrating gaze. She began to doubt whether she would enjoy this ritual called *panunuyo*. She was nearly tempted to tell him to stop gawking at her. It seemed forever before P.J. stood up to leave without saying a word. Relieved, she resumed eating, this time uninhibited.

The solitude was short-lived. The sound of the sliding door opening and closing caught her attention.

It was P.J. with both hands full like before. "I'm back."

In his tow was a uniformed maid carrying a huge tray of food. She didn't answer and continued to eat. And she thought her silence made the point clear to him.

The maid and P.J. laid a feast on the table. It was more crunchy *lechon* skin with a bowl of thick brown sauce to boot, a plate of *leche plan*, a mug of iced *sago*, a heaping bowl of pork and chicken *adobo*, some *menudo*, a steaming bowl of rice, and several scoops of mango ice cream. Plus another platter of her favorite *pansit palabok* and hot *bibingka* with a sprinkling of shredded coconut and goat cheese.

P.J. cocked his head to signal the maid to leave. "Eat some more. You're too thin." He scooped some *pansit palabok* to put on her plate.

"Stop. I can't eat all of this."

"Yes, you can."

"Why don't you?"

"Excellent idea. I'll get an extra plate. We can eat together. It'll only take me a minute."

P.J. vanished. Pearl hurriedly grabbed seconds on her plate. Taking the plate with her, she joined and mingled with the crowd, feeling relief.

Soon darkness set. The sea breeze turned cool. The uniform whoosh of swaying palm leaves competed with the crickets' call, the rhythmic sounds of rising tide, and the buzz of mosquitoes. Several help lit green mosquito coils to arm against mosquito bites. Bamboo lanterns were lit, transforming the place into a glittering gem. The maids began offering colorful *alampay* to serve as blankets to ward off the chill. Several male help arranged rows upon rows of chairs to surround a wooden stage.

Guests started claiming seats as *tambuli* horn blared to announce the beginning of a performance. A dance troupe marched to the stage to the delight of the guests. They started with *pandango sa ilaw,* a dance performed by women balancing votive candles on their heads and palms to lilting music that builds up to a rapid tempo. It was followed by *maglalatik,* an all-male ensemble displaying dexterity with halved coconut shells tied on their half-naked torsos. The men touched the shells in unison with the other halved coconut shells in each hand without missing a beat to frenetic music. Then there was the *sayaw sa bangko* with a pair of dancers performing without losing their balance on top of a narrow wooden bench.

For the finale, there was *tinikling,* named after *tikling,* a thin-legged bird indigenous to the island. It is performed by a pair of dancers crossing back and forth a pair of bamboo poles clashing rhythmically together without their bare feet getting caught. It was a sight Pearl had never seen before.

"There you are." It was Aurora.

"We've been looking for you," Mario said. "Where were you?"

"Are you enjoying yourself, *hija*?" Doña Esperanza sounded worried.

"Yes," Pearl said and meant it. "Aren't they awesome?"

"Yes," Dona Esperanza curtly answered. "Why are you by yourself? I told P.J. to keep you company."

"I'm fine, *Tita* Espe."

Doña Esperanza smiled, pleased. Pearl addressed her by her nickname. A man approached Doña Esperanza to compare notes with her.

"Yes, she is here. Make sure P.J. is here before you begin." Doña Esperanza approached the podium. "May I have your attention, please."

On cue, the band responded by rapid beating of drums ending with a clash of cymbals. The chatter faded. All eyes were on the podium.

"Thank you to everyone for taking the time to join me, Techie, and P.J. . . ." She paused. Her eyes surveyed the crowd. She smiled upon seeing Pearl. "To a special day of friendship and company. We have a special guest with us tonight, and this party is being held in her honor. It is our humble way of making her feel at home, our way of introducing

her to Filipino hospitality, our simple way of saying welcome. *Mabuhay!*"
Doña Esperanza clapped her hands, and the crowd joined her.

Excited silence followed. Pearl was startled when a hand reached
out to her. It was P.J.. Before she could show any resistance and before
anyone could start to be bored, a hissing sound cut through the night.
A spray of stars burst, lighting the sky. Then there was crackling and
booming sounds. More rainbow of colors and a spectacular display of
fireworks followed them. Oohs and aahs were heard.

Pearl felt P.J. squeezing her hand every once in a while. Behind them
were Techie, Aurora, and Mario. Pearl could feel their eyes riveted on
them, guarding their every move, like sentinel guards. More bodies
inched closer toward them to get a better view of the fire show.

The show ended with the letters M-A-B-U-H-A-Y—P-E-A-R-L
painting the sky. Pearl gasped, disbelieving what she had just seen. P.J.
nodded at her and once again squeezed her hand to acknowledge it was
indeed in her honor the party was held. She saw the same look from
Doña Esperanza, who snuck back to the podium. She couldn't hear
what she was saying as the woman began to clap, joined by deafening
applause from the crowd. Plus she was giddy from the unbridled
attention.

"I can't believe it. Why?" She gazed back at Techie and saw the
smiling face and the prideful look in her mother and Tatay. "This is
too much. It is awesome." She laughed. She was on top of the world.

Alone in the guest room, which she would share with her mother, as
proper decorum and modesty dictated, Pearl was busy peeling a ripe
mango. This time, she had mastered the dexterity of peeling one like
the locals, peeling the skin to form an annular ring without break. Her
mother was busy playing mahjong with Techie, Doña Esperanza, and
Tatay while P.J. made sure they had food and refreshments.

Pearl imagined P.J. lounging on a sofa across from her with his head
resting on his palms, legs crossed, face cocked sideways, and confident
eyes on her. She could see those light brown eyes, his lips that showed
even, white teeth, the smooth skin that wrinkled at the corner of his

eyes when he smiled, and the eyes disappearing in a slit bordered with dark, thick lashes.

She could see P.J.'s lips uttering, "You are just perfect for me. Grandma Espe says so. I think she's right."

"Yeah, right." Pearl blurted, mocking. Her half-finished mango landed in the garbage with a dull thud.

CHAPTER 7

LEAP OF FAITH

The old man and his wife gathered their three children: a pubescent sixteen-year-old girl with big dreams and huge appetite, a thirteen-year-old boy who hid his adolescent insecurity of sudden growth spurt with hunched posture, unsure smile, and constant fidgeting, and their youngest, the old man's favorite, an eight-year-old girl with happy disposition and a near clone of the wife. They were near Quiapo Church where they joined other families, some with their second- and third-generation members housed in temporary makeshift dwellings, where members toiled for a few nights to make fast money selling *palaspas* come Easter Sunday, the beginning of Lenten season. These are decorated coconut palm fronds that families bring to the church to be blessed by the priest. It commemorates the coming of the Messiah to Jerusalem where revelers carrying palm leaves greeted him. Believed to possess magical powers, these blessed *palaspas* were brought home and hung on doors or windows to ward off evil spirits. Some families kept them for a year to be burned at the beginning of the next Lenten season.

The old man's youngest child was his biggest asset. Gifted with beautiful tapered fingers that hid agility, she could easily cut open several *ibus* (palm fronds) and magically weave them into different designs, beating her older siblings and their parents. There was the *palapa*, which appeared to be a deceptively simple pattern of several French braids; the *binabig* with its base looking more like a mat; the *pinuso* folded into a heart shape; the *kinurus* in the form of a cross; and several more shapes such as *kidlat* (lightning), *espada* (sword), *bola* (ball), *ibon* (bird), *hipon* (shrimp), and bows. The man's family toiled the night away until the crack of dawn with their finished work displayed along the roads leading to Quiapo Church and sold to passing cars and vans who pulled over, the occupants never having to get out of their vehicle. Similar scenarios were repeated along church routes throughout the country. Some enterprising vendors carried samples of their wares by the church steps to catch last-minute business from churchgoers.

The Gomez family, led by Tatay, dropped off Aurora, who perused the displayed *palaspas* along the sidewalk. The car inched slowly to follow her. The man's oldest daughter glanced at Aurora, admiring the dress that must have cost a fortune, amazed that Aurora kept every strand of her hair in place. Her skin smelled sweet while she lay squat in front of her wares with her simple cotton dress sticking to her dried sweat and corpulent body. Cheap rubber sandal slippers protected her ugly, calloused feet. And then she saw Pearl.

Gazing up, she saw her arm dangling from the window, wearing a simple bracelet with fingers painted with clear polish. Like the older woman, she was well dressed. Unlike the older woman, her skin was very fair, her hair was the color of corn husk, and her eyes were the palest shade of brown with trace of green, a mestiza. The old man's daughter swallowed hard.

The woman inside the car was blessed. Unlike her, her parents were pure natives, brown-skinned with black hair and brown eyes. The daughter felt a tap on her shoulder. It was her father. He was smiling at her. His teeth were stained from chewing betel nut. His face was leathered, deeply lined from constant exposure to the elements.

"Can you break this fifty pesos for me?" the old man asked. "The lady needs some change."

As it was Palm Sunday, the Santuario de San Jose was overflowing with the faithful. A parade of expensive cars dropped off the well-heeled crowd in elegant attire and dresses. Some wore expensive perfumes that sweetened the air. There were a few nodded heads and smiles to acknowledge an acquaintance or a friend.

That summer, the temperature was in the nineties, but inside the confines of their air-conditioned cars, neither Tatay, Aurora, nor Pearl appeared to be sweating while navigating the short distance from the front step to the main door of the church, a clear glass door with its frame reminiscent of a stylized wooden cross.

Aurora wore a simple one-piece pale blue dress accented with a choker of Mikimoto pearls. Her hair was pulled in an elegant bun to Pearl's more youthful two-piece, short-sleeved white blouse and printed skirt with flat Ferragamo shoes. Her hair was tied in a severe ponytail with matching kerchief. They were walking hand in hand, each one carrying *palaspas* they had bought from Quiapo Church. Mario was walking not far behind, carrying an equally elaborate *palaspas*.

Inside the church, the attendees carried those palm leaves like badges of honor. The next one seemed more elaborate than the previous, waiting to be blessed. The church smelled of burnt incense and candles, though later it began to smell faintly of humanity even with the air-conditioning on as the mass was long, not unusual for the occasion.

It was a beautiful church, decorated this time in royal shades of purple. Though there were several rows of wooden pews between the center aisle, the church was jammed, with shoulders and elbows touching their neighbors. Donated from a prime piece of land from the prominent Ortigas family, surrounded by exclusive Wack Wack Club and White Plains and prime shopping malls, it was a modern church with simple façade and clean lines with gold and wooden accents, stained-glass windows that afforded a play of light, and vaulted ceiling. The altar had a human-sized figure of Jesus Christ in the crucifix, flanked on the left by images of young Jesus with St. Joseph, his father, on the right by the Virgin Mary with cherubs by her feet.

As the mass ended and the crowd began to wait outside, a long line of cars began to appear to pick up the same passengers they dropped off. Some went to their parked cars.

"What's with the traffic?" Aurora noted the unusually heavy traffic.

"Imelda Marcos entertaining some European royalties," Mario said.

"Really?" Pearl said.

"It's a joke. I don't even know if she's in the country. She shops in Beverly Hills in a chartered Philippine Airlines plane if you didn't know. Or being the Holy Week, she probably is holed in her own room or private chapel in the Malacañang Palace, reciting the Hail Mary or the passion of Christ with her diamond rosary."

"Wow," Pearl said. She gazed outside her window. Her eyes were entertained looking at the local scenery of a passing jeepney. It was covered in vivid hues of blues, greens, oranges, and purple tassels attached to its antenna and window corners with blaring music from a local artist.

How could the driver see? she thought. What a revel. She was positive the music was nothing pious.

"May God bless her soul. We shouldn't be thinking bad of our fellowmen this Holy Week, right, Tatay?" Aurora asked.

"Sure. In fact, I can treat you to lunch if you want. It's on me. A penitence for your *lolo*'s badmouthing a holy woman."

"Not today, Tatay," Pearl protested. "I asked Juling to make some *lechon kawali* and *pansit luglog*."

"Since when did you learn Filipino food?" Mario asked.

"I know how to cook them too."

"Now you really have my attention. Well, a fruit doesn't fall far from the tree, like your mom."

"Thanks, Tatay," Aurora said. "And remember, no more meat after this."

"Well, okay. It's true. Mother taught me how to cook. I perfected them."

The two women laughed. There was a brief silence.

"How come nothing is showing in the movies except religious films? And the radio." Pearl asked.

"It's the Holy Week, *hija*," Mario said.

"So . . ."

"It would be sacrilegious," Aurora said.

"Really?"

"Really," Aurora said in serious tone.

Tinay, if she were alive, would be busy organizing *pabasa*, the Gomez family sponsoring the three-day vigil of singing and chanting of the reading of the passion, death, and resurrection of Christ beginning Holy Monday through Holy Wednesday. It was now Aurora's obligation to carry on the tradition. *It was a tradition Pearl needed to know,* she thought. Participants, mostly women, some coming all the way from province of Pampanga, stayed with them. A free meal and a place to stay were these women's only compensation.

During *pabasa*, Tinay would have Juling serve meatless meals like *rellenong bangus* (deboned milkfish), *hipon sa gata* (shrimp in coconut sauce) with added squash or green chili peppers, stuffed squid, *pinangat na pompano* (pompano, a toothless fish in silver with blue black tiny scales) poached in *calamansi* or lemon squeeze, tomatoes, together with ginger and spices, or fried *hito* (catfish) with *buro* and *mustasa* (fermented rice and mustasa vegetable). She would recall occasionally joining these women having lunch. These women would wash their hands in wooden *mangkok*, gingerly dipping their fingers and wiping them clean with towels before eating with their bare hands, sharing communal food among them. Tinay and she would use the silver spoon and fork they had been used to. Her mother pretended she did not notice anything unusual and avoided looking these women in the eyes.

It was the same group of women Aurora joined this Holy Week without Nanay. Not wanting to appear like a sore finger, she grabbed the *mangkok* wooden bowl and washed her fingers like the rest before passing the wooden bowl to the next woman. She imitated these women eating with their bare hands. The trembling of her hand showed her uneasiness. This time, it was the women who pretended not to notice, looking straight ahead, avoiding the previous incessant talk among them in their dialect. Everyone ate in complete silence. Toward the end of the silent meal, the women gathered, wearing colorful *saya* that reached their ankles and their ears elongated from years of wearing the same heavy silver or gold hoop earrings. They huddled in a corner, unmindful of anyone, with their legs folded close to their withered breast as they lay squat. The leader unfolded a soiled handkerchief hiding brown betel nuts. She cut them in tiny chunks, sandwiched them in tiny, folded green leaves, and crushed them with a tiny pestle that miraculously materialized, hidden among the folds of her *saya*. Then she shared the treasure, munching them in silence. Their gums appeared to bleed, their teeth was stained blood-red. It was a private ritual among them.

Aurora stood up, leaving the women in peace. For three days, their place would be enveloped with unending singing and reading of the passion of Christ. Come Holy Thursday, Tinay and she used to do *Bisita Iglesia*, a tradition where they would visit at least seven different churches to pray the Stations of the Cross. Except now she had to do it alone.

The heavy cross inched slowly, pausing every once in a while, leaving a mark on the graveled road. It was carried by a man naked except for his loincloth. His face was soaked in caked blood, and some fresh blood dripped and bathed his torso. A crown of thorns pierced his scalp. His body would convulse every once in a while as a whip holding several pieces of tiny bamboo sticks landed on his back, marking the spot with red welts. Plasma mixed with onyx red liquid gushing from a fresh wound, inflicted by a fellow penitent.

He was not alone. Ahead were about a half-dozen half-naked, barefoot, or flip-flopped men in tattered shorts or denim pants splattered with blood and drenched in sweat, punishing themselves with single or solitary whips. Some wore kerchiefs around their heads, a flimsy protection against the burning sun, perhaps to catch the sweat dripping from their foreheads. Others wore thorns too. Some shielded their faces to hide their identity.

Crowds peppered both sides of the street. While most men braved the sun, most women carried dark umbrellas. Women flinched and covered their mouths, looked the other way, or blinked as whips landed and tore naked torsos. Women participants wore long tunics with veiled faces as Virgin Mother or Mary Magdalene, while male participants wore Roman attire as soldiers. Some oglers retreated as penitents looked for a kind soul for water. The rest of the crowd appeared stoic, quizzical, amazed, disbelieving, and disenchanted. A smattering of European and American tourists photographed or filmed the bloody spectacle. Street urchins followed the participants or led them like town criers.

These young boys expected the same men fulfilling the annual *panata* or holy pledge while a few new recruits replaced aging ones, the unfit, or the retired the following year. To these impressionable boys, it was something some imagined participating in when they reached the right age, marking Easter Friday as a red-letter day.

Most were eager for the penitent who carried the cross, called *Kristo* or Christ, to reach the end of his journey. They watched others tie his wrists and feet on the cross, surrendering his body to be crucified, mimicking their Christian Savior year after year, approximating the traditional time the actual crucifixion occurred, three o'clock in the afternoon, when the sun was at its blinding peak.

Young as these boys were, they adroitly maneuvered themselves in front of the crucifixion, watching every fall of the hammer as it tore the flesh, seeing the nail disappear in the palms and feet, save for its head, hearing the groan of pain, smelling the sweat, and tasting sputtered blood. The rest of the crowd mingled around the scene, some with raw emotions on their faces. Their ears rang and hearts dropped as the scene unfolded, hearing their own rapid breathing and the palpitation of their hearts. A few jostled for a better view, their thirst for blood hidden under the cloak of this unsanctioned pagan Christian ritual.

That night, under duress, Pearl accompanied Aurora to a procession done all over the country of the dead Christ, *prusisyon ng Santo Entierro.* The image of Christ was paraded on a lit carriage decorated with flowers, followed by images of crying ladies, Mater de Dolorosa, Mary Magdalene, Mary of Cleophas, Mary of James, Salome, and also John the Evangelist. Following tradition, the last one to be paraded was Mater Dolorosa. Aurora wore a veil dressed in black. Pearl compromised by wearing black dress without the veil.

Pearl was not hungry. She was thirsty. While Aurora rested in her bedroom, she went to the kitchen, poured herself some ice-cold water, took off her shoes, and raised her feet to relieve her aching legs on a stool. Darkness shrouded the kitchen. She did not mind. The stillness of the place and privacy was something she craved for after these unending ceremonies she was obligated to be a part of—those she could not refuse after some failed impassioned plea.

The parallel band of lights from the window blinds facing the servants' quarters caught her curiosity. That was unusual. This time, darkness usually covered the servants' quarters. The helpers were fast asleep to get ready for another day of unending chores. She finished the glass of water, put on her shoes, and went to the servants' quarters. It was a short walk from the back of the kitchen to a nondescript building. A light in one of the windows was on, a sharp contrast to the rest of the building. As she drew closer, she heard some murmuring, a chorus of voices interrupted by silence, mostly children's voices. Inday, the laundry woman, was the only helper with young children. It was late for the children to be awake. She was about to knock and then realized she could see the inside through the window.

It was the laundry woman's bedroom. The woman and her two children were busy attending to a man naked save for his underwear. The woman was wringing some towels and then washing the man's body. Blood stained the basin.

The man's knees had cuts and scrapes. The laundry woman chewed some green leaves, spit them in her palm, and applied as a liniment to the wound. The back of his torso had wounds and welts visible when she rolled him on his side.

He was quiet, though he grimaced as he was rolled to his back. The starched bedsheet rubbed his back. It was stained with his bodily fluid. The older child kissed the man on his cheek and caressed his arm to ease the pain. The younger child, a girl, combed the man's hair with her bare fingers. The laundry woman cradled his hand, kissed each finger, and then spread them to kiss the wound on his palm.

Pearl blinked. She wanted to make sure she was seeing right. A fresh wound was in the center of the man's hand. Basic instinct made her examine the other hand. Pearl saw the back of his other hand, which confirmed her suspicions. At the center of this hand was another fresh wound. His wrist had linear ligature cuts.

What am I seeing? Pearl thought.

Her eyes examined the rest of his body. She saw some caked blood near his hairline with what appeared to be puncture wounds. His lips were chapped, probably from prolonged exposure to heat. The front of the torso had fewer wounds than the back. His legs were scraped and bruised. The ankles had similar ligature wounds. Pearl's eyes widened seeing fresh wounds at the center of each of his feet. She stepped backward. Her mind was urging her to knock at the door and get an answer to myriads of question brewing inside her, yet the sacredness and the privacy of the moment with this family made her think twice.

She ran back to the house with her skirt billowing in the night. She knocked impatiently at Aurora's bedroom.

"You look ashen." Aurora closed the bedroom door quietly. "What happened?"

Her daughter appeared fearful of being uncovered.

"There is a man in our laundry woman's bedroom. He's wounded. He needs a doctor."

"That's Ansel."

"You know him?"

"He does that every year. It was his *panata*, to experience God's suffering. A way of asking forgiveness."

"What?" Pearl noticed all the religious images in Aurora's altar were all shrouded in purple.

"Yes, he is crucified every Good Friday. And yes, they are covered in purple, mourning the death of our Savior."

"Why? The Church. What does it say?"

"It is not sanctioned."

"He is a religious zealot."

"Maybe. There is nothing the Church could do to stop the tradition. It's done for years now. It's . . . the culture to some."

"It's wrong. It's insane."

"What's not wrong, Pearly? What's not insane?"

There was a long pause of silence between the two women.

"You are tired. Go to bed now. Or you can sleep with your mother."

"No, Mother. G'night." Pearl saw the *palaspas* hanging by the bedroom door as she turned to leave.

"They ward off bad spirits."

"I get it."

"I asked Candida to put one *palaspas* in your bedroom door. So don't be surprised."

Pearl turned her head toward her mother. *So that was why the palaspas was left hanging on her door.* "Is that also sanctioned by the Church?"

Aurora covered her mouth. Her eyes watered. She did not say a word. Pearl's words stung. She closed the door to her bedroom.

Pearl woke up to Aurora gazing down on her.

Her mother appeared in good spirits, smiling at her. "Wake up. Time to dress up, Pearly."

"What time is it?"

"Eleven."

Pearl saw it was dark outside. "It's nighttime. Where are we going?"

"Didn't I tell you we are attending Easter Sunday mass? Hurry up so we make it to *Salubong.*"

"At midnight? Who are we meeting?"

"Yes. Tatay is waiting downstairs." Aurora ignored her other question.

"All right. Give me fifteen minutes." Pearl jumped out of bed. It was useless arguing with her mother. It was one of those lost battles. "I need to freshen up."

The driver dropped them off at a street two blocks away from the church. A throng of women and girls were already lined up behind a veiled image of Virgin Mary. Hushed voices were heard. The crowd appeared somber, most wearing black veils. Otherwise, they were all dressed up. The driver sped up, taking Tatay with him.

"Where is Tatay going?"

"He'll join the procession with the image of the risen Christ at the other street. That's where the men and boys are. The two processions would end in front of the church. You watch, Pearly. You've never seen anything like this before."

The procession inched slowly. The women and girls huddled close together with their body heat keeping them warm as the night was cold. Participants who were late occasionally broke up the long line. This rite of meeting or *Salubong* began with the choir singing "Alleluia" as Mary moved toward Jesus. Finally, in front of the church, as the two images met, a girl dressed as an angel was hoisted from a flower-shaped platform to descend on top of the head of the Virgin Mary and lifted her black veil. It was a procession of joy and triumph, light and festivity, as Jesus met his mother. An angel of the Lord removed her *lambong* or veil of sadness. The choir continued singing.

The church bells rung to announce the beginning of the Easter mass as the procession of the image of Christ and Virgin Mary ended up inside the church. The crowd marched inside, filling the church to capacity.

Aurora squeezed Pearl's hand. Pearl looked at her mother. She was no longer sleepy.

Her mother's warm body and natural scent were comforting, reminding her of her childhood.

CHAPTER 8

FLORES DE MAYO
(FLOWERS OF MAY)

She was the first of the three Reyna Elenas (Queen Helen) to arrive in a gleaming black Mercedes-Benz that balmy night. Her entourage included two maids in white uniforms who were skittering around like frightened mice. A matronly woman with glittering diamonds and flaming-red nails and lips was shouting directives. A uniformed chauffer opened the back door wide to assist the Reyna Elena.

She gingerly stepped out, ushered by one leg clad in expensive designer shoes with fluffy layers of underskirt obscuring her face and body. The diadem on her head glittered as she leaned forward to step out, stretching her bony hand for the driver.

She finally got out of the car to stretch to her full height, which wasn't much. Her eyes, which appeared like perfect black holes, surveyed the curious crowd, devotees with heads covered with veils or white handkerchiefs. A majority were in simple cotton dress, wearing flat shoes or open sandals, holding unlit candles or sparklers to guide the parade. Some recited the rosary while waiting for the procession to start. The men were in simple short-sleeved shirts, long pants, and dark shoes or slippers. Several groups of barefoot boys, shirtless or wearing faded undershirts with unmatched short pants, were gawking in awe. Some were giggling bashfully, whispering among themselves with eyes wide open with excitement. The brave ones shoved their way up front, causing some belligerent protests and threatened cuffed fists silenced by a loud "Shhh" from parade participants.

The Reyna Elena pouted her lips, which appeared to be in a proverbial pout and smirk. With disdain, she threw her eyes toward the other *sagalas* who were also dressed in floor-length gowns, sizing them up.

The well-dressed elderly woman nervously directed the crowd to give way to the vision that had just appeared before them, frantically hissing under her breath, dismayed the maids were too slow to assist her daughter.

"The cape . . . the cape," she said, continuing to hiss. "Hurry up, lest it get soiled, *ano ba* (What the heck)?"

The light from the generator flooded the young woman, emphasizing her bony face, tiny nose, and long neck bedecked in glittering jewelry. An elaborate arch carried by sturdy men inched toward the young woman. It was festooned with fresh flowers. The sweet smell of *ylang ylang* and *sampaguita* permeated the air. She continued to survey the crowd like they were her subjects. Her tilted head accentuated her slightly protruding jaw. With her black hair pulled in a chignon, her head appeared bigger than the rest of her. Under flashing flashbulbs, the mother took a foot-long crucifix from a satin-lined box and presented this to the Reyna Elena. She would cradle this during the procession.

A slight commotion distracted the crowd. A heavyset woman weaved in front of the crowd. The woman was catching her breath while she carried her five-year-old son who was attired in a princely medieval outfit, complete with his own cape that reached the back of his mid thigh. He was Prince Constantine to the young woman's Reyna Elena.

A few eager participants lit their candles early, blossoming against the dark night, punctuated by a few who also began to light their sparklers, called *luces*. Some of the crowd formed a line behind the Queen Elena and her consort, though the parade had yet to officially begin.

Hushed comments were exchanged, punctuating the religious procession.

"How cute! See how he looks like the Niño himself," said one.

"*Mestizong-mestizo*," said one, gushing.

"Did you notice her jewelry?" Another exclaimed.

"*Tunay*, I know they are genuine when I see them."

"Beautiful dress. It must be quite expensive," said another, hushing.

Flashing cameras continued to record the event for posterity by a paid photographer while a partner recorded the event on film. Satisfied with the attention she was receiving, the young woman opened her mouth to reveal a toothy grin, a trace of a smirk remaining like she was born with it.

"She looks like a crocodile," Techie whispered to Aurora in Tagalog inside their waiting car. "Her family must have donated a fortune to the parish."

The comment didn't escape Pearl who was seated between the two women. She saw everything from her vantage point, though she couldn't hear the noise created by the arrival of the first Reyna Elena, as the air conditioner was on full blast to protect her from sweating. She giggled.

Caught red-handed, Techie feigned embarrassment by her comment. "I'm sorry. I was just telling the truth to your mother, *hija*." She patted Pearl's forearm. "Nobody can even hold a candle beside you, Pearl. Nobody."

Aurora smiled. She was proud to say she agreed. Even the third Reyna Elena, who she heard was a rising movie star, could not compete with her Pearl. Pearl kept quiet, savoring the compliment. She was used to that. She was intrigued, curious, and surprised by all the cacophony and frenzy with the tradition. She had to admit that being part of the festivity and being the center of attention was quite intoxicating. Her friends, if they could only see her, would be salivating.

The Santa Cruzan is traditionally held in May when flowers are in full bloom with the season's generous rain and full sun. Young girls dressed in dainty white or pink frocks, or embroidered clothes to honor the Virgin Mary by offering baskets of fresh flowers to the altar. The festivity ends with the Santa Cruzan, a religious procession to honor and celebrate Queen Helen and her son's, Prince Constantine's, discovery of the cross, the symbol of Christianity. A parade of young maidens, the *sagalas*, who represent prominent female biblical figures, including infamous ones, walked the main streets in their finest gowns. Devoted churchgoers trailed each *sagala* with lit candles or tiny firecrackers called *luces*. They recited the rosary or chanted prayers to the Virgin Mary printed on tiny booklets while accompanied by the strains of band music.

Through the years, Santa Cruzan had evolved to include legendary heroines, historical women, and fictional characters from local lore and legends that had nothing to do with biblical times. There was Mariang Makiling—a fictional character about Mount Makiling parading with biblical figures such as Salome, the woman whose sultry dance caused John the Baptist to lose his head—carrying a platter with John the Baptist's head. There was Veronica, who parlayed a veil with Jesus's three images on it, a miracle that happened when she wiped the Messiah's bloodied face while he carried the cross at the Calvary. Then there was the Reyna Abogada, the defender of the poor and oppressed carrying a tome. Then there was the Reyna de las Flores marching with a bouquet of flowers.

The parade starts with Methuselah, a bearded old man riding a cart while preoccupied toasting some grain of sand in a pan over a fire. He was supposed to remind us that all that glitters will end up as dust, like what he was toasting. The parade would not be complete without the traditional Reyna Fe to symbolize faith, Reyna Esperanza for hope, Reyna Caridad for charity, Reyna Banderada for the flag symbolizing the coming of Christianity, Reyna Justicia for justice, and Reyna Mora to symbolize the Muslim princess from the southern part of the island who converted to Christianity.

Every prominent family with young daughters wished that their daughters would be chosen one of the *sagalas*, if not the Reyna Elena, the most coveted part. It used to be there was only one Reyna Elena chosen from a parish district. Through the years, with pressure and clamor from prominent families who contributed substantial donations or *abuloy* to the Church, the richer parishes with more elaborate Santa Cruzan evolved with not one, not even two, but not uncommonly three Reyna Elenas to appease most everyone.

Pearl recalled a few weeks prior that the Women's Auxiliary from the parish church that Doña Esperanza belonged had requested an audience with her and her mother. One of the officers was reed thin, wearing clothes like she was a hanger. Her serious mien was suddenly radiant at the sight of Pearl. The other was a plumpish, middle-aged woman with a perpetual grin on her face, reminding Pearl of a fairy godmother.

"*Ang ganda!*" blurted the plumpish woman uninhibitedly. "Doña Esperanza was right. You'll make a very beautiful Reyna Elena."

"*Kita mo naman, hindi maikakaila* (No doubt. White blood is obvious in this woman. Perfect blend)," said the thin one.

"Mestiza," said the plump woman. "No doubt, I agree." Her voice was proud, and her tone was jubilant. "She would add prestige to our Santa Cruzan."

"It's local tradition, *hija*," the thin woman said. "It's a yearly event to honor the discovery of the cross. Young maidens parade in the main street to honor the cross. The part of the Reyna Elena is the most important one."

The woman straightened her back to stress her point. "We want the Reyna Elena to come from a very good family, one with impeccable background." She hastened to correct herself. "Of course, just like the rest of the *sagalas*."

"With Doña Esperanza's recommendation, who could go wrong?" the plump woman asked. "Not only is she of good family background but ravishingly beautiful as well. You could be in the movies, *hija*."

"Absolutely."

"They want your permission, Pearl." Aurora's eyes were excited, and her voice was expectant and hopeful.

"Everyone would be delirious. The chosen Reyna Elena is kept a secret until the day of the parade to surprise the people. We have three these year."

The reed-thin woman sighed. "Well, we have to please everyone. Someone complained about Rosario Rosales as the Reyna Elena, the movie actress. The auxiliary had an emergency meeting. It's too late to retract the invitation for Rosario. So the council decided to add the daughter of this family as the other Reyna Elena with the understanding we would have a third one of the council's own choosing. That's it. It's only fair."

"So *hija*, will you be our third Reyna Elena?"

The commotion outside interrupted Pearl's reminiscing. The generator that shone an eerie glow to the first Reyna Elena began to putter and finally died, to the dismay of the mother in particular. Relative darkness enveloped that section of the road while the crowd was getting ready for the start of the parade. There was a rabid exchange of words as the mother addressed a group of men in charge of the generator. Bony knuckles knocked impatiently at their closed window. It was the mother. Up close, she was a mature version of the daughter, down to the proverbial smirk.

Aurora and Techie got out, leaving specific instructions to Pearl.

"Stay in the car, *hija*," Techie said.

"Pearl, wait inside," Aurora reiterated. "We'll be right back."

P.J., who was in the driver's seat, chuckled. "Whoa. What does she want?" He threw admiring glances from the rearview mirror.

Pearl pretended not to notice. Seated at the front passenger seat was Pearl's Prince Constantine, P.J.'s seven-year-old cousin. Like the other Constantine, he was in the ancient attire of a prince. The boy looked ill at ease with the bulky costume, though bearing the discomfort in silence as well-behaved and well-bred children were expected to. Unlike the other Constantine, he had narrow eyes, black hair, and brown skin. Aurora and Techie came back wearing frowns and knitted brows. The car shook as they slammed their door. It startled the young Constantine.

"That woman," Aurora said, "I could wring her neck."

"She wants her daughter to be the last Reyna Elena to march so they could fix the generator," Techie said, dismayed.

"My Pearl should be the last Reyna Elena to march," Aurora said. "We have already agreed to this."

"What does it matter?" Pearl asked.

Techie and Aurora exchanged glances and then rolled their eyes.

"Where is the president of the Auxiliary?" Aurora uttered. "She should tell the woman to stop making petty demands."

"I thought everything was settled. I'm so embarrassed." Techie gazed at Pearl. "To think it was the Auxiliary who convinced you to become Reyna Elena. I am sure she was the only one who wanted her daughter to reign as Reyna Elena. The gull."

P.J. got out of the car without being noticed while his mother and Aurora continued to vent. Meanwhile, the crowd continued to swell while the other *sagalas* took their assigned spots. A few cars cruised bearing other *sagalas* who arrived in the nick of time. To call attention to their importance, some blared their horns. The lead band began to play a tune to the boom of the drum, the blowing of the trumpets and clarinets, and clash of cymbals. The rest of the devotees, the so-called *manangs*, the eager participants, and the few revelers at the head of the procession began lighting their candles with round paper sleeves to catch the drippings, choosing specifically or at random which *sagala* they elected to follow and light her way—friends, relatives, admirers, and strangers.

"*Dito . . . Dito,*" an eager relative of a *sagala* stage whispered to her company, enticing the crowd to join in.

"*Ayoko diyan. Gusto ko rito.* Not there. I prefer to light this *sagala*," somebody said.

Each *sagala* had arches under which they marched to the band. One arch more elaborate than the next, each one equally competing for attention and scrutiny as the rest of the *sagalas.* Toward the end of the procession, the commotion continued to unfold. Under duress and visibly near tears was the movie actress who was forced to march ahead of the indisposed Reyna Elena. Some movie fans could not contain themselves from shouting her name, while others took pictures for posterity. Somehow that smoothed the actress's rumpled feathers. She started to smile for the camera, worried her tears could ruin her makeup. The fan magazines would carry the event the following days. She'd better not appear ugly. She prayed no reporter took notice of her placement among the three Reyna Elenas. A uniformed sigh of relief was heard. The group of men hovering around the generator gradually dispersed. P.J. was among them with hands soiled and beads of perspiration dotting his forehead.

The generator was revved to its full power for the skinny Reyna Elena. The mother smiled awkwardly. She was unsure whether to feel relief the generator got fixed a tad too soon, thus losing her daughter's chance to march last versus parading without the extra light source to display her daughter's exquisite gown that cost a fortune, a Ben Farrales original, she was proud to say, not to mention the heirloom jewelries her daughter wore and, of course, her daughter's ethereal beauty.

P.J. knocked at the car's side window. His hair was rumpled with beads of sweat on his forehead. He signaled to the three women that it was time for Pearl to step out of the car. Techie lowered her window.

P.J. nodded to his mother. "It's fixed."

Techie took a deep sigh of relief, along with Aurora. Indeed, the glaring source of light once more illuminated the demanding and imperious Reyna Elena.

"A few more minutes, *hija*," Techie said to Pearl. "As soon as she begins to march, we can get out of the car."

The crowd was beginning to feel impatient. The hired men carrying the arch were gazing at each other, waiting for the cue. There was a widening gap from the first Reyna Elena and the procession. Finally accepting defeat, the mother motioned the men to bring the arch further toward the middle of the road to catch up with the parade. The daughter grudgingly positioned herself under its shadow, her Constantine hobbling beside her to keep up with her pace. The dispersed crowd resumed to queue behind her with their glowing candles and sparklers, forming a band of light.

Another elaborate four-poster arch was ushered under the cover of a tall acacia tree to the middle of the road. It was made of bamboo and rattan. Its roof formed a cupola with a round tiara on its top made of tiny *sampaguita* buds. The tiara was a close replica of the one Pearl was wearing. Curlicues, elaborate vines, and rare white orchids with a hint of light pink in its center clung to the lattice from each post. Numerous tiny lights flickered on the roof, and clandestinely hidden light sources powered the four posters. The whole arch was a glittering gem against the dark sky. It was commissioned by Doña Esperanza from skilled artisans with no expense spared.

Pearl began to march as sparklers held by devotees and candles lit her way. The cross was held close to her bosom. Her Prince Constantine walked by her side while flashing cameras and film recorded the event, just like the other Reyna Elena. Pearl was soon followed by the carriage of the Virgin Mary, elaborately dressed in gold finery, floating in a bed of flowers. A coterie of devotees could be heard murmuring words from tiny prayer books following behind. The rest of the devotees sang "*Dios Te Salve*" while walking with the procession, a tone-deaf woman's voice drowning the rest.

Llena eres de gracia
El señor es contigo
Bendita tu eres
Entre toda las mujeres
Y bandito es el fruto
Y bandito es el fruto
De tu vientre Jesus
Santa Maria Madre de Dios
Ruega por nosotros
Pecadores ahora
Y en la hora
De nuestra muerte amen. Jesus.

The last band began to play its music, drowning the prayers, chants, and singing. There was palpable held breath as Pearl marched to the plaintive and slightly syncopated tune of the band and admiring glances from the pious crowd. The solemnity of the occasion was observed without the previous circus show. At the front of the parade, the crowd continued to grow although most had already claimed prime spots when Doña Esperanza's car arrived. Her driver found a vantage spot, a quiet side road lined by mature acacia trees that intersected the main parade route. Sturdy branches of trees fronting the parade were occupied by children for a bird's-eye view of the Santa Cruzan. The driver had to shoo some of them as they claimed spots at the car's front bumper like miniature soldiers.

Inside the car, Doña Esperanza was gazing through her binoculars. She could see some church leaders, a man in embroidered *barong tagalog* holding a clipboard and two women in exquisite *baro at saya* comparing notes, giving orders which *sagala* should march first and when, guiding the pious *manongs* and *manangs* to queue behind. The *sagalas* were young, some teetering between childhood and early womanhood with faces dolled up and painted and bodies still unripe but revved up to look mature. Their gowns competed with one another for attention and lavishness. Their dark hair was made fancy, adorned with exquisite costume jewelries and genuine ones in some.

They all marched under the strains of bands spread out at the beginning, middle, and end of the parade. Doña Esperanza witnessed the smooth transition from one *sagala* to the next, gliding and marching slowly past her. She was spared the spectacle involving the three Reyna Elenas. She took notice of some *sagalas* whose families she knew and eyed the rest with passing curiosity and impatience. She was mainly interested in the three principal Reyna Elenas toward the end of the parade. Finally, there was an unusual huge gap in the parade as the rest of the *sagalas* passed through. The crowd began to gawk, straining their neck in the same direction.

What is going on?

Her curiosity piqued, Doña Esperanza got out and positioned herself in front of the car's bumper, squeezing herself among the young urchins who, like mushrooms, kept sprouting and materializing before her and her driver's eyes. The children giggled upon her sight and made room for her. They were careful not to touch her arm or clothing, aware she must be "somebody" with her coiffed hair, heeled shoes, and nice smell.

The Santa Cruzan was just the icing on the cake to these children. They were waiting for the *pabitin*, the culminating activity. *Pabitin* is a square trellis where goodies such as candies, fruits, and toys are hung by strings. The trellis is tied to a rope suspended on a pole or a strong tree branch. The children would gather under the trellis and compete with others, picking up the goodies as the trellis gets lowered, pulled up, and lowered again until eager, yelling youngsters claim everything on it.

Doña Esperanza meticulously inspected the first Reyna Elena with discerning eyes. This Reyna Elena was a *morena*, not fair-skinned like Pearl. She was not bad looking. *A little odd though*, she thought, *this uncultured* bakya *crowd would consider somebody not fair-skinned or mestiza worthy of adulation and popularity.*

She heard that she was a popular Tagalog movie actress. She did not keep up with Tagalog cinema. She would rather see Stateside movies. *What is wrong with these people?*

She held her breath at the sight of the second Reyna Elena. The hum of the generator was overpowering. It was a comedic sight to behold, the young woman's attire clashing with her. Doña Esperanza blinked her eyes and gazed far to obliterate nasty thoughts percolating in her mind. She knew the mother of this Reyna Elena, an occasional participant in her mahjong crowd.

Forgive me, God, but her daughter is ugly.

She continued to gaze far. She was more interested at the final Reyna Elena, Pearl. As the familiar figure she was waiting for gradually drew close, her heart raced. *Why not?*

Without exaggerating, she was the arbiter of all of these. It was her blood, sweat, and tears. There she was, Pearl, nearly reachable with her hands, beautiful beyond her imagination, every inch the Reyna Elena she envisioned her to be. The heavy ornate arch over Pearl's head was just perfect, (every cent worth it), not to mention her nephew who was cute in his attire as her Prince Constantine.

She felt vindicated. Her heart continued to throb. She was right the very first time she saw Pearl. Pearl would be a perfect match to P.J.'s dark good looks. *Where's P.J.?*

Pearl would be a perfect addition to her late husband's Bisayan roots, the Lopezes, to Pearl's Tagalog and Ilocano roots, widening their political base and clout. A smile crossed Doña Esperanza's taut and unlined face. Her late in-laws would be livid with her. They didn't want to be lumped with the rest of the Bisaya. They were Ilonggos, a higher ethnic group among the Bisayas. *Where's P.J?*

She wasn't wrong. She was stubborn. But she was right choosing her late husband of the Lopez clan over her parents' choice of a Tagalog lawyer who was the sole heir to a vast rice granary in central Luzon. Her parents were wrong, paranoid, and prejudicial of her late husband's Bisayan roots (Ilonggo, please don't forget the Ilonggo), who her parents considered were of inferior ethnicity to their Tagalog forebears. Her Techie married a Romualdez from the Leyte province's political dynasty, also a Bisaya. *Mother and daughter could not be wrong at the same time*, she thought.

She waved to catch Pearl's attention. She stage-whispered Pearl's name, but Pearl continued to march. The crowd began to disperse and thin behind the last band as the head of the parade continued to snake through the main roads. The children followed, some miming the trumpet and band player while the rest marched to the band's tune. The sound of music gradually ebbed with the beat of the drum fading last.

Doña Esperanza was left standing in front of her car, captivated, mesmerized, and enthralled.

CHAPTER 9

THREE WOMEN

The dusty road led to the town mayor's house. It was facing the town plaza with a veranda on the second floor framed on both corners with huge windows, welcoming visitors. It sat on a tiny lot. A short driveway ended with a single garage. Every available spot in the driveway was occupied, bumper to bumper. Several men were idling around them, gossiping, puffing cigarettes, some drinking San Miguel beer, and occasionally bursting into lusty laughter.

If you looked at them closely, you would notice most had guns hoisted in their belts, while others had rifles slung around their shoulders. Their lusty laughter halted when they saw P.J.. Recognizing him, they parted to allow him to pass through. They bowed their heads to show respect. P.J. led Pearl as an old woman was trailing Pearl with a protective umbrella to shield her from the piercing noon sun. Their eyes traced their steps.

The ground floor was bare earth. The space was dedicated to several prized roosters in bamboo cages. It obscured the view of the rest of the ground floor.

An old man was holding one of the roosters, puffing smoke in the fowl's face while rubbing its shiny black-and-brown feathers. He did not notice them until the roosters began to make noise. The man ignored them. A steep front stair led to the upper floor. The stair creaked under the weight of P.J., Pearl, and the old woman.

The door at the top of the stair opened. A woman in her early thirties greeted them with a smile. She did not say a word but signaled them to come in and motioned for them to take a seat. Her hair was slightly disheveled. She was finishing buttoning her blouse, which was slightly rumpled. The woman had fine features. Her graceful long neck and slender yet strong arms and shapely legs gave her the appearance of a gazelle, arresting and majestic in her bearing. Though tiny, she made anyone notice her and give her a second or even third look. She did not seem to notice the effect she had on first encounter, which made her more attractive.

Seeing them seated, she excused herself and disappeared. A tall, portly man appeared from a bedroom. He was barefoot. His shirt, unbuttoned at the top, a size smaller than his frame, seemed ready to burst open with his pregnant belly.

His eyes, bulging like headlights, lit up on seeing P.J. "*Putang Ina*. I know it. Esperanza told me to expect your company. And here you are. Obedient young man. You are learning fast. I like that."

P.J. stood up and extended a hand.

The man squeezed P.J.'s hand, pulled him, and gave him a bear hug. "You look and smell just like your *lolo* (grandpa). A good sign. I can see you stepping right into his shoes. Join me. And we'll be an unbeatable force to our enemies."

The man stood in his tract, gently pushing P.J. to his side to inspect the two women who accompanied P.J.. With a wide grin, he examined Pearl, who remained seated, from head to toe. He did not hide the lust in his eyes.

"Is she one of them? You got good taste in women, like me."

"He likes to joke. He doesn't mean anything, Pearl. You'll get used to him. *Ninong*, she is the granddaughter of Mario Gomez. Pearl, he's my godfather. *Ninong*, Pearl."

"Should I know her grandpa?"

"Gomez, Yulo, and Perez law firm. He is the senior and founding member."

The man pulled P.J. close to him, whispered in his ear, and shared a secret. Grinning from ear to ear, he kept his eyes on Pearl. "I have heard about your grandpa. Excellent lawyer. P.J., we could use him. I am beginning to be unhappy with my lawyer." He extended his massive hand, squeezing Pearl's hand tight.

Pearl remained silent. Crinkling her nose, she managed a forced smile. Candida, her mother's *yaya*, pulled Pearl's legs protectively near her. The woman reappeared, bringing several desserts with empty plates, some forks, and a pitcher of chilled pineapple juice. She gave empty plates to Pearl and Candida. She helped fill their plates without waiting for them to make choices. She put some ice in the glasses and filled them with already chilled pineapple juice. The woman smiled at them, satisfied she was the perfect host to these two women, the mayor's guests.

"Hope you like them." At last, she broke her silence.

"Good. Entertain them while I give my godson some advice. Good advice. Come on P.J.. Leave these women. Woman, open that bottle of whisky and bring some more ice. We'll be at the balcony. And hurry up."

The woman excused herself. She soon reappeared to bring a tray with alcohol and some sweets for the man and P.J. at the balcony. She once more disappeared and came back bringing her own glass of juice. She sat across from Pearl and Candida. She eyed them with curiosity.

"Where are you from?"

"Forbes Park," Candida said, interrupting. She kept her protective hand on Pearl's thigh. "Pearl's from the States. Visiting."

"Her *yaya*?"

"Her mother's. I am chaperoning her, like good girls do."

"Must be his girlfriend?"

The woman looked at Pearl before throwing a glance toward the balcony where the two men disappeared. "I'm not good at remembering names. Or faces. I know he is his godson. I have seen him a few times."

"Not yet," Candida answered. "P.J. is showing her around. Doña Esperanza wants her to experience a town fiesta."

"I am curious. My first time to attend one," Pearl said, ignoring Candida's comment. "Doña Esperanza, that's his grandma."

"You do speak with an accent. Your Tagalog, though, is pretty good. Then you should keep your stomach ready."

"I warned her. She knows we would probably visit several homes. Offered food at each place," Candida said. "It would be impolite to refuse." She gazed at the woman, expecting her conspiratorial nod, and then tapped Pearl's thigh. "It only happens once a year. To honor the town's patron saint. Try a bite of everything. I would be offended myself if you do not finish what was served."

The woman again smiled, wider to show an even row of teeth. The sudden loud playing of a band in front of the house interrupted the conversation. The woman stood to signal them to follow her to the balcony. Candida's arthritic frame took a while to follow. At the balcony, the mayor raised his and P.J.'s hands, acknowledging the band who assembled in front of the house to show their respect to him. P.J. turned his head to Pearl and smiled at her. She feigned not to notice. The woman also waved her hand at the crowd, blowing them kisses.

Colorful *papel de hapon* triangular buntings hanging from tree branches or utility poles festooned the streets. A century-old baroque church across from the house began to peal its bell. After rendering a few select pieces, the band marched toward the main street facing the mayor's house, again parading to festive music. The town plaza, which was right in front of the church and visible from the house, sprouted several makeshift stores selling trinkets, souvenirs, games of chance, cotton candies, popcorns, *halu-halu*, *palitaw*, and rice cakes. There were a few rides, which included a carousel and a Ferris wheel. Most of the crowd were dressed casually to ward off the hot weather. The three women settled back inside and claimed their seats.

"You should stay. There will be fireworks tonight. The town's patron saint will be paraded too." The woman pointed to the tray to remind Pearl and Candida to replenish their plates. "Pablo will lead the parade. A yearly tradition since he became the mayor. You must have noticed the decorated top-down car in front of the house."

The sound of firecrackers interrupted their conversation.

"You will be riding with the mayor," Pearl said.

The woman smiled. "It would be nice, isn't it?" She looked down. "It's only right. But then, it's the mayor's decision."

Candida shrugged her shoulders. Living with the Gomez household for several years, she felt privileged to speak her mind and be part of the conversation. "It's up to Pablo, the mayor. He's been the town mayor for several terms, isn't it? I would insist though, being the wife. You campaigned for the man for sure. You were there. Joining him in the parade is only right."

"Undefeated." The woman's eyes brightened. She smiled. There was something sad about her smile. "I'm worried about him. Last election, he almost got killed by *galamay* (cronies) of his opponent. He missed the bullet that killed one of his bodyguards. He has added more bodyguards since, but . . ."

"That's politics," Candida said. "Dirty, dirty politics."

"But kill?" Pearl's eyebrows furrowed. "Why?"

The woman and Candida looked surprised at Pearl.

"It's the cultural norm here," the woman said. "Not much in the bigger cities, though occasionally it happens."

"Particularly if it's a tight race." Candida said. "Ballot boxes get lost, replaced by the opponent's name."

"People like my Pablo. Never been defeated. Even with rumor of vote buying from the other side. Or voters voting more than once. My knees got calluses from my *panata* (religious pledge), walking to the altar on my bended knees to spare my Pablo from harm. Especially near election time."

"Which one do you go to?"

"I always have my faith with the Virgin Mary in Guadalupe."

"*Ay, naku,* we're the same. So far, she's heard my prayers."

"I still keep telling my Pablo to be careful. If something happens to him, I would die. What about his children?"

"How many do you have?" Pearl asked, interrupting.

"I'll show you her picture." The woman showed a wallet-sized picture of a girl in school uniform. "Doesn't she look smart?"

Candida grabbed the picture. She scrutinized it for a long time. Without comment, she passed it on to Pearl.

Pearl saw a young image of the mayor gazing at her. "She's . . . pretty."

"No. She looks like *my* Pablo." The woman's eyes shone with pride. "I see him in her."

"And I don't need to share her with anyone else except Pablo. I insisted she go to private Catholic school. Like his other children. She's the mayor's daughter, his favorite and the youngest. I gave him the daughter he has always wanted. This picture is a year old. She's now in fourth grade."

"Of course. She's the mayor's daughter. And his favorite," Candida repeated. "And the only girl."

"How many other children do you have?" Candida beat Pearl to the same question.

"She's my only child." The woman grabbed back the picture. "His three boys are from his wife."

Just then, an armed guard barged, startling the three women. He stage-whispered to the woman, "Let's go. She's here."

A loud commotion was heard downstairs. A woman's voice was heard, sounding belligerent. The sound of rushing steps shook the stairs. The woman leaped to her feet and rushed toward the back of the house. She threw a glance at Pearl. Pearl couldn't read her eyes.

She waved at Pearl. "Thanks for coming. I'll see you next year?"

The guard followed close behind. There was a loud banging at the door.

"Open the door. Pablo, I know she's there. Open the door."

The mayor ambled from the balcony and took his time. He was holding P.J.'s arm. A voluptuous woman with coiffed hair, tight-fitting dress, and overdone face with strong perfume came rushing to the mayor. She clawed her long, painted nails at the mayor's face, which the mayor grabbed.

"Walang hiya ka! Where is that woman? Where is she?" The mayor embraced the woman. The woman turned her face when he kissed her. "Kiss of Judas. I know you. Where is your woman? I'll kill her. Where is she?"

"We have visitors. Please, please . . . behave. What will they think of us?" The mayor's voice was soothing. He whispered in her ears, "Why would I do that? I'm done with that woman."

The woman was inconsolable. "P.J., don't do this. Don't be like your *Ninong*. How could you? How could you bring that woman in our house? That *kerida* of yours. See what kind of mayor we have? Do you see?"

The mayor didn't let go of the woman. He showered her with kisses, caressed her hair, and led her toward the bedroom. "P.J., I know you understand. Women don't understand us. They'll never understand us. I am sorry how your *Ninang* is behaving today."

The door to the bedroom closed. The woman continued to rant. She was sobbing. Her cry reached a crescendo, stayed there, and then quieted down. There were few more loud cries, some sobbing and gradually fading. Then there was silence.

P.J. remained standing. "Well . . . Want to go to other houses? I do know other families here."

Pearl stood up. She remained quiet. P.J. stepped ahead of her and reached for her hand as they got down the steep stairs. She obliged. Candida followed behind, not a word spoken like before.

"Now you could say you have been to a fiesta." P.J. gazed back at Pearl, who sat at the back of the car. He turned on the AC to ward off the heat. "Any favorite kind of music?"

Candida, who occupied the front passenger seat, remained quiet. Pearl ignored his question.

"You're close to the mayor?"

"He is my *Ninong*." P.J. turned on the radio.

"What exactly does that mean?"

"He is my baptismal godparent. My mom chose him to be my second parent. If something should happen to my mom, he would assume the role of my parent." P.J. cruised the stations.

"And the mayor's wife?"

"She's his wife. So . . . she would also do the same." P.J. settled on a light classic on the radio. "Like this?"

"Your mom, Techie, was she the only one who chose the mayor for your *Ninong*? What about that woman? What's her say in you . . . if . . . something happens?" Pearl continued to ignore P.J.'s question.

"Well . . . Nothing really. She doesn't count. She's just the *kerida*."

"Your Grandma Espe, she must be influential too in choosing the mayor."

"I would say so. *Ninong* was the running mate of my *lolo*, my Grandma Espe's husband. He was running for mayor when my *Ninong* was his vice mayor candidate. They were close to my family."

"What did your grandpa die from?"

P.J. was quiet for a moment. "He was killed," he finally said.

"Why? How?"

"Well, I am glad you've finally showed some interest in my family," P.J. joked.

"You haven't answered me."

"He was assassinated. It was election night. It was a close mayoral race. I was just a young boy. I was probably six or seven. I can't be sure. I don't remember much."

"Is that why your *Ninong* has armed bodyguards?"

"He is a prominent person in this town. He needs protection."

"Your immediate family doesn't have bodyguards."

"No, we don't. Being in politics is a different ballgame."

"And you want to go into politics?"

"My mom's side has always been in politics. The Lopezes and the Romualdezes. It's a family tradition. I am the only son from my mother's side. They expect me to follow in my grandpa's footstep. My father, if he hadn't died, was also geared to be in politics. Both his sides of the family are in politics too."

It was Pearl's turn to be quiet.

"Don't worry. I won't make you a widow."

"I'm not interested in being your widow."

"Marry me for my money then. You'll have a comfortable life. You'll have dozens of maids. You will be well provided for even when I die. I will be good to you. You may even cry at my funeral."

Pearl's and P.J.'s eyes locked in the rearview mirror.

"You will learn to love me. I am easy on the eyes. Women would envy your position. Lots of women are vying for my attention."

"I don't want to be like those two women."

P.J broke into a lusty laugh. The traffic coming back to the city had slowed down to snail's pace. P.J. opened the window on his side. He signaled a young boy peddling flowers. The boy rushed to the window and showed P.J. his wares. Like bees, it didn't take long for others to rush toward the car. Two older teens came shoving each other, vying for his attention. Each showed P.J. *sampaguita* leis, pushing the boy to the side. P.J. signaled the two to hand him all their merchandise, each receiving generous payment. He signaled the young boy to come near him, took all the leis he was peddling, and handed him money. The young boy told P.J. he didn't have enough change.

"Keep it." P.J. waved the boy away and handed all the flowers to Candida. "Put one lei on, Candida. Pearl, they're yours." P.J. closed the window on his side. The intoxicating smell of *sampaguita* flooded the interior of the car.

* * *

"*Hija*, try something else. The place is noisy, smelly, crowded. It's not for women. Go shopping with your mother or Techie. You enjoy shopping," Mario pointed out.

It was the weekend. He was casually attired, a short-sleeved polo, a comfortable though expensive pair of jeans, rubber shoes, and a fedora. The driver, *Mang* Tomas, had several small cages, each housing one of Mario's prized cockfighters in the van. Pearl saw at least four. It could be more. Her grandpa was actually retuning to the town P.J. had brought her to earlier. Being the town fiesta, cockfight marathons were primetime events.

P.J. would join them if he were free, Pearl thought.

P.J. himself raised prize-winning roosters. He had even gifted her grandpa one. While it ingratiated P.J. to her grandpa, it kindled her curiosity about the sport. The driver eyed Pearl with an amused look. Pearl looked funny in Mario's loose, long-sleeved shirt. She wore a pair of jeans. Her long hair was tucked inside a baseball hat. She wore a large pair of sunglasses to hide her face. She could pass for a thin, young lad. Her camouflage should work as long as she didn't talk and stayed close to her grandpa.

"You hate blood."

"I want to see one, Grandpa. Please." She ignored his warning.

"Women, you don't see them. It's a male sport."

"They wouldn't know, looking at me. I won't talk. I'll stay close to you. I could be between the two of you." Pearl winked at the driver. "Right?"

Mario kept quiet. It was what Pearl was waiting for. She knew her grandpa. It was a sign. He was beginning to give in. She rushed to him and showered him with kisses and bear hugs.

"Please, Grandpa, please."

The inside of the arena was indeed cramped. It resembled a miniature coliseum with narrow tiers of hard, wooden planks for chairs. At the center was bare earth where a pair of roosters were being readied for a fight. An older man, which Pearl assumed was the referee, was talking to two men who were each holding a rooster. Colorful ads of cigarettes, banks, soda pops, and private businesses, including a funeral home, a doctor, and a dentist were plastered around the arena, some totally alien to Pearl.

The crowd began to make noise. Hand signals floated. Some had thumbs up; others had thumbs down. Some had hands raised parallel to the ground to indicate how much money was involved. And her grandpa was right. Except for the woman handling the tickets to get in, the crowd was all male. The two men began to let the roosters peck each other's head, shoving them forward while holding them, taunting them to fight the other. Knowing they had kindled the killer instinct in them, the two men released their candidates. At the start, the two protagonists appeared to be sizing each other, approaching then retreating, scratching the ground with their feet. They flew a few feet in the air and spread their wings to appear bigger and menacing. Their claws were geared to attack. They croaked their best warrior noise. They repeated the ritual, meeting at midair, landing, and retreating to gauge the opponent. Then they attacked with fury. Feathers flew as they kept their bodies close to the enemy, biting, clawing, and poking at each other.

The crowd continued to yell, encouraging their candidate. It was hard for the novice to judge who was winning as they clashed in midair. Their bodies pivoted in tiny circles. They appeared as one pulsating, violent mass. Pearl saw blood squirting, sputtering. A shiny sliver caught her eyes. There were razor-sharp, crescent metals anchored on one of their legs, their lethal weapon. One rooster began to spin around, appearing dazed. It appeared barely harmed compared to its opponent, whose feathers were soaked in fresh blood.

They again retreated, scratching the ground. Then with fury, they lifted off the ground with their feet ready to give a final blow. Their wings spread out while they launched against the other with feathers hurling and falling softly to the ground. The less bloodied rooster landed on the ground, barely moving. The bloodied one continued to attack, piercing the opponent's body with its sharp knife. The crowd was in a frenzy, shouting at the top of its voice.

The winner, croaking with victory, moved around the arena, cocking its head while its owner came to retrieve him, lift him off the ground, and remove its weapon. Though his body was soaked in blood, it was the blood of the defeated. The owner claimed the defeated one. Its limp body was removed from the arena. Its owner's dream dashed, the rooster probably ended up on one's dinner table. It was quite a short spectacle. This bloody sport probably lasted a mere two to three minutes.

Pearl assumed that must be the reason why her grandpa had to bring more than one rooster. It was Mario's turn in the cockpit. The crowd turned quiet. His opponent, a popular movie star, walked in a confident stride and wore expensive attire and gold watch that glimmered as the light hit its surface. Stage whispers broke the silence, the crowd again betting with their hands. A lot of hands pointed down to indicate betting was in the thousands. The crowd knew these two opponents were aficionados, spending hundreds of thousands for each game.

Mario's hired hand got inside the arena. A master of his trade, he was paid a handsome fee by Mario to make sure the *tari*, the rooster's weapon, was placed just right on its leg. Not to be outdone, the actor's own assistant began to do the same. Pearl saw the blades sparkle as the roosters were released in the center of the arena. The excited voices of the crowd took hold as the two roosters spread their shiny brown-and-black feathers to make them look bigger, the peacock in their head standing stiff, menacing, their pupils dilated. They began to scrape the bare earth with their bare feet and stood tall in warrior stance, gauging their opponent and gearing for a fight to the end, one of them maimed or more likely dead.

That night, Pearl's journal read:

I attended a town fiesta. It is in honor of the town's patron saint. Each house prepares food. Lots of it. There were fireworks and carnival, and the town was decorated. I missed the parade of the patron saint, though. We stayed at the mayor's house at the fiesta. He is married, though he has a mistress. It seems it is accepted custom. A predominantly Catholic country, they do not have divorce here. I also saw a cockfight for the first time. It's a bloody sport. It could last for a few minutes to almost half an hour, depending on the prowess of the opponents. It is held in an arena where men bet who wins. My grandpa raises roosters for the sport. I am not sure if I like it. P.J even gave him a rooster as a gift. P.J. himself raises roosters. Not that I care.

The roosters fought till one of them dies. The crowd, which were all male shouting in revelry, somehow reminded me of the mayor's wife and mistress. P.J.'s family is currently courting me to be his wife. Do I expect the same fate if I do marry this man? The wife shares her husband with a kerida, *a kept woman. Right now, I am in an enviable position. Until when? I feel I am being groomed for the same fate. And yet women yield power in family affairs, a contradiction. Perplexing, you might say.*

CHAPTER 10

THE QUEEN OF DIAMONDS

Pearl pirouetted in front of the floor-length mirror, admiring herself. She paused, undecided whether the designer cloth she had on did her justice. The color did go well with her hazel eyes, that she knew. She pulled stray hair away from her face. Eyes seemed to gravitate toward her when her hair was pulled in a simple ponytail. She hated it, but she put up with it to please those eyes. It pleased her no end too.

The proprietor, a middle-aged woman was admiring her. "You can't seem to make up your mind, *hija*. Any color would look fabulous on you."

"Well, then I will get them in all shades."

She made it sound like an imposition. She looked for her mother to gauge her response. Aurora was busy talking with Techie, though. She browsed the glass-walled *escaparate* (display case) where the latest designer bags were. She wrinkled her nose, a shared mannerism with Aurora when things displeased them. They were more suited for mature women like her mother, *Tita* Techie, *Tita* Espe, or this woman. She wished a magical wand would bring her pronto to a place more fitted to her age. She heard laughing. The three women were talking animatedly. They walked toward her.

"Here she is. Are you done shopping, *hija*?" Aurora asked.

"Yes," she said softly to hide the annoyance in her voice. "Can we go now?"

"Of course. We didn't want to rush you," Techie said. "But if you're ready, we're ready."

There were several more boutique stores, each one as opulent as the previous one if not better. Each one carried exclusive merchandise, mostly imported ones. Pearl did not find anything to excite her.

"You seemed bored," Techie said. "Want to bite something?"

They were cruising around the shopping complex with Techie's driver.

"Not really."

"I have an idea."

Techie talked to the driver in Ilonggo dialect. The driver made a U-turn, exited the shopping mall, and whisked through a busy highway. It did not take long for them to leave the highway as the car entered a gated community. After announcing their presence to the guard house, the iron gate let them inside. Palatial homes with manicured lawns dotted the landscape. The driver parked in front of a circular driveway surrounding a tiered fountain. A uniformed maid ushered them inside.

A heavyset woman dripping with diamonds greeted them. *"Amiga.* What a surprise. Pleasant surprise."

Gifted with porcelain skin, she looked like a Dresden doll. It was hard to guess her age as she walked with unusual agility in spite of her corpulence. After the brief introduction, they were ushered into a cozy but well-appointed parlor. A white Siamese cat with arresting green eyes sat motionless on an antique chair. On its neck was a gleaming diamond necklace. Upon seeing them, it gave them an imperious gaze and then noiselessly left the room. The woman opened a safe hidden behind an oil painting, an Amorsolo original. She took out a huge leather case, laid it down on the empty, large, round table in the center of the room, and opened it. Exquisite gems made mostly of diamonds took Pearl's breath away.

"For you, *komadre,* I recommend this," she said to Techie. "You know I won't charge you a fortune." The woman showed a diamond brooch on a display case. "Just a tiny bit of profit for my friend." She flashed an engaging smile.

"Fabulous. What do you say, Pearl . . . Aurora? I brought them to show your collection."

"You made the right choice. *Hija*, this pair of earrings and necklace would be perfect for starters." The woman then gingerly took off her own earrings and necklace to model the merchandise on herself. She gracefully moved her head. The jewels sparkled as they caught the light, displaying their luminous beauty. "It's perfect on your daughter's flawless skin . . . and yours, of course." She again flashed her winning smile to Aurora and then to Pearl. "I used to have flawless skin like hers." She threw a feigned envious look at Pearl. "How I envy youth."

"*Komadre*, you still have beautiful skin," Techie said.

"You think so? You are very kind. I thought I saw a beginning of an age spot here." She pointed to a spot near her ear. She sported a sudden look of anguish.

They were interrupted by the maid who brought some *empanada*, fresh from the oven, their buttery smell wafting in the air. There were steaming mugs of hot chocolate to wash them down. The woman motioned the maid to put down the tray and waved her away.

"Please, help yourselves."

A soft knock was heard.

"What?" The woman did not hide her annoyance. "Didn't I leave instructions?"

A well-built man, probably not even thirty, walked into the room. He flashed a smile and showed gleaming white teeth. Every strand of his hair appeared to be in place. Though casually dressed, his long-sleeved cotton polo was pressed, matched with an expensive brand of jeans and unblemished pair of canvas shoes. He wore an expensive watch. On his ring finger was a huge diamond ring of obscene size, the only vulgar accoutrement on this otherwise well-dressed young man.

He went straight to the woman. He planted a long, lascivious kiss on her, embracing her tight, ignoring the presence of the other women.

"My boyfriend," the woman said, catching her breath.

The man flashed another smile and waved to acknowledge Techie, Aurora, and Pearl. He pulled the woman to a corner, exchanging whispers while his eyes continued to explore the woman's eyes, lips, and face as she talked.

"That Lazaro, he never fails to surprise me," the woman said as soon as the man left. "He wanted me to see a new condominium he bought me in Makati. Ah, men, they are like bees. Always wanting a taste of honey. He could wait. He knows I'm busy."

"You never changed," Techie said. "Pearl, she used to appear in the movies."

"I got tired. I am always offered the role of the other woman, the *kerida*. The truth is, I've never stolen a husband in my life. Never. They are the ones who come to me."

"Can you blame them?"

"Exactly. Can you blame them. *Hija* . . ." She looked at Pearl. "When I was your age, I had a long line of admirers."

"You still do." Techie threw a glance toward the door where the man left.

"I still do. Funny is, when I was younger, older men were the ones going gaga over me. Now that I am older, the young men are crazy about me." The woman pirouetted, displaying the jewels adorning her. "This may not be right for every woman. For me, this is. Everything provided for, compliments from these men. Men are like babies. Feed them. Burp them. They sleep like a log. Then you can ransack them dry. And why are we talking about me?" She broke into a contagious laugh.

She took off her bracelet and put on a new one to show Pearl and Aurora, daintily waving an arm to display the merchandise. "Any takers? This is the newest in my collection. This would look good on either one of you. Even you, *komadreng* Techie."

The rest of the afternoon was spent with the three women admiring and trying on exquisite pieces of jewelry. Pearl tried a lot. They seemed to sparkle more and were more desirable trying on.

"Your grandpa would spin on his head when he sees how much I spent," Aurora said as she handed a check to the woman.

Pearl couldn't be disturbed, still admiring a full-carat diamond ring on her finger. It fascinated her to no end moving her hand to catch the fire on the ring.

"Let me tell you. She's worth it." The woman asked, "Should I set that aside?"

Pearl threw a pleading look at Aurora. Aurora took a deep breath, nodded her head, and crinkled her nose. She grabbed her check and placed her reading glass to see the price tag.

"Pearly, only this one, and then that's it."

Writing the amount, she raised both hands to signal they were done shopping.

"Of course," Techie said. "We could always come back."

"I'll have more in two weeks. Just between us, I can give you the first showing. Don't tell anyone." The woman wasted no time giving her business card to Aurora and then to Pearl. She flashed her winning smile.

"And can you give us some reading?" Techie asked. *"Por pabor."*

"But of course. Give me a minute." The woman turned her back to them and returned the leather case inside the safe. She joined them, pulling a chair out in no time. "Who will be first?"

"Not me," Techie said. "You just read me."

"I don't mean you. I'm talking about these two women. Mother first or daughter?"

Pearl spread out her palm before anyone could answer. "Me first." Unlike her mother and Nanay, palm reading and its kind were all a game for her.

The woman grasped Pearl's hand. She examined it and ran her soft fingers on it, tracing the lines, crevices, and tiny mounds. Her face showed a myriad of emotions. Her lips quivered as she spoke, "You're not from here, are you?"

"My mother is."

"I was right. You're . . . visiting."

Pearl nodded. She was not sure where this was going. She crinkled her nose, like her mother. She found it boring.

"You have a brother?"

"No, she's my only child."

"I'm confused. I see there is a man who will play a very important role in your life."

Techie and Aurora exchanged glances.

"And where is this man from?" Techie could not hide the excitement in her voice.

"Let me run my finger on your hand again, *hija*. He's somebody foreign. I can sense that."

Pearl took a deep breath. *Brian, he is foreign. To them, he is foreign.*

"You'll travel far."

"Yeah?"

"You mean both of them," Aurora said.

"Is he the future husband?" Techie continued to press.

"Possibly. I can't tell from what I could read."

Aurora cradled her hands and kneaded her fingers. Her lips quivered. "Could you tell how many children they would have?"

"I can do that." The woman closed her eyes. She continued to hold Pearl's hand. After what seemed like eternity, she spoke, "I can see the number three. That's right, three."

"Three grandchildren," Aurora whispered, disappointed. Her mother, Tinay, if she were alive, would like more.

"I can also see she's traveling alone. All over."

"How is that possible? If they are married, they are supposed to be together."

"She will be a success. Business . . . something. Has to do with barter. Numbers. Has to do with lots of people. Lots of round things. I'm not sure what those round things are. What they mean."

"Money?" Techie said.

The three older women laughed.

"I never imagined you, *komadre*, thinking about money."

"I never judge people by their money," Techie said, feeling slighted.

"*Komadre*, I know. None of us do. It would be an insult to insinuate we are *mukhang pera* (money conscious). But . . ."

"But what?" Techie asked.

"What?" Aurora asked almost in unison.

"There's another man. He keeps popping up."

"A rival?" Techie asked.

"Maybe," the woman said.

Aurora gasped. Techie was probably right.

"I don't know. Very strong influence. I can't tell what his role is. He will only be present for a brief period. His influence, though, will be huge. He will be a huge influence in your life, Pearl. Be careful."

The session lasted nearly an hour. Though Aurora and Techie were fascinated, Pearl remained unconvinced. She thought the woman was a charlatan. She was using her customers' gullibility to foster her business. The woman's smile was from ear to ear while leading them to the door.

"Isn't she good?" Techie said. "She was describing P.J.. I can tell." Techie spoke to her driver, "Berto, they must be famished. Madrid fine with you ladies?"

"The woman said foreign." Pearl pointed out, which neither Techie nor Aurora noticed or chose to ignore.

"Yes," Techie said. "And P.J. is foreign. Pearl is from the States. That makes P.J. foreign to her." Techie motioned her driver to proceed to Madrid restaurant.

Aurora looked up and made the sign of the cross.

Pearl ignored the two women while she admired the diamond ring catching light, its brilliance nearly blinding her. She knew its rightful owner—her.

"Oh, it's you." The woman got off from the divan. "I didn't expect you to come. I'm resting."

The visitor remained quiet. Unlike the other man, he appeared nervous. He was sweating, even with the AC on. He pulled the woman close to him and planted a warm kiss to her lips. She pushed him away.

"I'm tired. I need my rest."

He ignored her, tightened his embrace, playfully bit her lower lip, and then kissed her neck and nibbled an earlobe.

"I said I'm tired." She shoved him hard to distance herself. "What do you want? I'll have her make you supper, and then you can leave."

"What's going on?"

The woman laughed. It was full of sarcasm. "I'm done with you. That's what is going on."

A slap landed on her cheek. She reeled from the force. The woman tasted salt and saw fresh blood staining her fingertip. She wiped her cracked lip, disbelieving that a man was capable of violence toward her. The door to the parlor opened wide. It was her maid.

"You heard her. She asked you to leave. *Manang*, I'm sorry. I shouldn't have let him in."

"It's fine. Now show him the door. Don't ever let him inside again—ever."

The man turned toward the door. His head and shoulders were down like a defeated warrior. He was mumbling to himself. The maid followed close behind. Without warning, he turned back, startling the maid. His eyes burned with rage, his nostrils flared, and his face contorted in anger. The maid did not see his hand suddenly raised high, holding a lethal knife. With precision, he aimed it toward the maid's chest. Bloodcurdling screams echoed through the room, along with the shuffling and desperate fleeing of feet, the heavy thud landing on the wooden floor, moaning, some desperate plea for mercy, and then eerie silence.

The double murder landed on the front page of most tabloids, the inner pages of major newspapers. Still, it made waves among the upper crust of the society. The woman was considered one of them, one of their favorite and trusted jewelers. There was no immediate suspect. Robbery was not the motive, as there were no valuables reported missing. However, the police knew it must be somebody known to both victims, as there was no sign of forced entry.

Techie and Aurora were horrified. They felt sorry for the woman. But more so, they lamented the loss of the soothsayer to predict the future. Pearl couldn't care less. She was more convinced her predictions were all bogus, the woman failing miserably to foresee her own mortality. School would open soon, and Pearl was eager to fly back home.

CHAPTER II

THE FAMILY ALBUM

Pearl pretended to be startled by Brian's presence beside her. She saw him seconds before, while she was placing her stuff in her locker.

A warm glow washed over her body as she looked at him. "Hi." Her pulse quickened.

She quickly checked herself in the mirror at the back of the locker door. Satisfied, she broadened her smile and locked the door.

"Hi." Brian was flushed and nervous. His smile was awkward.

"Yes?"

Brian swallowed. His Adam's apple rose. "Are you free tonight?"

Pearl feigned not to notice his discomfiture.

"Care for a movie?" Brian cleared his throat. "*Star Wars* is showing at the Cineplex."

She had seen it twice. Harrison Ford and Carrie Fisher. Her mind went to overdrive.

"I'd love to see the movie. Heard it's great."

Gaining confidence, Brian inched closer. "How about the last show tonight? I can pick you up."

Pearl could imagine Brian at the front door smelling fresh with a dab of cologne, holding a bouquet of flowers—red roses—for her. She suddenly pictured Aurora appearing out of nowhere, arms akimbo, shifting gaze between her and Brian and checking him from head to toe.

Pearl's smile faded. "How about meeting you at the lobby? It will save you the trip."

There was an awkward look on Brian's face. "Sure."

"I'll see you then, before eight forty. In the lobby."

Pearl bit her lips. It was too late to retract what she said.

"Eight forty?"

"I looked up the schedule before."

Pearl silently cursed herself at her gaffe. "It's long, I heard."

"Yeah." Brian retraced his steps and smiled sheepishly, unsure of his next step. "I heard that too."

"Listen, my mom's car should be here any minute." She began to race toward the school lobby, quickening her pace. "I got to go."

Out of the corner of her eyes, she saw Brian mulling what to do. He ran after her. At the lobby, the driveway was full of cars coming and going, picking up students. She was hoping her mom's car was there, but at the same time, she was hoping it hadn't arrived yet. Brian wasn't far behind. Just then, she saw the familiar car as Aurora pulled over. She felt a twinge of regret, though at the same time, she felt relief. She glanced at the lobby as the car sped away. There was no Brian.

"Did you hear me?" It was Aurora.

"What?"

"I asked how's school today."

"Fine."

"You don't sound it. Something happened in school? I can tell."

Pearl's face reddened, annoyed at her mother. "I'll watch a movie tonight, Mother," she spoke softly. She didn't want to jeopardize her plan. "Can you drop me off and pick me up later?"

"Who are you going with?"

"Joy, Michelle . . ." Pearl looked straight ahead, maintaining a relaxed tone. "And Donna." Her stomach was in a knot. She had never done this before.

"Which movie?"

The sting in her face spread to her neck. *Why did Mother have to ask? Why did she need to know?*

"*Star Wars?*" Aurora asked.

"Yeah." Pearl felt relief. "*Star Wars.*"

Aurora kept quiet. She hadn't seen the movie and wasn't planning to. She was not a fantasy film buff. *Seeing the movie for the third time? These teenagers.*

When she dropped off Pearl that night, there was no denying her daughter's excitement. Aurora hid a smile. It wasn't that long ago when she was the same age, was it? There was quite a crowd. She failed to pick out Joy, Michelle, or Donna from the crowd.

"Enjoy."

Pearl barely acknowledged her. Pearl was rushing. Her ponytail swayed as she jaunted with spring in her steps. Aurora craned her neck for one last look. Pearl was already lost in the crowd. Inside the car, Aurora waited until the crowd thinned out. She stepped on the accelerator to drive home and get some rest before picking up Pearl later.

The phone was ringing as Aurora entered the house.

"Hello?"

"Hi. Can I speak to Pearl?"

"She's not home. Can I take a message?"

"Yeah. Tell her Michelle called."

The girl did sound like Michelle, but Aurora wasn't sure.

"I thought you're going to see . . ."

Michelle had already hung up. Aurora sighed. How different her Pearl was from her friends. They barely acknowledged her when they dropped by to visit, not even a polite good-bye when they left the house or even announcing they were leaving. Her daughter was growing up the way she was brought up, she hoped. Either she was too old-fashioned or nostalgic of tradition back home. *Wasn't Michelle supposed to go with Pearl?*

She went to her bedroom and sat at the side where Red used to sleep. Aurora caressed the pillow and raised it to sniff a remnant of his smell. Her eyes blurred. She scolded herself, stood up, and rummaged through her movie collection. She had quite a few Tagalog films, most of them courtesy of her Cousin Boy who regularly sent her copies of films of her favorite movie stars, Amalia Fuentes, Susan Roces, and Charito Solis.

She had settled down on the bedroom lounge chair watching a Charito Solis tearjerker when the phone once more rang. It was Pearl's friend Joy.

"She's not here, Joy."

"Could you tell her to call me back?"

"I'll do that."

"Bye."

She barely acknowledged Joy's good-bye. *Wasn't Pearl supposed to be with Joy, Michelle, and Donna?* Two of them had called and seemed to have no idea of the plan. Charito Solis was crying herself out on the TV screen, but Aurora's mind was somewhere else. Unable to contain her mounting curiosity, she grabbed the school's directory, found Donna's number, and dialed her phone.

"Hello." It sounded like Donna.

"Hi. This is Mrs. O'Neil, Pearl's mom. Can I talk to Donna, please?"

"This is . . ."

Aurora paced the floor. Amber Pearl would not lie to her. Her daughter was a good daughter. She had always been. There must be some explanation to this.

"Calm down," she said, repeating to herself.

She took some deep breaths. "Calm down, Aurora. Calm down."

She ended up in the living room. She slumped on the sofa, feeling exhausted. She pulled a couple of family albums off the shelf. They should perk her up, calm her, and clear her mind. They always did. There was Pearl, Red, and her in front of their home when Pearl was just a baby. There was the christening photos, Red's thirtieth birthday, Pearl's grade-school graduation pictures, Pearl's piano recital, their family vacation to Disneyland, Nanay and Tatay, and Nanay and her posing for her wedding pictures. She touched Nanay's picture.

Memories began to flood Aurora.

It was a sweltering summer afternoon. There was just the two of them, Nanay and her. Tatay was out for some errands.

"Auring, how are my orchids? Are the flowers in bloom yet?" Nanay was swathed in a thick sweater. A long skirt covered her emaciated legs as she sat in a wheelchair. "Remind Dionisio that too much sun would kill them. Too much water will drown them. Dionisio can sometimes overdo things. Take care of them for me, will you?"

Aurora pretended not to hear her mother's *habilin* (last wishes). She busied herself by unfolding a thick blanket on her mother's lap. "Nanay, you're shivering."

She covered Tinay's legs. Even with the AC turned off, her mother was drenched in cold sweat. Aurora pushed the wheelchair into the elevator shaft. Its hum accompanied them as it brought them down to the main floor of the house. They didn't talk. The soft echo of Aurora's feet broke the silence as they passed the wide hallway down the *narra* floor of the formal dining room, the adjacent office of Tatay next to the billiard room, the library, and then out the flagstone-covered path overlooking the marbled living room floor. The sun's glare greeted them on their way out. The covered path ended inside the green house.

Tinay's eyes roamed. She inhaled to smell the moist earth, the lush vegetation, and the clay pots with their budding young plants in the nursery. "I miss the smell. It's been a while."

Outside, the garden was in full bloom. At a distance, the gardener, Dionisio, was busy tending the plants. Several sprinklers hissed spouting water intermittently.

"Yes, it's been a while, Nanay."

Aurora pulled up an iron chair to sit on and anchored it beside the wheelchair. Tinay gazed at her, unflinching. Tinay opened her mouth a few times, but no words came out.

"What is it, Nanay?"

Tinay shut her eyes. The ensuing silence engulfed them. Aurora assumed her mother was either tired, sleepy, or both. Aurora savored the remaining time they had by keeping quiet too. It didn't take long, and

Tinay opened her eyes again. Aurora saw the dying ember in those eyes. It wouldn't be long before those lights would finally be extinguished.

"Forgive me, Auring." Tinay feebly squeezed her daughter's hand. "Forgive me for all the troubles."

Aurora reciprocated her mother's squeeze tightly. It felt like squeezing brittle bones. *Did Mother just flinch?* Aurora released her grip.

"Anything hurt?" Aurora rubbed Tinay's arms and legs.

They were cold. The skin was pigmented, even jaundiced, from chemotherapy. The flesh appeared like parchment, ready to be peeled off the bony arms and legs.

"I've been rude to your husband. I may never have the chance to ask for forgiveness." Tinay paused, catching her breath. "Tell him forgive me."

Aurora squeezed her mother's hand, this time softly, afraid of causing pain.

"Time is running out. I had planned on telling you this a while ago, Auring. I never had the courage." Tinay coughed. Exquisite pain registered in her face.

Aurora rubbed Tinay's arms. Tinay smiled to assure Aurora she was fine. "Either I carry this to the grave or—"

Tinay broke into a paroxysmal cough. Her smile vanished. Aurora rubbed her mother's back. Worry creased her forehead. After what seemed like an infinity, the cough subsided. She wiped the sweat off Tinay's forehead.

"Whatever I tell you . . ." Tinay paused to catch her breath. Her eyes appeared sharp and alert. The dying ember suddenly ignited. "Promise me you won't tell Tatay. He doesn't deserve to be hurt more." Tinay struggled to say between dry coughs. "He's a good man."

Aurora's brows knitted. *What does Mother want to say?* She held Tinay's hand to her cheek.

"Remember, you are his daughter. Not a minute did he think otherwise. From the time you were born, he treated you like his own flesh and blood. Tatay blessed you with his name. I want you to protect that name. He's a good man." Tinay reiterated before breaking into another bout of coughing.

This time, Aurora didn't seem to notice her mother's unrelenting cough. Her mind was preoccupied. She had heard ugly talks, subjected to meaningful looks and whispers growing up. They were all rumors— malicious falsehood, empty assumptions, and just plain envy. *Were they?*

"They say I look like you," she asked him while seated on his thigh.

She was about seven. There was the sudden nervous jerk of Father Francisco's thigh. She giggled. She traced the priest's nose and touched his wavy hair.

"I have curly hair too. Like you."

"A lot of people look alike, Auring." Father Francisco was blushing. He always did so when he was drunk, though he wasn't drunk that time. "And they are not even related."

"Are we related?" She felt Father Francisco's hands on her waist to get her off him. "What does related mean?"

"Tatay is looking at us." Father Francisco pointed toward Tatay. "He wants you to go back to him." Father Francisco gently tapped her behind to usher her back to Tatay.

When she was about ten, she cropped her long hair close to her scalp. Nanay was livid. Tatay looked perplexed.

"Why did you do that?" Nanay's lips were trembling.

"I want to see if I really look like Father Francisco."

Nanay burst into tears. Tatay's color faded. Though he didn't say a word, the pained look remained etched in her memory.

"Is it true, Nanay?" Aurora sought the truth in her mother's eyes. "Tell me if what I am thinking is true."

She waited. It seemed forever. With tight lips, Tinay nodded. The ensuing silence was deafening.

"I always liked him." Aurora broke the silence. "Now I know why. Now I understand why he needs to know everything about me, why he insisted on knowing everything about Red like Tatay did."

Aurora shook her head in disbelief. She would like to believe Tatay was her father, yet she was glad to know who her real father was. She broke down. Her sobs intermittently broke the stillness of the afternoon. Tinay confided the rest and relieved Aurora's curiosity.

Dionisio remained busy tending to the garden from a distance.

Tinay and Mario were childhood sweethearts, growing up in the same affluent neighborhood. Both sides of the family approved of the relationship. Soon they were talking about marriage. Needless to say, both the Gomez and Tinay sides of the family were excited. It was a perfect match. A few months before the wedding, Tinay and Mario had a spat, one mundane issue about the wedding that Tinay could not even recall the specifics of. She was young and impulsive. Mario would do anything to show his unconditional love for her. He would be sorry for what he did. He would ask for her forgiveness. She would play hard to get. She would love to see him suffer a bit. She was the woman. The man should be the one to court her, giving in to all her whims and caprices. She planned on having an audience with Father Francisco. Father Francisco would be officiating at their wedding. Who should be privy to how inconsiderate her future husband-to-be other than this priest?

Father Francisco could give Mario some lessons and teach him how to behave to his future wife. She asked the family driver to drop her off at the rectory and wait for her. The rectory was quiet. Father Francisco's car was the only one in the driveway. The church secretary was gone for the day. Father Francisco was extremely popular in their parish, especially with the young crowd. In his early thirties, he was young, good-looking, and charismatic. Both his parents were from Madrid, Spain, and had settled in the Philippines. His foreign accent was actually considered an asset. His Hispanic heritage was a premium like any other white race among the locals. He made everyone comfortable.

She was positive he would listen to her, side with her, and comfort her. Plus, Tinay's family had given substantial donations to the church. Indeed, Father Francisco was waiting for her.

He greeted her warmly. "How are you Kristina? You're looking good today."

He invited her to go upstairs to his private quarters, where he supposedly had his office. She felt completely at ease with the priest. He let her talk and vent. He even chided her. He placed an arm on her while she blubbered about Mario's shortcoming. He stroked her hair and caressed her arms. He was like a second father to her. She was brought up to treat men of God with unconditional respect. They could never do her harm. The arm embrace tightened. The stroke became more exploitive.

Startled, she resisted. The rectory, which was a sanctuary, became a fortress, guarded no less by Father Francisco. Though the family driver was just a few hundred feet away waiting for her command, he was too far to hear her cries, too far to stop what was the unthinkable.

After what seemed like an eternity, she was left by Father Francisco, shaken. Part of her skirt was torn in the struggle. She camouflaged it by rearranging the pleats and tucking it under her belt. She smoothed her disheveled hair. The hair bun metamorphosed to a simple ponytail. Getting out of the rectory was a lesson in fear. Though soon she was left to herself, somewhere in the building was Father Francisco.

The stillness of the afternoon was frightening, portending evil. Her ears sprouted antennas. Her eyes grew an extra pair behind her head. Her nose smelled body heat. The hairs on her neck and arms stood up, magnetized by imaginary ogres and monsters hidden behind every door and closet, one of them hiding the master of them all, Father Francisco.

Though she literally flew to reach the front door, to her, it seemed she moved just inches at a time. Her heart choked her throat. It took her forever to unlock the door. The glare of the sun was a welcomed relief. The interior of the car was a haven. She slammed the door. The driver's eyes widened, surprised. She avoided looking him in the eyes from the rearview mirror. She felt naked in front of him.

"Drive me home!" Tinay bellowed, furious.

Why her parents would hire a feeble-minded moron who couldn't even think ahead was beyond her. She wanted to be driven home immediately. He should have anticipated it. The driver drove her home with eyes darting from side to side, stealing looks at her, and studying the sudden change in Tinay's composure.

Home at last, she took refuge in her bedroom. She felt dirty and washed herself for a long time. She nearly skipped dinner until she heard her father's call for dinner. Her father was always soft-spoken, but the sound of his voice always commanded fear and respect in his two children. At the dinner table, her mother commented on her picking on her food, which was not like her. She ignored her brother Doming's words, "I'll eat her share."

As soon as dinner was done, she retreated back to her bedroom, ashamed of her misfortune, aware she was no longer worthy of Mario's affection. Her mother knocked at her room to ask what the matter was, but she did not have the courage to tell the truth, assuming she probably would be blamed. Who would believe a man of God could do such a terrible thing to her? Nobody.

She did cry her heart out. Her mother soothed her, calmed her, and concluded it was a trifling fight she had had with Mario. Tinay became moody and unpredictable the ensuing weeks. Her mother rationalized that it was the usual premarriage jitters. When she began to lose weight and had morning sickness, her mother became suspicious. Their family physician confirmed she was indeed pregnant. Even then, she let her parents assume the father was Mario. Because she was betrothed to Mario, their indiscretion was considered acceptable and forgivable. They had faith Mario was man enough to make an honest woman out of her by marrying her.

Except she had never been intimate with Mario. She was a virgin until then. A firm believer in the sanctity of marriage, Mario expected her to remain clean and pure, untouched and lily white like her wedding gown until she was ready to surrender herself to him on their wedding night, like any respectable woman should. Would Mario, a fresh law graduate, buy that the baby was his, especially if she prematurely delivered a full-term baby? What if the baby took after Father Francisco with light-brown hair, well-formed nose, high cheekbones, large hazel eyes, and olive skin?

She finally got the courage to confide, first to Mario. Devastated, Mario would have nothing to do with Father Francisco. Tinay's family was more receptive to compromise. They did not want public humiliation. As strict Catholics, abortion was out of the question. They allowed Father Francisco to remain the priest officiating at the wedding. Any self-respecting man worth his salt would have backed out of the wedding. Everyone would have understood. Mario would be the laughingstock if they knew he married Tinay to save her from public disgrace, covering for somebody's mistake, even if it were a priest's mistake. He would be without honor. The unassailable truth was that he married her because he loved her.

During the wedding, Father Francisco had a sudden bout of illness and had another priest take his place. Nobody seemed to notice. Tinay and the rest of the family thought the storm was over and she could start fresh. Nobody knew except her parents and Mario. Not even Tinay's brother, Doming, known for being a rebel and short-tempered, knew about the 'incident.' They were wrong.

The family driver, whom they fired after repetitive alcoholic binging and not showing up for his work, had other things on his mind. Vindictive, he spread a rumor about Father Francisco and Tinay that spread like wildfire. He had witnessed Tinay emerge distraught from a private audience with Father Francisco. He was smart enough to notice Tinay come out of the rectory with a sudden change in demeanor, along with a change in her hairdo, a hair bun to ponytail. The family paid the driver a substantial sum to keep mum and disappear, but some damage had already been done.

When she delivered Aurora, the family hoped nobody noticed the early visit from the stork or the striking resemblance to the parish priest. They hoped the euphemistic premature delivery would be accepted without raised eyebrows or meaningful looks. The family pretended that nothing happened, kept their noses up, and went about their daily lives with their prominent social status remaining unblemished.

Aurora was startled by the clock's chime, breaking her reminiscing. She was almost fifteen minutes late in picking up Pearl. She rushed to her car. On the way to the cinema, she opened the car window to ease the stifling feeling in her chest. Aurora's mind was racing. Questions kept popping in her head in rapid sequence. Should she confront Pearl about lying? Or shouldn't she? Her daughter had learned to lie. What else? Where would this lead? P.J. crossed her mind, along with Techie and *Tita* Espe. The image of Father Francisco flashed. She imagined people whispering behind her back, laughing and mocking her. The whisper got louder.

"Anak ng pari (a priest's daughter)."

It was true. She was indeed a priest's daughter with all its derogatory connotation. She grew up hearing those whispers. It was the loudest whisper she had heard.

She slammed on the brakes. She nearly missed the road leading to the cinema. A few cars were still leaving the theater complex. Their headlights blinded her as she drove the wrong way in front of the theater lobby. A few blew their horns. Pearl was alone, anxiously waiting.

On the way home, Amber Pearl kept telling her how great the movie was, how she had picked up certain subplots or images she had missed, and how Donna, Michelle, and Joy enjoyed *Star Wars* for the third time.

Aurora remained quiet. She decided not to say a thing. She would think of what to do in the morning when her mind had rested and she could think more clearly.

CHAPTER 12

ENCHANTED EVENING

Aurora had less than a year preparing for Pearl's debut. It was a tradition back home that she owed her daughter. Plus, she had promised Nanay that her only grandchild would have a proper one, befitting of a Gomez, as her mother pointed out.

For starters, Aurora had already reserved the Grand Orrington's main ballroom for the occasion. The historic hotel in downtown Evanston could accommodate their guests and the overflow in adjacent hotels. It was convenient for their guests since it was only about a half-hour drive to Chicago. She preferred the old-world charm of the hotel with its dedicated elevator for special events, its main ballroom with its baccarat crystal. Three hundred some mother-of-pearl custom-made seven-by-five picture frames from Manila had already been ordered and delivered. Aurora already had the guest lists, though she knew it may swell or shrink. She painstakingly printed the guests' names in calligraphy and placed them in individual picture frames that would double as placement cards and party giveaways. Eighteen of Pearl's closest classmates and friends (nine pairs) had been practicing diligently the last three months prior to the debut, perfecting their cotillion dance. This ballroom dance would be performed to officially introduce a young maiden to adult society when she reached eighteen.

Aurora hired a seasoned dance instructor for the cotillion, a Filipino immigrant, thus familiar with the tradition. She collaborated on the design for the invitation, the menu, the flower arrangement, and the décor of the ballroom. She hired two bands well in advance, including scripting the program with the help of the dance instructor. She also hired a photographer who would videotape the event. It was a formal affair. Aurora was doing for Pearl what Tinay had done for her. Red would introduce their daughter, as tradition dictated.

Aurora had to bite her lip and swallow her pride to allow Mary, Red's wife, as a guest. Mario, who was footing the bill, reluctantly agreed. The O'Neils would be amply represented: Martha and Oren, Aunt Millie and Uncle Larry, Red's two siblings and their spouses, and a few close relatives. The Gomezes had Tatay, Nanay's brother Doming and his wife, *Ka* Lucia from Canada and her significant other, Fe, Cousin Boy and his girlfriend, plus more than a dozen relatives who would be willing to spend the money to travel abroad.

A week prior to the event, Doña Esperanza, Techie, and P.J. had checked in at the Hilton's The Grand Orrington. Its lobby became a hubbub of raven-haired, brown-skinned visitors who spoke accented English. All spoke Tagalog plus several Filipino dialects. From the northern part of the country, Tinay's relatives spoke Ilocano while Mario's side of the family spoke Tagalog. There were a few intermarriages with different ethnic groups from the southern part of the country who spoke Cebuano, Ilonggo, Waray, and Chabacano, each with its own distinct regional mores, cuisines, and traditions. The cohesive force between these ethnic groups was their predominant Malayan race and Tagalog language.

Aurora heard a lot of good comments about a certain Manila couture designer, Joe Salazar, to execute Pearl's gown. Pearl preferred one with more international flair. They finally settled on Valentino. The designer was insanely expensive, but Mario insisted on abiding his only granddaughter's wish. Pearl planned on wearing a red gown, and Valentino was ecstatic. Red was his signature color. Aurora was steadfast that the color was inappropriate for a young debutante. With Valentino's nod, they finally settled on a pale-pink gown befitting of the occasion, while the rest of the entourage would be in all-white, long gowns. Aurora was also adamant who would be in the welcoming party: Martha and Owen, Mario, then Red, and Aurora. The guests would be ushered to a private room where drinks and hors d'oeuvres would be served. Later, they would be led to a hallway where numerous pictures, medals, and awards of the celebrant were on display. An adjoining long table had the seating cards inside the picture frames for guests to locate their assigned seats. An elaborate arch bedecked with pale-pink flowers would greet the guests as they passed through on their way to their seats. Two live bands in opposite corners would provide the music.

Tatay made the opening remarks. They were followed by a welcoming note from Red. Cousin Boy played a jazzy rendition of "Some Enchanted Evening" on the grand piano, setting the tone for the evening. The guests were quiet, listening attentively. Tatay interrupted on the microphone, pointing out Cousin Boy as the perpetrator, introducing Aurora to Red. Laughter erupted from the audience.

As food was served, a surprise guest artist from the Philippines, Rico Puno, wowed the audience with native songs, accompanying himself on the guitar. Red's family joined in the revelry, even when the lyrics and tune were alien to them. The audience clamored for more as he sang his finale.

Then the lights dimmed. The crowd quieted down. A drum played to announce the appearance of a pair of teenagers in white gown and tuxedo. A spotlight shone on the first pair as they sashayed to the opening music and stayed in their assigned spot, then the next pair joined them. With the nine pairs in their designated sports, the cotillion began with them dancing in unison. They finished their dance with each pair parting at the middle, the young women forming a line parallel to their partners. A trumpet blared to signal the first official public appearance and introduction of Amber Pearl Gomez O'Neil to polite society.

Pearl appeared resplendent in a floor-length pink gown, escorted by her father, Red. Aurora and Tatay appeared briefly surprised. Recovering, they both applauded with approving smiles. Father and daughter danced to the strains of a waltz while surrounded by her escort.

Pearl's eyes searched the crowd as she swirled. *Where's Brian?*

Brian was supposed to be her escort. He had been present with the rest of the cotillion entourage earlier in the room provided by the hotel.

He had been very visible, continuously playing pranks with everyone, laughing at the top of his voice, and helping himself to the finger food in the hotel room. The girls in the cotillion, all schoolmates of Pearl, were busy primping themselves, doing last-minute checks on their makeup and hairdos in front of the mirror while the tuxedoed young men nervously glanced at their reflections without making it obvious.

There was a short knock at the door. The bellboy had brought a stunning flower arrangement for Pearl. The men did a few chuckles. Admiring comments from the girls led by Michelle, Joy, and Donna were heard.

"From Brian!" yelled one of the tuxedoed young men.

Pearl eagerly looked at the card. Her smile lingered.

"Well . . ." Joy was dying of curiosity.

"It's from P.J.." Pearl answered, dampening everybody's expectation.

"Who the hell is P.J.?" One of Pearl's tuxedoed classmates blurted. "We want Brian!"

He cartwheeled an arm repeatedly, signaling everyone to join.

Every male followed, whistling and yelling, "We want Brian! We want Brian!"

There was another quick burst of knock at the door. It was a different bellboy.

"Ma'am . . ." He paused and spread his five fingers to Pearl.

Pearl nodded and glanced back at the rest. "Guys, five minutes to go."

The entourage excitedly left the room and squeezed themselves in the private elevator to get to the ballroom. They could hear somebody singing in a foreign tongue behind the door leading to the main ballroom where they were hiding. Curious, they took turns peeking.

"Who's that?" asked Michelle.

"Rico Puno!" Pearl stifled a squeal upon recognizing the voice, herself surprised. She had heard him perform once while visiting Manila and commented to Tatay how she liked his style. *It must be a surprise from him.*

"Rico who?" blurted Joy.

"He's a very popular singer in the Philippines."

"He's good," said Donna. "What language is he singing? I could hear some English words, sometimes mixed with a foreign language or dialect. Am I right or what?"

"He's singing in Tag-lish," Pearl answered, bemused. It was spoken mostly by teenagers from prominent families, an affectation.

"What's that?"

"It's like . . ." Pearl groped for words. "Like Pidgin English."

"A mongrel?"

"Kind of . . . oh, well. I don't know."

The song faded; hearty applause followed. Then the lights dimmed to signal the first pair to pass under the arch. The rest of the pairs followed as their names were announced. Pearl panicked. Brian was nowhere to be seen.

The light squeeze on her hands broke Pearl's reminiscing. She nearly missed a step. Red caught her waist and smiled. Pearl smiled, catching up on her step. Nobody seemed to notice her—their—miscue.

As they sashayed, her eyes continued to search. Instead of Brian, there were the smiling faces of Techie and Doña Esperanza, an excited gaze from P.J., and the proud look from Tatay. *Ka* Lucia and her girlfriend looked at her with equal pride. There was *Tito* Boy, her mother's cousin, seated with his girlfriend. Smiling from ear to ear was Aunt Millie to Uncle Larry's stoic stare. The music ended.

As she curtsied to acknowledge the applause, straight ahead was Brian, smiling awkwardly at her. He whistled with his two index fingers in his mouth and yelled at her to stay frozen in the curtsied position while he fumbled with his camera. The flash blinded her while he took her picture. Red led Pearl to the main table where Aurora was already seated and waiting. She took the vacant spot between her parents. Rico Puno serenaded them with a few more songs while they enjoyed the sumptuous meal.

A tiered birthday cake with an abundant spray of pink flowers was later carted in. The crowd gathered close while Rico Puno once more sang to the strains of his guitar. He invited the crowd to join in. The band resumed playing after the guests had sampled the birthday cake.

P.J. approached Pearl and asked her to dance. She obliged.

"You're beautiful." P.J.'s eyes glittered. They settled on her.

Instead of being annoyed, he made her smile. She noticed he looked equally arresting in his tuxedo. She kept quiet. He held her gently and guided her steps with aplomb. He exuded confidence. And he smelled nice. P.J. felt a tap on his shoulder. It was Brian.

"My turn." Brian grabbed Pearl's waist without waiting for a response and brusquely dashed her out of P.J.'s arms.

Brian signaled the orchestra to change the tempo to a fast beat and began to dance with abandon with arms and legs flailing in the air. Brian didn't seem to tire, unperturbed and later ignoring Pearl's signal that she was exhausted.

When Pearl finally left the dance floor, he followed, sulking. He barely waited for Pearl to be seated, left her, and grabbed Michelle to dance with. When Michelle got tired, he grabbed another girl and then another, monopolizing the dance floor. Finally spent, Brian returned to his table where Aunt Millie, Uncle Larry, Boy and his girlfriend, *Ka* Lucia and Fe, and Mary were seated. Wearing a rental tuxedo, he was confident he looked spiffy and at the top of the game.

His food, though, was cold from waiting. He was obviously flustered which utensil to use.

Aunt Millie saw his predicament. "Start from the outside," she stage-whispered.

"What?"

Boy, seated to Brian's left, said on a quieter tone, "Use the outer fork and knife."

"Thank you," Brian said, snapping. "Thank you. And who are you?"

"An uncle of the celebrant," Cousin Boy responded in thick English.

"Are you a brother of Aurora?" Aunt Millie queried.

"A cousin."

"How many are you here?" Aunt Millie hadn't seen so many of Aurora's relatives at one time and in one place. *Actually, there was, though many moons ago. It was Aurora and Red's wedding.* She recalled.

"I can't tell you exactly how many, but a lot."

"And you are all staying at the Hilton?" Aunt Millie asked. "Each of you must have spent a fortune. We are at the Hilton, correct? Hilton's The Grand Orrington. Wow!"

"For Auring and *Tito* Mario . . . and Pearl, of course, it's nothing. It's worth it."

"You Filipinos are very closely knit, aren't you?" Aunt Millie leaned sideways toward Boy, squeezing a very quiet Larry who was between her and Brian.

Brian remained busy with his food.

"Clannish," Aunt Millie said, summing it up.

"Yes." Cousin Boy nodded. He was not sure where this talk was leading. "Sort of."

"Lots of extended family," Aunt Millie said.

"I've never attended a party this big," Brian said with food in his mouth. "It's awesome."

"Pearl's an only child. It's not unusual for a family to spend a fortune for a daughter's debut if they can afford it," Cousin Boy said.

"Her family can afford it." Aunt Millie straightened her posture. *She was family.*

"I second that." Brian said in between food bites and wine. "I can just imagine her wedding." He chuckled.

"It will be a while yet," Cousin Boy added.

"Definitely." *Ka* Lucia was quietly observing, breaking her silence. Fe elbowed her.

"I don't know about that," Brian said. "What's the point of waiting? I am ready whenever she is ready."

"You're Pearl's boyfriend." Aunt Millie gasped and smiled with delight. "Why, I am certainly honored to be seated at the same table."

"Yes, ma'am." Brian proudly cocked his head. "This is the man, the future husband."

Cousin Boy nodded. *Did Auring know about this?* "What do you plan after graduation, Brian? Did I catch your name right?"

"My dad works in a body shop. He already spoke with the owner, and I am promised a spot," Brian uttered with confidence. He looked at Aunt Millie and then Cousin Boy, *Ka* Lucia, and Fe, ignoring Larry. "With a very good starting salary. I can start working tomorrow if I want."

Cousin Boy continued to nod.

Mary remained quiet in her seat. She appeared bored, and did not hide it. She wasn't even part of the receiving party. And she was the stepmother of the celebrant.

"The pay's big," Brian continued. "My hourly rate would be something like this." He wrote the sum in the air.

Aunt Millie gasped. "Really? Did you see that, Larry?"

Ka Lucia, Fe, and Cousin Boy and his girlfriend exchanged quick glances. Uncle Larry's mouth was full. Rushing to answer, he began to cough hard.

"My goodness, Larry, are you all right?" Aunt Millie began to rub and smack his back.

"Here's some water," Brian offered.

"No." Cousin Boy took the glass of water. "You'll make it worse. Can you talk?"

Uncle Larry nodded. He continued to cough, clearing his throat. His ruddy complexion gradually returned to its normal sallow color.

"I . . . I'm fine."

"Who's trying to be a hero here?" Brian met Cousin Boy's eyes. "Are you a doctor or something?"

Cousin Boy nodded. His girlfriend looked relieved.

"You are?" Aunt Millie's eyes rounded. "Larry, why don't we swap places so I can be closer to the doctor? I do have a medical question I want to ask. I am sure he wouldn't mind."

Aunt Millie stood up and flattened the creases in her dress, waiting for Uncle Larry to trade places, like nothing happened.

"What's your name, doc?"

"Call me Boy."

"Is that your last name, doc?"

What's taking Larry so long? She kept her smile on.

"No. It's my first name, my nickname."

"Boy?" Aunt Millie's eyes wandered.

"Yes, Boy."

Brian ignored the conversation, grabbed his wine glass, gulped its contents, and raised his hand to signal for more. The dance floor remained packed. Some female members of the cotillion changed into short gowns from an all-white ensemble. Pearl danced a few more slow numbers with P.J. and once with Tatay before hobnobbing with the rest of the guests and her friends. The party didn't wind down until past midnight. For the finale, the two bands played a fast number. Nearly everyone joined. Conspicuously absent was Brian. There was no sign of him when a group picture of Pearl and her entourage was taken. Aurora discovered Brian's whereabouts.

"He's in the men's restroom," Aurora whispered to Pearl. "Must have drank more than he should. Probably needs a ride home."

Aurora turned her back to go, obviously flustered. Pearl was left alone. Her confused and worried look didn't escape P.J.. Pearl told him what the matter was. P.J. excused himself. He came back with Brian on his arm, obviously inebriated.

"Hi, hon," Brian managed to say to Pearl.

Pearl ignored him. She saw P.J.'s soiled tuxedo. It was wet, crumpled, and stained. "Did he . . ." She hesitated.

"It's okay," P.J. answered. "We need to bring him home."

"Yes, I know," Pearl said.

Aurora was back with Cousin Boy in tow. "Your *Tito* Boy will bring him home."

"We're fine," P.J. reassured everyone. He smiled when Aurora and Cousin Boy noticed his soiled clothes. "*Tito* Boy, you don't want your clothes soiled too. Pearl will show me his place."

Brian's place was quite a drive. Except for the occasional barking of dogs, the place appeared deserted. There were rows of cookie-cutter-sized dwellings. Brian's place was in the end row. There was a security light at the front door. The front lawn, though small, appeared well tended.

Totally intoxicated, Brian needed help with his steps. Pearl watched from the car and saw P.J. ring the bell. A middle-aged man appeared at the door. P.J. disappeared behind the door to bring Brian inside.

"Thanks for bringing him home." Pearl broke the silence as they drove back to the hotel.

"It's no big deal."

There was another period of awkward silence.

"Thank you for coming," Pearl said.

"My pleasure. I had a great time. So with Mom and *Lola* Espe. Did you enjoy Rico Puno?"

"Sure did."

"My mother was worried Rico wouldn't be able to squeeze your debut into his busy schedule."

"I thought Tatay arranged for Rico Puno's appearance."

"Tatay mentioned to Mom that he is your favorite. He said you enjoy his music. We thought it would be a very nice surprise for your debut."

"It was. It's very generous of you."

"Thank my mom," P.J. answered. "I have my own gift for you."

"Rico Puno was more than enough gift from your family."

"That's my mom and *Lola* Espe's gift."

Pearl remembered the flowers. "And thank you for the flowers. They are beautiful."

P.J. nodded to acknowledge her. "My gift . . . I had it sent to your place. You'll see it when you go home tomorrow. Hope you like it."

At the hotel lobby, Pearl politely declined P.J.'s offer to see her to the door of the hotel suite she was sharing with her mother, *Ka* Lucia, and Fe.

"Are you sure?" P.J. asked. "I can drop you off at your room."

"I'm fine. Go to your room. You need rest."

"I am not tired."

"I said go," Pearl said. "I need to check on something." She waved her arm. "Go."

P.J. walked to the elevator with his eyes constantly stealing glances at her. He waved reluctantly at her as the elevator door closed.

As soon as P.J. was gone, Pearl raced back to the main ballroom. She wasn't expecting her mother or any visitor would still be there. Aurora must be up in the complimentary guest suite the hotel management provided them. It was a relief they didn't need to rush home that night. Though tired, Pearl felt ecstatic and happy at the turn of events.

In spite of Brian's behavior, it hardly caused a ripple to her.

The ballroom was nearly deserted except for the cleaning staff as she entered the ballroom with its sweeping staircase. A male staff looked at her. She waved and smiled at him. She giggled when he ignored her and turned his back on her. It didn't matter to her. Pearl ran the length of the ballroom, lifting her gown to avoid tripping, her feet feeling light. There was inexplicable peace and quiet in her that she wanted to capture forever.

She sat on the carpeted floor. She closed her eyes. She imagined P.J.'s eyes that nearly disappeared when he smiled, the sound of his voice, and the feel of his warm body. She imagined sashaying and being lifted by him to the tuneful sound of *that* music played by *Tito* Boy on the piano, the two bands playing louder and louder as they danced solo to dizzying heights, just the two of them. Above them the ceiling was replaced by sky dazzling with stars. It was magic.

Pearl took a deep breath but kept her eyes closed. It was indeed some enchanted evening.

CHAPTER 13

A Sack of Rice, a Jar of Salt, a Pound of Sugar

Mario swallowed hard. He removed his glasses to wipe the smudge.

"You're sure about this?" His chest heaved from frequent shallow breathing.

Pearl nodded without blinking. "Yes, Tatay." Her mind was already made up. Tatay, without a doubt, would understand, would be on her side.

"Have you told your mother yet?" Mario continued to wipe his glasses.

Pearl shrugged her shoulders. "She wouldn't mind." The truth was that she wasn't sure.

Mario was not expecting this. If this were the courtroom, he could have kept his emotions under wrap. But this was his granddaughter. He put his glasses back on. His lips and mouth were dry.

"Talk to her, Tatay. She'd listen." Pearl knew Tatay would do as she said.

"P.J., what did he say?"

Pearl's eyebrows arched. "He has nothing to do with this, Tatay."

"He would be disappointed."

So would Techie and Esperanza, Mario thought.

"Everybody's expecting you to go to college, like everyone else." He thought about some girls back home going to extreme, prostituting themselves to afford a good education like exclusive private Catholic schools. It was not unheard of among his colleagues. He thought it was a rumor, an urban legend, until he ran into one. A colleague, a judge, was actually a sugar daddy to one of them. He had met the girl, passing herself off as the judge's niece when they went out. There were more.

"I've got a year of college," Pearl pointed out.

Why do Tatay and Mother always think alike? She was wrong thinking he was on her side.

Mario could sense Pearl was undeterred. "Why?" That single word summed up his disappointment. He needed to light a cigar. *Every girl or boy back home dreamed of going to college. It was expected of every decent family. It was not unheard of for families to go into debt just to send their children to college.*

"I want to travel." A flight attendant would be a start. The truth was that Pearl had already sent a few applications. "I've always wanted to travel."

Aurora was hysterical when she heard the news. "Your grandpa told me about your plan."

Aurora held her breath. It was hard to keep her emotions at bay. *Please say it was all a mistake. She really meant to go back to school this fall.* Aurora prayed to herself that Pearl would acknowledge it was all a misunderstanding. *What would everyone say?* Pearl avoided her eyes.

Aurora's hope rose. "Now, you really didn't mean it. I know." She inched beside her daughter. Aurora dreaded to say the word "quit."

"I do, Mother." Pearl looked her in the eyes.

Aurora failed to see the look of submission in her daughter's eyes. And she thought she knew her daughter quite well. She sensed the panic building up in her.

"P.J. would be visiting. How would you explain—"

Pearl interrupted her. "Stop, Mother." Pearl squeezed her arm. "This is my decision."

Aurora couldn't believe what she heard. Except for a few flaws in judgment, Pearl had been a good daughter. She was proud to say that Pearl grew up not unlike her. She listened to her. The thought renewed Aurora's confidence. Her hope sprang eternal. Pearl was and still is her mother's daughter.

"Why would your mother think you need to consult P.J.? P.J.'s family are all professionals, just to remind you." And then for the coup de grace, Aurora bowed her head and covered it with her hands. "Go ahead. Do what you want. I'm just your mother anyway." Her sobs filled the room. "After all the sacrifices I've done for you. Had I known this, I could have just pinched your nose when you were a baby."

Aurora was surprised at herself. She was talking just like her mother.

Aurora's sobbing faded. The shaking of her shoulders ebbed. She did not detect any movement beside her, not even the quiet breathing of Pearl. Raising her head, she spread her fingers. Between the webs of her fingers, she caught a glimpse of Pearl's shadow disappearing behind the door, followed by the click of the closing door. Aurora's heart sank.

"Come back here, Amber Pearl. I am talking to you. You hear me. Your mother is talking to you!"

Aurora's loud sobbing filled the room. This time, her anger and tears were real. She heard the click of the door opening. She held her breath and controlled her sobs.

It was Tatay.

Pearl turned on the ignition to her two-seater, red convertible BMW, a gift from Tatay for her eighteenth birthday. She pushed the accelerator. The car glided out of the driveway, gathering speed as she pushed harder.

The steel machine yielded, pliant under her command. *Is that how Mother expected me to be? Malleable like those rice papers she uses to create sumptuous meals, giving like those purple yams molded into diamond shape, and yielding like that thick coconut milk extracted from grated coconut meat?* She needed space. Had she stayed, she would probably crumble and give in to her mother.

Guilt gnawed at her. She had been raised by her mother, raised the way Aurora knew was the proper way for a daughter to behave. The same way Nanay and Tatay had raised her mother, a tradition handed down, polished, and perfected through one generation to the next. The other side of her told her to be independent, assert autonomy, set aside filial obedience, and think for herself. She did not recall when the silent voice began to be heard. Like a bud, it grew and flourished, rooted, and began to claim its place without her wanting to or nourishing it. Pearl was in a quandary.

The blare of the siren and throbbing lights jolted Pearl. Her speedometer recorded nearly ninety miles per hour. She released her foot off the gas and guided her car to a complete stop, the police car not trailing far behind her.

Whereas before a day wouldn't pass without mother and daughter exchanging notes and idle talk, the ensuing weeks were a succession of quiet unrest in the O'Neil household. For several days, Aurora's eyes were nearly shut from her constant crying. Her voice had turned hoarse. Even when Pearl would initiate talk to mend the rift between them, Aurora was steadfast and adamant, ignoring her daughter. Mario was hapless in patching up the two women's differences. From then on, Aurora made it a point to avoid running into her daughter as much as possible. If they did run into one another, Aurora ignored her, looked the opposite way, or cast her eyes downward. Anything they needed to communicate would be through Tatay, the go-between, whose short visit got extended indefinitely due to this development.

Several weeks passed. Aurora remained steadfast until she heard the news from Mario.

"She can't do that, Tatay."

"You pushed her, Auring."

"This is her house. She belongs here."

"You treat her like rubbish, I'm sorry to say. She is an adult, Auring. And raised here in America. Remember?"

"And the way she treated me?" Aurora's voice squeaked. "Tatay, how can you forget the way she treated her mother."

"How did she treat you, Auring? Tell me."

"Tatay?" Aurora could not believe what she heard.

Tatay had always been her *sandigan*, her defender. She was wrong.

"It's time you stopped foolish pride, Auring. Accept that Pearly is a grown woman now."

"And leave her mother alone?"

"Her job requires that."

"She didn't have to—"

"I don't know about that, Auring. Pearl is moving out by the end of this week."

"She won't do that."

"Ask her."

Aurora was dumbfounded. Tatay was telling the truth. Her Pearl was leaving home for her own apartment. In New York yet, where the airline's headquarters and training school were. Pearl, she wouldn't do that, or could she? She was quiet for a long time. Then finally summing up courage, Aurora rushed to Pearl's room for the first time in weeks. Mario trailed close behind, worried about a possible confrontation. The door swung open as Aurora was about to knock. Pearl was standing by the door as if she was expecting her. The women's eyes locked.

"You're moving to New York." Aurora's tone was measured with a hint of diplomacy palpable.

Pearl nodded.

"Are you doing this to slight your mother?"

Pearl's eyes registered surprise. She shook her head vigorously.

"Then why are you doing this without even letting me know?"

"But—"

"What do you know about apartments? You didn't even let your mother help choose the place."

"Mother—"

"Exactly, I am your mother. Had you told me earlier, I could have helped you buy the furniture."

"It's furnished, Mother."

"The more you should ask your mother's advice."

Aurora glanced at Mario. But her father's face remained blank. She couldn't mirror anything in those eyes, just when she needed most an ally on her side.

"Have you moved any of your stuff yet?" Aurora's tone changed to concern.

"I was planning to."

"Good." Aurora felt relief. "We're not late, Tatay."

Mario was not sure he understood what Aurora was implying. He was relieved that the two women had started talking.

"Salt, a sack of rice, and sugar. We need to buy those." Aurora was empathetic. "The first three things you should bring inside your new place for good fortune. Tatay, you remember that, I'm sure."

Mario agreed with a nod, anything to maintain peace between these two women in his life.

That weekend, Aurora and Tatay flew with Pearl to New York. Aurora didn't waste time helping her daughter get settled after the rice, salt, and sugar were neatly tucked in the apartment. Aurora made sure of that.

"It's nice this apartment faces the east," said Aurora.

"And why is that?" asked Pearl.

"Didn't you know? It means grace can enter your apartment. It's good luck."

"If you say so, Mother."

Aurora didn't waste time doing groceries for Pearl while Pearl and Tatay busied themselves moving Pearl's personal belongings. Armed with a measuring tape, she bought and changed the curtains and hung some pictures and art pieces to decorate the place. She even checked where the apartment complex's laundry room was. She and Tatay bought a new vacuum cleaner for Pearl. It was close to midnight when the three finished with the move.

After a quick shower together, the two women settled in the single bedroom in the apartment. Mario slept on the living room sofa bed. He barely closed his eyes. The constant talk and intermittent laughter from the adjacent bedroom kept him awake.

The following morning Aurora was up early, busy cooking. She prepared pork and chicken *adobo* because any leftovers would not spoil easy, Aurora pointed out. She would have cooked other food except Pearl insisted that she did not. Aurora then resumed checking on everything, even rearranging the furniture. For lunch, Tatay treated them to a fancy restaurant. Back in the apartment, Aurora continued to meticulously check on everything again. Before anyone could realize it, it was late afternoon. It was time for Aurora and Mario to finally leave.

"You're sure you're okay now, Pearl?"

"I'm fine, Mother."

"How long do you have to fly domestic?" Aurora was hoping Pearl would soon fly international, get the travel bug out of her system once she got her fill, and then come back home.

"I'm patient, Mother." Pearl could certainly read her mind. "Once I gain enough experience and seniority, I'll have more options." Pearl spread both arms. "Then I can really travel."

"To places your mother would just dream about."

"I love to travel, Mother."

"Well, I guess I have to live with that. Just remember, you reserve every other RON . . . is that what you call your days off . . . to stay with your poor mother. Your room will always be ready. I'll make sure nothing is changed. I'll miss the sound of you playing the piano."

Pearl laughed, a noncommittal one. She did not bother to correct Aurora.

"P.J. would be surprised . . ." Aurora bit her lower lip to control the urge to lay down a guilt trail for Pearl. Her voice began to falter.

Mario cleared his throat. "Auring, the traffic . . ." He lit his cigar and cleared his throat again. "We want to avoid the traffic." He puffed on his cigar. "Our flight."

The two women embraced, tight and long. Pearl pecked Mario on his check and then gave him a bear hug. Aurora rushed to the elevator while this was happening. She didn't wait for Mario. She didn't want Pearl to see the look on her face. In the lobby, Aurora was seated, waiting for Mario, staring blankly into space.

Contrary to what he thought would happen, there were no histrionics from Aurora. She was quiet, extremely so. Aurora remained sullen on the ride to the airport.

"Want to come home with me?"

Aurora shook her head.

"P.J. will be visiting. It's embarrassing if I'm not even here to entertain and show him around, Tatay."

"How are you by yourself?"

"What can I do? It's my *kapalaran*, my destiny. First, my husband . . . now, my daughter."

"Don't pity yourself, Auring."

"I was a good wife. Didn't even work so I could take care of Red and Pearl. This is what I get in return."

Mario decided to keep his thoughts to himself. He drove quietly. Aurora was soon deeply asleep, with her mouth drawn on both sides and worry lines creasing her forehead.

CHAPTER 14

MOTHER-OF-PEARL

The spicy aroma of the *salabat* stung Aurora's nostrils. Steam escaped and billowed from the teapot's nose. As the ginger roots danced in the boiling water, their bleeding colored the crystal-clear water a strong brown. Aurora brought the platter to her bedroom. Pearl was lying on her bed. In a fetal position, she was facing the east-side window, her back to Aurora. With her rhythmic breathing, Aurora wasn't sure if her daughter was asleep.

"*Anak.*" Aurora addressed Pearl with endearment. "I boiled some *salabat*. It is good for upset stomach. Green guava also helps."

Pearl kept still. Aurora circled the bed to face Pearl and sat the platter on the bedside table. Filtered bands of light flooded Pearl. Her eyes were shut; her lips were tight. Aurora saw dried tears on her daughter's cheeks. She gently stroked her daughter's hair while she gazed at her face. A lump grew in her throat. Her eyes began to sting. She straightened her spine and closed the blinds to protect her daughter's pale skin. The noise startled Pearl, her body recoiling and retreating. Her eyes registered terror.

"It's me," Aurora said. She resumed stroking her daughter's hair. "It's me."

Recognizing her, Pearl closed her eyes. Her shaking began to ebb. Aurora pulled the bedsheet up to Pearl's neck. She sat beside her daughter and reached to rub her daughter's back. In no time, Pearl was back to a deep sleep. There was a silent rise and fall of her chest, in synchrony with her soft snore. Aurora kept rubbing her daughter's back until her arm ached. It was an effort to keep her head up as her eyes began to feel heavy. She didn't even remember lying in bed beside Pearl.

Aurora floated in space. Ironically, her feet felt like they were cast in lead, so it was a struggle to walk, much more to run.

With the wind blowing in her face, she found herself inside Pearl's apartment. A mirror materialized in front of her. She touched her clothes, surprised that she was wearing Pearl's flight uniform. Reflected in the mirror was a stranger standing behind her. Aurora turned to face the stranger. Her scream and the stranger's laughter mingled, filling the tiny apartment. The stranger had an angelic face, marred by a diagonal scar on his upper lip, a hairless strip in an otherwise trimmed moustache. His eyes were azure blue. His smirk showed a perfect set of teeth. She retreated backward, gearing to distance herself. In a last desperate effort, she took cover behind the three-paneled screen separating Pearl's living room from the breakfast nook. The screen was made of *narra*, varnished in its rich, natural, deep brown mahogany. It was intricately carved. The embossed paneling showed young bamboo branches guarding a winding brook, tiny *maya* and *pipit* birds perched on its branches, and a regal peacock strutting by the water's edge. Rows of spindles guarded the top and the bottom. The native flora and fauna were made of semiprecious stones and mother-of-pearl. It was P.J.'s gift, flown all the way overseas for Pearl's debut.

Powerful hands toppled the heavy screen that came crashing to the floor. The force decapitated the tiny *maya*, broke the colorful plumes of the proud peacock, and tore some spindles from its hinges. It nearly missed her as she stepped backward and then cowered at the corner of the piano for refuge, balling herself. He yanked her arms and pulled her legs, sprawling her on the cold floor. Aurora screamed as the stranger caught her blouse, ripping it open. She clawed his face as he tore her undies. His brute strength overpowered her resistance. She shut her eyes to avoid the look of victory and satisfaction in those sinister eyes. His hungry lips muffled her shouts. His tongue slithered like a snake inside her mouth. The pain in her groin felt like a knife cutting her flesh repeatedly.

In desperation, her one hand clung to the side of the piano, banging the notes randomly, the syncopated sounds a desperate call for help.

Aurora woke up, gasping for air and sweat drenching her. She covered her mouth to stifle a scream, not wanting to wake up Pearl. Her daughter needed rest. This wasn't the first time she had had this dream. It always showed her being chased by the assailant, hiding behind the *narra* screen, desperately banging on the piano as Pearly narrated to the authorities.

With slight variation, the event played over and over like a movie reel. At times, Pearl would be sprawled on the floor about to be ravished, and Aurora would suddenly appear as an onlooker. She would stage-whisper to the assailant to look her way. Getting his attention, she would tear her blouse to expose her breasts and poise her hips seductively, pouting with the "come hither" look in her eyes and tempting him to get her instead.

"Take me. I'm better. I promise. Take me, not her."

She fought tooth and nail not to report the assault. She lost. Pearl was adamant. Her daughter had a good look at her assailant and could positively identify him in a lineup. Aurora had her lingering doubts. How many rape crimes were solved by the city police? Not many, she assumed.

P.J. was also insistent. Disappointed, Aurora felt betrayed by P.J.. Was his insistence partly to assuage his guilt? He saw the man standing by the anteroom of the main lobby. The man was fidgety, shifting his gait with rings of smoke from his mouth. Seeing P.J. walking toward the door, he smiled at him while leaning his body against the glass door. The man acknowledged P.J. by nodding his head as he let him in. The man wore a thick, dark jacket.

To P.J., that was nothing unusual, as he was unfamiliar with the four seasons. The police noted its peculiarity. It was still summer, though cold air and occasional gusty rain began to lately signal an early fall. That day in particular was not cold at all. It was, in fact, hot and humid. To P.J., the weather was just right as he headed to his car, a couple blocks away. He was walking fast, pretending to act like he belonged, a local, though feeling conspicuous and claustrophobic with the skyscrapers surrounding him, dotting the cloudless sky. He did not expect to see a parking violation on his windshield. On unfamiliar ground, P.J. decided to go back to the building and ask Pearl what should be done with the citation on his rental.

In a way, Aurora was grateful to P.J.. The ticket probably saved her daughter's life. A kitchen knife in the apartment was later reported missing. It was intended for Pearl, no doubt. Pearl was crawling to the phone while the intruder was occupied ransacking the place. After one ring, Pearl immediately answered. She recognized P.J.'s voice. She didn't waste time pushing the intercom button to let him in. The intruder had already escaped through the back exit when P.J. came knocking hard on the main door, hearing desperate yells from Pearl.

Aurora took a deep breath. She removed the blanket that covered her and got out of the bed, careful not to stir it and wake her daughter. She reached for the silver platter on the side table. The *salabat* had long been cold. The green guava rolled freely as she walked down the stairs on her bare feet to the kitchen. She went back upstairs to her room. Pearl was still sleeping. Aurora took a quick shower to get rid of the sticky, dried sweat and put on fresh clothes.

Done, she again went downstairs and turned on the TV just loud enough to keep her company. She barely listened to what was on. Listless, she went to the kitchen, rinsed the already clean cups in the dishwasher, and put them back to dry. Finished, she took the kitchen mop, soaked it in a pail of soapy water, wrung it to drain excess fluid, and then went about cleaning the kitchen floor. Having done that, she went upstairs to check on Pearl. She saw that she was still asleep. She traipsed to her walk-in closet, scattered the clothes that were already neatly folded, and began to fold them meticulously as before, placing them back where they belonged. She had to keep herself busy, or she would go berserk.

The phone rang. It startled Aurora. Recovering, she rushed to grab the phone in the adjacent master bathroom so as not to disturb Pearl. She cupped the receiver to tone down her voice.

"Hello?"

"It's Tatay. How's Pearly?"

"She's sleeping right now, Tatay. She's on leave. Would you like to talk to her?"

"Not if she's resting. Any updates?"

"Nothing." Aurora still thought it was a mistake that the police had a report of the event. It would be a permanent record of her daughter, Pearly. "They're done with the usual questions and lineup of usual suspects. Interviews. Why does she need to go through all of these?"

"It was her choice, Auring," Mario said, interrupting. "I expect the authorities will not disappoint her . . . or us."

Aurora felt some resentment but didn't say a word. Being her father, he deserved respect, outside of the privilege of being older. And Tatay had his reasons. She was hoping he was an ally and would convince her daughter to not file a police report. And she could just imagine the callous way the emergency room doctor probably probed her daughter's private parts, took specimens here and there, and likely referred to Pearl as "alleged rape victim." An intruder had violated her daughter. There was no question about it.

"I'm done packing, Tatay." Aurora changed the topic, erasing painful thoughts, even momentarily. "Pearl wouldn't let anyone do hers. What else is new with your granddaughter?" She forced a shallow laughter.

"I know," Mario answered. "Our summerhouse in Baguio has been cleaned and repainted. Take Candida with you to help. Just be patient with her. Now that she's old, she has become ornery. Plus, her arthritis has been bothering her a lot. I can relate to that."

Aurora laughed, a genuine one this time.

"Baguio is already much colder during this time of the year. I shouldn't forget that Pearl is used to that kind of weather. You too. Regardless, that would give Pearl and you some privacy, away from *tsismis* (gossip)."

"Remember the birthmark I have on my right shoulder, Tatay? Nanay kept reminding me that it's in a bad location. It portends bad fortune, *pasang Krus* (bearing the cross). I didn't want it removed. She was right. More than ever, I believe bad luck is written in the palm of my hands."

Mario's barely audible "uh-huh" did not escape Aurora's sharp ears. Tatay didn't believe in any of that crap. How right was Nanay about Tatay or men in general. When did they listen to a woman's hunch? Aurora did not want to argue her point to her father.

"Pearl has an appointment with her psychiatrist tomorrow."

"She does not need one!" Mario's voice rose. "I thought she already saw a rape crisis counselor in New York?"

"The rape crisis counselor recommends a regular visit. She will see this one while she's here."

Aurora didn't believe in it either. She agreed with her father. *You rely on your family for support in times like this. That's why they are family. Not a paid professional*, she thought. Who would understand Pearl better but her own mother, her grandfather, and, if Tinay were alive, her.

People back home didn't go to a psychiatrist for a personal crisis. They went to their best friend, their favorite aunt or uncle, or their immediate family at the least. But then she had to bend to pressure from Red, from his side of the family, the American side of her daughter.

"Nonsense," Mario said emphatically. "Pearly has her family. She has our complete support. What she needs is plenty of time off and rest to keep her mind off what happened. Not strangers giving her cookbook advice." He echoed Aurora's thought.

"Wish we were home this minute, Tatay," Aurora said to appease Mario.

She didn't want him riled. It was not good for his blood pressure. And the noise he created might wake up her Pearly.

"Pretty soon, Auring," Mario said, placated. "I promise that things will be a lot better here. Pretty soon . . ."

Aurora could still hear Tatay's last words as she ended the conversation. Tatay was probably right. They needed a clean break from this nightmare, a place familiar and comforting, her warm bed as she remembered it, the friendly faces of the household help they had for years (most of them anyway), her *yaya* Candida who, at the ripe age of seventy-five, remained a permanent fixture in the Gomez household, their cook Juling, and their washerwoman Inday. She longed to revisit and rekindle friendship. She even missed the flooded Manila streets like España during the rainy season, where even Malacañang Palace was not spared the overflowing banks of Pasig River, flooding its ground level while crystal chandeliers hung as silent witnesses to Mother Nature's dominance.

Her palate ached for *halu-halu* and *pansit palabok* served in Little Quiapo across from Universidad de Santo Tomas where she had finished schooling. Too bad it was rather too late to do a pilgrimage to Antipolo where they had luscious golden mangoes with *suman* wrapped in banana leaves for dessert or shoot the rapids at Pagsanjan Falls, places Pearl herself had learned to love.

Newly energized, she resumed cleaning her closet, rearranging her numerous shoes and dusting her drawers, anything to keep her busy. She began to hum a native ditty to herself, *"Dahil sa Iyo* (Because of You)" in her soprano voice. She had a beautiful voice. It soothed the gloom that came in surge like the tide, threatening to conquer her spirits now and then.

CHAPTER 15

MOONLESS NIGHT

"We're here, Pearly," Aurora said, ecstatic.

She cupped her daughter's face as the plane taxied Manila International Airport's runway. Surrounded by familiar sights of towering coconut trees and intense greeneries, she was home.

"Yes, Mother," Pearl answered. This was her second home. Soon they were at the airport's lounge. The clock's face read six in the evening. When they landed, the sun was still up, but it didn't take long for it to hide in the shadows. Night came fast on this side of the world. The transition from day to night was rather abrupt. Floodlights replaced the wide span of vegetation from the glass windows as evening took hold. The terminal was teeming with activities with excited families and friends welcoming arrivals and subdued noise from those departing.

Among the crowd, Pearl's fair skin and light hair attracted side glances and admiration. Her look was a contrast to the native's ebony hair, mostly olive and brown skin, and unhurried pace. Pearl's face brightened. Tatay was coming their way. He looked older, though, with his hair suddenly white. His face came alive upon seeing them. His shoulders snapped to attention. A middle-aged but burly man walked with him. Pearl recognized him as one of Tatay's household help. Though he had a name, any male household help was always called the Boy. And as the Boy, he had the duty of helping not just with the household but with his fellow help (who were mostly women) running errands, helping with heavy stuff, doing minor household repairs, and acting as an extra driver when the need arose. Nobody could explain the reasoning behind it to Pearl.

Though the burly man, whom she later recalled was *Mang* Tomas to the Gomez household, the *Mang* was a sign of respect. To the outside world, he was the Boy, like a title bestowed. *Mang* Tomas, the Gomezes' household's Boy, was there to help with the luggage. She smiled at recognizing him. *What a short memory I have.*

Mang Tomas had been the driver to the town fiesta with Tatay. Pearl's face clouded when she didn't see anyone else. Tatay gave them both a bear hug. He looked contented seeing them. Calmness replaced the worry lines he had sported earlier. His voice echoed excitement. As they left the confines of the air-conditioned lobby, the hot, humid air greeted them. Though Pearl had grown up in a different place, the transformation was comforting, not totally alien to her. The smell and movement of the air had a familiarity she had experienced before.

P.J. came to her mind. Would she be willing to relocate and settle down here? Marry and have children with P.J.? The idea didn't seem farfetched to her, not like before. After all, this was her mother's birthplace. Though she wasn't raised here, she had her ties.

Soon, *Mang* Tomas was navigating the busy thoroughfares, the unforgiving traffic, and the cacophony of colorful jeepneys blaring their horns impatiently early that evening, not a few with deafening radios playing the latest Tagalog and Tag-lish, that mongrel of Tagalog and English-language hit songs, while some cars and buses zigzagged to get ahead, ignoring traffic lights when they could. It seemed forever before they finally entered the guarded enclaves of the exclusive residential park where Tatay lived, where everything seemed to be of another world, with immaculate and magnificent homes, well-tended manicured lawns and gardens, and the hiss of garden sprinklers the only sound in an otherwise quiet place, each family cocooned in its own private quarters, unmindful of the chaotic traffic and hand-to-mouth existence of the remaining three-quarters of the population, and that was by far a generous estimate.

With their arrival, Tatay's household suddenly came alive. There was organized commotion among the household help. Candida was giving directions to everyone, ignoring Alma, the Gomezes' *mayordoma*, the titular head of the household help. In spite of her arthritis, Candida helped the two women, Pearl and Aurora, unpack and get settled, to the chagrin of Alma, relegated to the role of follower to Candida's domineering ways. Juling, excited and blubbering, was making excuses for receiving short notice of their arrival in her central Luzon dialect, Kapampangan, nevertheless she came up with several main courses for their special guests in about an hour—hot *pansit palabok* noodles, *mongo* bean soup with generous garnishing of whole shrimp, crackling *chicharon* with vinegar and diced hot *sili* pepper, and broiled tilapia fish with tart green mangoes paired with sliced fresh red tomatoes. There was the steaming *milagrosa* rice to tie the dishes together. Then there was the chilled dessert of lychees mixed with golden jackfruit and cubed sea gelatin, a fitting repast for a balmy evening.

Pearl's bed was freshly made. Ironed cotton sheets and fluffed pillows with crisp hand-embroidered pillowcases and several striped woven blankets of primary colors from Ilocos region were neatly folded for her own disposal, enough to seduce one to fall asleep. Pearl, though, remained awake and restless. It wasn't the jet lag. Tatay promised he would notify P.J. and his family of their . . . her . . . arrival.

Pearl was eager to call P.J. or talk to *Tita* Espe or Techie. She had to forgo the idea when she realized it was almost midnight when they finally settled down. She could barely wait until the following morning. Her bed creaked from her continued tossing and erratic movement through the night. Her unwavering excitement kept her eyes wide awake. Her room remained flooded with light, an acquired habit since that fateful day.

It was nine the following morning when sleep finally won. She woke up with her room in pitch darkness. Hair began to rise on her nape. She imagined whispers in her ears, eyes looking at her in the dark, and someone poking her cheeks, pinching her feet, and pulling her bedsheet. Unable to contain her fear, she jumped out of the bed. Somebody had turned off the lights. She nearly tumbled in her rush to turn on all the lights. She shrieked. The four walls of the bedroom shuddered as she shut the windows. She inspected the walk-in closet and made sure nobody was there. She swung the bathroom door open and reached for the switch to turn on the light. She waited before stepping inside and then opened the shower curtain before closing the door behind her. Only then did she feel somewhat comfortable taking off her clothes. She took a quick shower.

Her eyes remained open as soapy water cleansed her face and body. She hardly recognized herself in the mirror after wiping the steam with her bare hand. Her cheeks were sunken, her eyes sad, dark circles surrounded them, and though she recognized some sparkle, they were the glitter of fear. She touched her breasts. They were firm yet they had been explored. She ran her hands on her tummy, her thighs, and her legs, feeling their tautness. They all felt the same, but they were no longer sacred. As her mother said, a woman's body is an altar that should be honored, a perfect gift to its rightful owner. Like a delicate vase, once it is broken, regardless how meticulously restored, it is damaged.

Inexplicable emptiness gripped Pearl. She again turned on the faucet to wake up her face and pacify the burning in her eyes. She had brought a couple books but couldn't get herself to read. She was in the middle of controlled chaos, her mother rabidly preparing for their trip to Baguio in a couple days and Tatay busy conferring with his private secretary regarding a major meeting with the local lawyers at the Peninsula in Makati. The household help of the Gomez compound was in constant commotion, to assure that their honored guests, Aurora and Pearl, wouldn't want for anything. They owed that to Mario Gomez, the master of the house, their benefactor, their bloodline.

Another night passed. She still hadn't heard from P.J.. By midmorning the next day, Pearl phoned P.J. against Aurora's advice. *A well-bred woman doesn't call her boyfriend. She waits for his call.* Aurora's voice echoed in her mind. A maid took her message. When she asked for Doña Esperanza or Techie, neither was available.

Bored, Pearl took a long swim in the heated pool. The water's buoyant force cradled her, enveloped her like a cocoon, and eased her anxiety. She kept her eyes closed. A ripple startled her. It was Aurora. Her mother swam toward her. A graceful swimmer, her mother sliced the water quietly.

"Have you talked to *Tita* Espe yet, Mother? *Tita* Techie?" Pearl continued to feel awkward calling both women *Tita* but Doña Esperanza refused to be called *lola* for grandma.

"No, not yet." Her mother disappeared from the surface, only to reappear at the shallow end. "I am having lunch with my friends from college. Want to join us?"

"I don't think so, Mother." Her mother did not seem interested in what she had to say. Pearl stayed at the deep end.

"Call your friends—Chato, Bubut, Maggie, Zeny," Aurora said. "Go shopping with them. Eat out, perhaps see a movie. Invite them to join us in Baguio."

"Yes, Mother."

Why was everyone not listening? Had her mother forgotten? School was not yet over for her local friends. They were still in the middle of their schooling. Prostrated, she swam the length of the pool, ignoring Aurora until her legs tired. She pushed herself up and sat at the edge of the deep end. Her mother was getting out of the water. Her mother had barely wet herself. Aurora disappeared inside the house. She reappeared fully attired in a simple silk dress accented with a printed scarf and black stilettos. Dark glasses hid her face. Juling appeared with a tray of snacks and placed it on the table shaded by thatched roof. Earlier, she had sent *Mang* Tomas to pick up *merienda* (snack) from a specialty store. It was *pinasugbo*, a Bisayan dessert of thinly sliced caramelized banana wrapped in a paper cone, plus the thirst quenching *buko* juice. Pearl stayed at the pool's edge. She ignored Aurora's repeated invitation to join her.

Done with her snack, Aurora walked toward the pool's edge. "Sure you don't want to come with me, Pearly?" Aurora shouted one last time. Even from a distance, her mother had never looked more beautiful.

"No, Mother."

She would be out of place with a group of middle-aged women, reminiscing on their lost youth and reliving the past. Blessed with youthful genes, her mother would be the one privileged to indulge.

"Enjoy." She barely was able to say the word.

The truth was that she didn't want to miss P.J.'s call. It was late that afternoon when the maid brought the phone to Pearl. She hurriedly put down the book she had just started. It was a welcome distraction. She couldn't concentrate anyway.

"P.J.?" Pearl said, excited.

"*Hija*, it's *Tita* Espe. How are you?"

"I'm fine. How's everyone?" She was hoping it was P.J.. She wondered if disappointment were palpable in her tone.

"Everyone's just fine and dandy. It's you I'm worried about." Doña Esperanza emphasized the "you."

"I'm okay, *Tita* Espe. Really. Is P.J. home?"

"No, he's not."

"Can you have him call me?"

"Sure." There was a momentary lull. "So . . . how's Aurora?" Doña Esperanza resumed. "And Mario?"

"Tatay's busy as usual. Mother's meeting some old friends. We're eager to see you all."

"There's really no rush. Whenever you've both fully rested and gotten over the jet lag, we'll get together sometime." There was a short pause, followed by the clearing of a throat. "*Hija*, I'm really on my way out. Promise to call me back sometime, and we can talk for hours on end."

"Like before," Pearl hastened to add.

Pearl imagined Doña Esperanza and Techie fussing in her presence, attending and catering to Pearl's every need and want, as she had gotten used to.

"Yes." There was another pause before Doña Esperanza spoke again. "Like before."

There was a soft click at the other end. Hearing the dial tone, Pearl put down the phone. Something didn't feel right. Or her mind must still be foggy from the flight, the jet lag. It was then that she heard footsteps.

Aurora was back. *Had it been that long?*

A woman, probably in her early or midthirties, was walking with her. The local woman wore clean but rather inexpensive clothing. Although Pearl had no doubt she had not seen the woman before, there was something vaguely familiar about her, though she could not place it. Something about the way she walked, her face, and her physique, Pearl couldn't say. The woman was gazing at her sandaled feet or, rather, looking at the marble floor.

"Perfect timing, Pearl," Aurora said. "I'd like you to meet your *Tita* Baby. Baby, this is my daughter Pearl. Tatay prefers to call her Pearly."

The woman awkwardly offered her hand. It was a phlegmatic grip, hardly responding to Pearl's firm shake. She didn't speak nor look Pearl in the eyes.

To end a rather awkward scenario, Aurora pulled Baby toward the living room. "Pearly," Aurora called, "tell Juling we have a visitor. Baby will have dinner with us. Juling will be surprised. Inday, Alma, and *Mang* Tomas are still here. They will be happy to see you."

Baby profusely shook her head and hands to decline the offer. "I already ate. Thank you for the invitation."

"We seldom get this chance," said her mother, pleading. "Please join us for dinner."

"*Naku, huwag na. Nakakahiya. Ayokong mang-abala pa* (It's embarrassing. I hate to be a bother)," Baby said, retracing her steps back.

"*Sige na* (Please)," her mother repeated. "Please join us."

Pearl kept a straight face. She was becoming too familiar with this social vignette, a game of false modesty. The voices of the two women mingled and became unintelligible as Pearl left for the kitchen. Juling and her two juvenile assistants were nowhere to be found. Pearl ventured to the adjacent door near the kitchen that was always closed. The strong odor of preserved fish greeted Pearl as she swung the door wide open, a habit she had acquired. There was a commotion, a thud of a pan landed on the bare floor. Juling's two young help stood up, spilled some beans, wetted the table while crashing a bowl, and knocked over their seats. Juling remained still with mouth agape. The live poultry from the crate croaked with vigor, startled. Pearl was an intruder, an unexpected visitor.

Herself surprised, Pearl clutched her throat to stifle a cry.

"Yes, *Ate?*" The cook said, recovering. She stepped forward and signaled her two helpers to do the same.

Juling did not expect anyone would dare peek at the "dirty kitchen," not the master's granddaughter, for that matter. The boy and the girl, older then but still younger looking than their real ages, gawked at their unexpected company with the white of their eyes showing.

"Have an extra plate, Juling. We have a visitor."

"*Opo, Ate.* Would that be all, *Ate?*"

"Uh-hum." Pearl had to strain her eyes to get used to the dark surroundings.

Compared to the main kitchen, the place was a poor cousin with its dark-soot pots and pans, the smell of unfamiliar preserved food, herbs, and spices, and its suffocating surroundings. Somehow, somewhat, it evoked her mother's kitchen. Pearl saw the look of embarrassment from the cook and decided to spare the domestic help further suffering by leaving, gently closing the door behind her. Pearl returned to the living room and opened the book she was reading to the page she had dog-eared. Baby and Aurora had retreated to the covered porch with its lush potted green plants, hanging exotic orchids, ornate iron furniture, and marble statues scattered like sentinels. The two women were seated together, engrossed in serious discussion. Aurora would hold or pat Baby's hand as Baby would dab her eyes. They didn't seem to notice her.

The phone rang. Pearl quickly placed the book down. She didn't wait for the phone to ring a second time. The clock registered six in the evening.

"Hello." Pearl's voice was expectant.

"Pearl." P.J.'s voice was hushed like he was afraid to be discovered. "It's me, P.J."

"I know it's you. Did you receive my message?"

"The maid told me."

"Good. It's about time."

"I want to see you," P.J. said. His tone was pleading, secretive.

A lump formed in Pearl's throat. There was a twinge in her chest. "Nobody's stopping you. You know where I am." She wanted to stress that she would soon be leaving for Baguio but heard a familiar voice talking to P.J..

"So, *Tita* Espe is back."

"She's been home," P.J. said. "I'll call you right back."

Pearl's cheeks tingled. Her face flushed. "What's going on, P.J.? Tell me."

"I'll call you back." P.J. hung up before she could say another word.

Pearl needed to talk to anyone. She gazed at the covered porch. Aurora and Baby were locked in an embrace, oblivious of her. Aurora rummaged her bag and pulled out a wad of money, which she handed to Baby. They walked toward the main door, arms locked on each other's waist. The two women still hadn't noticed her. Baby embraced Aurora one more time before leaving.

"Have you been here long? She won't stay for dinner." Aurora loosened her scarf. She kicked off her shoes. "And how was your day?" Pearl did not answer. "Are you all right? Pearly, *anak* (my child)?"

Pearl ignored her mother. "Who is she, Mother?"

Aurora stopped walking in her stocking feet. She grabbed her shoes and motioned Pearl to walk with her. The winding staircase was a silent witness as they climbed the stairs to Aurora's bedroom. Pearl helped her mother unzip. She sat on the bed and watched her mother wiggle out of her street clothes, disappear inside the walk-in closet, and come back wearing house clothes. Aurora began pacing the bedroom floor. It was another habit they shared.

"Baby's mother used to be one of our live-in help. We grew up like sisters. I was several years older. It didn't matter. She was my playmate. In fact, Baby was born in this house, in the servants' quarters. Her mother was deadly afraid of hospitals." Aurora paused, taking a deep breath. "Nanay couldn't convince her, not even Tatay. A *komadrona* (midwife) delivered her. Baby married one of our servants. He wanted to try his hand in business and dreamed of owning a few units of jeepneys to manage. Tatay helped provide the capital. Tatay wasn't disappointed in helping him. He was a good man and treated Baby well. Aside from hiring other drivers, he also did his own route between Cubao and Quiapo. He was killed in a robbery attempt plying his route one night. Left Baby without any children. No children after five years. It would have been nice. She remarried one of his drivers, a bum who ransacked his business and bore her three children. He was a drunk and a womanizer, to top it all. Tatay and Nanay tried to convince her to leave him. Baby won't. A second heaven is really rare."

"She's no relation then," Pearl said. "*Tita* was just a sign of respect."

Aurora stopped pacing and looked her daughter in the eyes. "You would address her as an aunt. You will call her *Tita* Baby. Tatay would be offended if you don't."

"And why is that?"

"She . . . Baby . . . Baby is Tatay's daughter."

"What?"

The two women's eyes locked, gauging and reading their minds.

Pearl broke the silence. "Nanay, did she know?"

Aurora was lost for words. *How am I to tell my daughter that Baby has as much right to this house as we do, probably more?* In the end, Aurora settled for a half-truth.

"Nanay didn't know. Tatay told her later . . . much later."

"When did you know, Mother? Did you know it was really your sister you were playing with? Did she know? Her mother, did she stay?"

"No, she left. Soon." Aurora covered her face in shame. Lying would be saving one's dignity and her sanity, everyone's in fact.

How could she tell Pearl she was not even Tatay's real granddaughter? Save for Nanay, neither Aurora nor Pearl had a right to stay in this house. She wanted Pearl to continue to respect and recognize Tatay as her grandfather. They owed Tatay gratitude.

"And Baby stayed?" Pearl asked, more to herself, still in shock. "*Tita* Baby." She corrected herself.

"Baby's aunt and husband were also our household help then. They raised her."

Again, Aurora knew these were half-truths. Though it was true Baby's aunt and her husband worked for the Gomezes, they had left shortly. Baby's mother stayed. She was a hands-on mother to her daughter until she died of consumption.

"Tatay," Pearl whispered to herself. "Tatay? Nanay had him at her fingertips."

"Remember . . ." Aurora pointed out. "He's a man."

"What do you mean by that?"

"Men, it's second nature. They are just like that. It's nothing for a man to have a wife and a *kerida*."

That night, quite a few souls remained awake late into the night. Pearl's admiration for her grandparent's solid marriage had been shattered and disillusioned with Tatay's indiscretion and cheating. She was so upset with the discovery that she couldn't even think of bringing up P.J.'s and *Tita* Espe's peculiar behavior. And yes, that was the reason *Tita* Baby looked uncannily familiar to her.

And Tatay? He was not asleep either—grilling, searching, and questioning how to steer his granddaughter Pearl back to normal life. His intuition better be wrong, but P.J.'s clan hadn't even shown their faces since Pearl's arrival. Not for one second did Mario think of Pearl but his own flesh and blood, his own granddaughter.

Aurora continued to dread falling asleep. Those nightmares continued to haunt her, continuing to fester. Her waking hours continued to nag her, fearing for Pearl's future. What was in store for her daughter after that harrowing experience? She shook her head when Doña Esperanza, Techie, and P.J. came to her mind. She refused to imagine what they were thinking. She covered her ears like her head was ready to explode.

P.J.? He was also wide awake most nights, tossing in his bed and chasing sleep. He could hear his *Lola* Espe and his mother's voices, constantly reminding him. "Think hard, P.J. Think of what we have told you. We always have your best interest in our mind. The family name . . . Romualdez. Lopez from your *lolo's* side. Our reputation is at stake."

It was indeed a moonless night, a long one for these souls.

CHAPTER 16

BITTER MELON

"P.J., you're so quiet. Here." Dante handed an ice-cold beer to P.J.. He cocked his head to signal to the *barkada* (close male friends) to pass the bowl of fried peanuts and *chicharong bulaklak*. "Worried about that test? We're all in this together."

"I know why," Balbon, of Eastern Indian descent, said. "I know exactly why."

Balbon's father owned several jewelry and pawn shops, and his mother was a famous Bollywood movie star. Blessed with a matinee-idol's looks, he was a hirsute man. He took pride in wearing unbuttoned shirts to display his hairy chest. He wore his long-sleeved shirt three-quarters to display hairy arms. Nobody among his friends was blessed with abundance of hair. His name Balbon said it all. Balbon meant hairy.

The group was gathered in his parents' place, which housed his parents and fourteen younger siblings, a spinster aunt of his father, and both of his widowed grandmas from his mom and dad. It was a four-story palatial house with its own private worship place and an inner garden with a huge gilded cage housing his mother's collection of rare and exquisite birds and orchids hanging on several huge trees dotting it. His *barkada* occupied one of the smaller function rooms. Small was relative. It had its own kitchen, a restroom, a dining room to sit a dozen, and a living room dwarfed by an ornate, commissioned crystal chandelier in its middle. As a law student, his value as a groom exceeded the sky. He was betrothed to an equally prominent girl of Eastern Indian descent studying medicine in Metro Manila.

"Tell us," Dante said. He was the scion of prominent husband and wife physicians who owned a private hospital in the province. "Why?"

His hand reached for a handful of peanuts and shoved them in his mouth. A diamond ring on each of his ring fingers sparkled. A gold chain with a diamond cross dangled from his neck. A Rolex completed his attire.

"You two quarreled, right? What's her name again?" Balbon said.

"Pearl," Dante and P.J. said in unison.

"His *alaga* (ward) lost," Mestizo rationalized. Relative to the rest, no one had been to his place. They knew his father was an American businessman who traveled constantly. He never showed up on any of Mestizo's school affairs. Nobody knew if he had any siblings or who his mother was. He was the brain in the group, so he earned their respect to leave him alone and not pry into his personal life. Everyone in the *barkada* knew he would make it big with pale hair, pale skin, and grey eyes as a passport. He could marry rich, anyone to his liking. Plus, the name of their all-male school and his future alma mater was the final stamp of approval.

"Am I not right? A spat with Pearl is nothing. You're the man. Show her you're the man. Losing a bet on your rooster is different. Am I not right? Tell them, P.J.," Mestizo said.

"How sure are you?" asked Dante, taunting. "Have you seen him act in front of Pearl? Have you?"

"*Walang kuwenta 'yan. Balewala 'yan,*" Johnny said in heavily accented Tagalog.

Both his parents were Chinese. They owned a very popular Chinese place in Chinatown. The group always had a blast coming to his place. There was always a feast come lunch or dinnertime, occasionally everyone's favorite, shark fin's or bird's nest soup.

"Tell me. How much? How much money lose? Your mom rich. Can afford. Buy more rooster, right?" Johnny said, agreeing with Mestizo, talking in broken language.

"That question. What do you think?" Jay-Jay asked, ignoring Johnny.

Jay-Jay was the scion of a powerful political family. His family was a mortal enemy of P.J.'s family. Both were political rivals. P.J. and Jay-Jay knew about the family feud, ignoring it and soldering friendship between them. None of their family knew about their friendship.

"Unfair!" Balbon bellowed. "The premise was wrong."

"You make a case either way," Johnny replied. "It's a trick question."

"That's the mettle of a good lawyer. Anyone can make a case with that question," Dante said. "For or against."

"You can make a case about his body odor. I can smell him a mile away," Jay-Jay said.

"He thinks he camouflage his smell with nice *pelfume*," Johnny said.

The group burst out laughing. P.J. remained quiet.

"Perfume, Johnny, perfume." Someone corrected.

"P.J.?" Balbon gazed at him and bumped his shoulder.

The rest were riveted on Mestizo, waiting to hear his take on their exam. A maid bringing the phone interrupted them.

"*Manong*," the maid said, addressing Balbon to show respect and handing him the phone.

"Hello?" Balbon, recognizing the voice, stood up and walked away from the group while the maid exited in a huff.

They all quieted, exchanged glances, and smiled at each other. P.J. gazed far, looking though not seeing. It was a more serious Balbon that came back. He claimed his spot.

"So?"

"It's the boss," Dante said.

"Checking. Just checking," Jay-Jay said. He mimed making a phone call.

"Hah. Tell her nothing to worry. This one good boy," Johnny said. "We'll vouch for you."

"You can only stay for two hours," Balbon said.

"What?" everyone said except for P.J., who began to stir from his seat.

"That's not fair," added Mestizo.

"Get used to how it's going to play in the future, boys. This is the beginning of the end," Dante said.

Laughter drowned Balbon's protests.

"That's the *leason* P.J. so quiet," Johnny said. "He imagined same happens when he gets *mallied*."

"Reason," corrected somebody. "You mean married."

"We need a speech therapist here!"

"Yeah, reason. P.J., don't disappoint us. Tell them our *barkada* is solid. We'll be same. You can marry her. But the *barkada* is the *barkada*. Right?" Dante pointed out.

"I don't mind being holed with her 24/7," Mestizo said. "Pearl, that's her name, right?

"Any red-blooded man wouldn't," Dante said. His hands mimicked a woman's contour, followed with a loud whistle.

"What did she see in you?" Balbon tussled P.J.'s hair.

"Seriously, why two hours?" Mestizo asked.

"Haven't you heard of curfew hours?" Dante said.

"We're going out," Balbon reasoned out. "She forgot to tell me. It's her dad's birthday."

"Everyone heard? The future in-laws. *Hilaw na biyanan*. Okay, you are forgiven," said Jay-Jay.

The group's banter was interrupted. A male servant, the Boy, came with a steaming platter. The Boy nodded at Balbon and sported a mischievous smile. He placed the platter in the middle of the coffee table, occupying an honored spot among the peanuts and *chicharong bulaklak*. The platter smelled of fragrant spices, the tender meat peeling off the bones. Forks speared them. Balbon raised his San Miguel beer, and everyone did, including P.J.

"House specialty. Compliments from the Boy."

The clinking of beer bottles was heard. Accomplishing a mission, the Boy accepted the compliment, took a deep bow, spread his arms, and smiled from ear to ear. He took several steps backward with his head still bowed and then disappeared.

Mestizo grabbed a fork and took a big bite. He swigged some beer to nurse his burned tongue.

"Hot, hot, hot." His eyes watered.

Dante followed. "What is this?"

"Whatever, it is good," Mestizo said. He swallowed some more beer.

"I try." Johnny pierced a big chunk and savored its flavor. Munching, he closed his eyes.

Balbon, pleased, took his turn and tore some meat with his fingers.

"Taste like chicken," Jay-Jay said.

"It is chicken."

"It's pork. You don't know your meat," Dante said.

"Wild pig." Mestizo forked some more meat. This time, he made sure it wasn't too hot.

"You all wrong. It's beef. Good beef," Johnny uttered, confident. "Right, Balbon?"

"You're all wrong," Balbon said.

Everyone's eyes were on Balbon. Gradually, their eyes were wide open.

"Don't tell me . . ." Dante covered his mouth.

Balbon nodded to everyone, confirming their suspicions.

"*Aso-cena?*" Mestizo's eyes vacillated between the food and Balbon. *Aso* meant dog. *Aso-cena* was a euphemism for a dish made of dog meat.

"Right." Balbon pierced another piece of meat that disappeared in his mouth. "Good, right?"

"It is good. I thought I wouldn't like it. Damn, it's good," Mestizo said. "I'll stop castigating dog eaters. But don't tell. I won't own up to it."

The *barkada* broke into a loud laugh.

"We need more San Miguel." P.J. raised his empty beer. "I haven't eaten one myself until now."

"Coming." Balbon pressed the intercom. "Now you're talking. Did you hear that? P.J. is talking."

"*Aw-aw-aw.*" Somebody mimicked a dog's bark. "*Aw-aw-aw.*"

The platter was empty in no time. So with several San Miguel bottles, the bowls of peanut, and the *chicharong bulalak* consumed,

P.J. stood up to go to the restroom. He rested his hands on some of the *barkada*'s shoulders on his way.

"You okay?" It was Mestizo.

P.J. waved his hand, dismissing Mestizo's concern. P.J. closed the bathroom door and anchored himself against it. He had eaten a lot. The meat was tender with its spice and aroma intoxicating. Like a guilty pleasure, he indulged, awash with guilt. The bathroom floor swayed. He closed his eyes and whispered Pearl's name.

It was an unusually warm evening. Madrid restaurant was busy. His mom and grandmother were already waiting for him, tucked in a private corner, away from the crowd. He was not even sure why they asked him to meet them at Madrid.

"Everything's fine in school?" Techie broke the silence after he had asked for his drink.

"Of course everything's fine in school." Doña Esperanza grabbed and squeezed P.J.'s hand. "I already told our server what we are having for dinner. Is there anything you want, P.J.? I ordered the usual."

"He trusts you, Mama."

Doña Esperanza nodded. "There is no reason not to. There is nothing not good here. That's the reason it has been around and . . . for many more years without doubt. It's not just the food. There's nothing vulgar about this place. Very elegant."

Techie roamed with her eyes. She eyed the crowd. She was not disappointed.

"Your *lolo*, my husband, lived his life well. Nothing left to chance. Everything planned. It served him well."

"Served us well, Mama," Techie pointed out.

Doña Esperanza nodded. "I have no doubt, had he lived, he would have been a very successful politician. He could even have been the president."

"Don't be too modest, Mama. You were his secret weapon."

"I'm glad you pointed it out. Yes, I helped him campaign. I wasn't just the wife. I orchestrated his campaign, raised funds, and visited his supporters in person. Personal touch is very important, P.J.. A woman's touch is very important. With me, half the battle is won."

"You were still very young, P.J.. If you remember, your grandma gathered all her friends to campaign for your *lolo*, wearing a uniform so they stood out in the crowd. Everyone knew it was your *lolo*'s group."

"Visibility, Techie. It's very important."

"Papa married the right woman. You, Mama."

"He married the right woman."

"You hear that, P.J.?"

P.J. nodded and gulped his wine. He remained quiet, observing them.

"We have a saying. You choose your own bed." Techie locked her eyes on him. "Choose the right one."

"Just like every pan has the right lid. You've heard that saying, P.J.." Doña Esperanza's eyes lit. She waved her hand to a group being led by the maître d' toward them.

"They're here, Mama," Techie stage-whispered.

An elderly couple came to their table, a petite young woman with them. After the brief greetings, they joined the table.

"This is P.J.?" the distinguished-looking man said. "*Muy guwapo.*"

The elder woman said, "Good-looking man."

The couple chose to sit together, leaving an empty seat for the woman next to P.J.. The woman cast her eyes down and spoke softly. She had a tiny face framed by jet-black hair. Her skin was the color of pale brown. Her eyes were the same shade. Unless spoken to, she remained quiet.

"So, *hija*, I heard you're studying journalism," Techie said.

"*Opo.*" The woman coughed nervously. She stole a glance at P.J..

"Perfect for writing P.J.'s speeches," Doña Esperanza said. She raised an arm to signal the head waiter that they were ready to be served. "What do you say, *komadre, kompadre?*"

P.J. covered his mouth, he began to heave, and he had a sour feeling in his stomach. He lurched to kneel at the toilet bowl, relieving himself of the juicy, tasteful meat, purging his body of it, akin to washing his hands of guilt.

CHAPTER 17

PAST IMPERFECT

Among the sea of men, the smell of humanity mixed with cacophony of voices rose and fell with the undulating movement of the carriage of the Black Nazarene as it was paraded in Plaza Miranda in front of Quiapo Church, the heart of Manila. It was the Black Nazarene's feast day, Quiapo Church's patron saint, that muggy day of January.

During ordinary days, the church was always full, particularly on Fridays. People were from all walks of life. Some dressed in long, maroon tunics, the color of the patron saint, the Black Nazarene. The crowd feverishly prayed in unison, oblivious to the activities outside, the church smelling of burnt candles, human sweat, and incense. A few women threaded the aisles on their bended knees for devotion, reciting the rosary. During these days, the front of the church would be full of merchants selling amulets and magic potions for different maladies— from nonhealing ulcers to impotence to *kulam*, a curse inflicted on somebody causing body harm or pain—treated by applying a soothing salve, liniment, or miraculous oil or giving token money to a go-between to intercede by incantation and prayers in tongue. Side by side would be mendicants. Some were nursing their babies with their shrunken breasts for all to see. A bilateral amputee was on top of a mobile cart. The blind had dark glasses to hide grotesque, opaque, or protruding eyes. Thin toddlers and children with big bellies wiped their snot with bare hands. The adults held empty tin cans, appealing to one's tender spot for the unfortunate and the social outcasts, their plea for mercy occasionally punctuated by the clang of coins against the din of passing humanity. But then being the Black Nazarene's feast, the crowd appeared to be mostly outside. It was a sea of humanity, of menfolk, a parade exclusive to them, tugging ropes that carried the image, fighting for a chance to touch the Nazarene, kiss its hands, feet, or face in return for a blessing or favor, some satisfied with the clean, white towels that touched the image tossed back to them. It was a Catholic rite suffused with pagan overtones. Men of all walks of life participated in this annual rite with unwavering fervor. Some of them who otherwise would have no remorse robbing a stranger or molesting a woman shared a common bond with the learned and the well-off during this short span of time, the former group firm in their faith that any past misdeed or transgression to society would be purged and cleansed by this yearly ritual.

The Black Nazarene inched slowly among the throng. Sadness and suffering seemed permanently etched in its chiseled features—the deep-set eyes, the narrow nose, the full lips, and its pointed chin. Its Caucasian features were a stark contrast to its ebony complexion. Legend has it that it was burned, thus its color, while transported in high seas by a galleon to its final destination, the minor basilica of Quiapo. The paraded Nazareno actually was a replica of its head, the original head of the image kept inside the church.

Mario was among the crowd, pulling the rope tied to the carriage with the hope of getting closer. Bright red blood with plasma oozed from his blistered hands. He had done this ritual once, the first one when he was still a young man, confused, disillusioned, and devastated by his misfortune, imploring God to help him with his predicament—to marry or not marry Tinay, the woman he loved in spite of impurity of her body, pregnant of a child not his own. He asked the Almighty for strength in his faith, shattered by betrayal from one of the Church's very own—Father Francisco.

This time, he was repeating the ritual as a much older man, weaker in body with creased face and a crown of gray hair, asking favor for his grandchild, Pearl. Was God punishing him for past sins? Or was it God's jest? First Tinay. Then Pearl. Aurora's constant reminder of destiny flashed in his mind. What would befall Pearl? With her tarnished reputation, who would want her for a bride? He doubted there would be another man strong enough to do what he did, become the object of silent ridicule among men and share the fallen woman's humiliation and public scorn, a fate worse than death. Was this atonement for his weakness? He was human after all. And a man.

He did have weakness of the flesh while married to Tinay. It was one of their housemaids. For some time, this housemaid gave him nervous, meaningful glances that he tried to dismiss. One night with Tinay asleep, he ventured to the kitchen to quiet the growling of his stomach. Who should he run into but the housemaid who somehow knew his itinerary, wearing a thin camisole, subserviently offering him, first, a cold glass of water. And more. In a moment of weakness, he took the bait, consummating the fire in him. The first encounter, like water, quenched the thirst. Like water, it needed to be replenished, and it continued to fire their passion. The illicit liaison produced a healthy baby who uncannily took his nose, his mouth, his color, and his laughter, Baby. His daughter grew up knowing who her father was yet accepted that she would never be allowed to use his name or be acknowledged as his daughter in public. It was a lie, though Mario had no compunction bartering the truth with the lie. It was also a vindication. It proved his manliness. It proved to his *kompadres*, his male friends, and to society that he was not a henpeck after all. He was a man.

Mario suspected that Tinay knew of the affair, though she never confronted him. There were instances when Tinay would catch him carrying Baby in his arms, giving the child stolen kisses. Tinay would give him silent looks without batting an eye. There were instances Tinay would linger her eyes upon him after their lovemaking. No words would be uttered except her probing eyes, the loudest whisper. Its power made him blink and divert his gaze to ease the guilt. Nearly tempted to ask Tinay what she knew, he never had the courage.

The affair continued until the maid suffered from consumption. Before his eyes, he witnessed her body wither to a heap of flesh and bone, failing treatment that was sporadic. Seemingly favored by the gods, Mario remained healthy. When the housemaid died, he didn't know how to react. In all honesty, he couldn't say he was in love with her, except he lusted for her body until then. He didn't even bother to provide a decent burial for her. She was buried in an unmarked pauper's grave when none of her relatives claimed the body, too poor to pay the hospital bill.

Baby grew up under his shadow, in the servants' quarters, with the rest of the domestic help. She was treated preferentially by them being the "other daughter," the *anak sa labas* (illegitimate child), with hidden envy probably fearing of slighting him, fearful for their job.

When one of the domestic servants asked his permission to marry Baby, his daughter, it jolted Mario. His daughter, his *anak sa labas*, was already a grown woman. And yes, they knew he was the father. He paid for the wedding expense. As usual, Tinay remained silent. She even attended the ceremony and wrapped a decent present for the newlywed. It was a modest wedding. Baby wore a simple white dress to her groom's plain *barong tagalog*. The reception was in an ordinary, no-frills Chinese restaurant. Mario acted as the photographer and *ninong* (godfather) for the wedding. Aurora was the bridesmaid.

When Baby and her husband asked for money to support the jeepney business, he agreed with the caveat that he needed to tell Tinay. Again, there was no raised voice and no questions asked. All Tinay asked was to make sure he issued a sufficient check.

The sweat itched as it dribbled from the tip of his nose, breaking his reminiscing. Though it was warm, he felt cold and clammy. His vision dimmed. He felt somebody steady him. Then voices echoed like they were coming from a deep well. He felt numerous, warm, sweaty hands support his neck and head, raising him above for a gasp of polluted air. The steeples of the Quiapo Church appeared hazy, faint, and double from a distance. The crowd inched slowly past him, jostling and pushing to get closer to the carriage while some passed him from one pair of hands to another.

The hospital suite where Mario was confined had its own elegant living room quarter, a well-stocked kitchen plus a private bath. A portable coach was also available for family who wished to stay the night. It was on the upper floors of the imposing Makati Hospital, considered at the time one of the premier hospitals for the city's rich and famous, in the affluent suburb of Makati surrounded by fancy restaurants, hotels, shopping malls, and boutique shops. Mario's physician ordered bed rest, and he had IV fluids flushed in his veins for hydration. Blood tests were done to ensure he hadn't suffered a heart attack. The reports were negative. He had a twenty-four-hour private nurse to check on him. The room was teeming with fresh flowers. Some sent fruits. Doña Esperanza sent both. Neither P.J., Techie, nor Doña Esperanza came to visit.

"*Kumusta*, hija?" Doña Esperanza's voice was strained. Her color faded like she saw a ghost. Neither expected to run into each other at the hospital's cafeteria.

"I'm fine." Pearl noted that Doña Esperanza avoided meeting her gaze.

Unlike previous encounters, Doña Esperanza didn't offer her cheek. It was clear she was not there to visit Tatay. Pearl decided not to ask.

"It was nice seeing you, Pearl." Doña Esperanza quickly slipped past her.

"*Tita* Espe." Pearl caught up with her while Doña Esperanza continued to walk away. "We need to talk."

Doña Esperanza stopped in her tracks. Without a word, she retraced her steps and motioned Pearl to follow. She ordered a cup of coffee. Pearl ordered soda pop.

"It's on me." Pearl insisted on paying.

Doña Esperanza did not counteroffer and walked briskly to a quiet corner. They sat. Doña Esperanza took her time putting sugar and cream in her coffee like Pearl was not there.

"Why are you avoiding me?" Pearl asked. "All of you."

Doña Esperanza sipped her coffee and gingerly placed the cup on the saucer. She wiped her lips, took a deep breath, and then exhaled. "What made you think that, *hija*?" She reached for Pearl's hand.

Pearl pulled her hands away and tucked them under the table. She forced a smile. "Please, let's stop pretending. You know you do, so with P.J., so with Techie." Pearl corrected herself. "*Tita* Techie."

"Things happen, Pearl."

"Did I do something to slight you?"

"No, not that."

"Then what?"

Doña Esperanza craned her neck, gearing for an encounter. "I think it will be for everyone's benefit if P.J. stops seeing you."

"Isn't that up to him?"

"*Hija*, P.J. is a good son, a good and obedient grandson, we're very proud to say. We don't want him to ruin his great plans. P.J. knows we always think the best for him. Wouldn't you?"

"What's best for him, may I ask?"

"I am sure he has told you he wants to enter politics, like my late husband, his grandpa."

"What does that have to do with us?"

"*Hija*, you have no idea how dirty politics can be. Rivals will dig up dirt about you." Doña Esperanza emphasized the word "you." "They couldn't wait to rattle the skeletons in your closet."

"And?"

"In other words, *hija*, we want P.J. to start with a clean slate. No extra baggage to carry."

"I am extra baggage." Pearl could not hide the disappointment in her voice.

"If you say so." Doña Esperanza's cup shook ever so slightly as she sipped one more time.

"Let's cut to the chase," Pearl stage-whispered. "Suddenly, I'm not good enough for your grandson."

"Yes." There was a slight clink of the cup hitting the saucer. This time, Doña Esperanza looked Pearl in the eyes. Like a sleeping dragon, she woke up, ready to spit fire. "People talk. They want their leader above reproach. So with the wife. She should pull him up, not down.

If P.J. married you, can you in all honesty look him in the eye, naked before him, without shame?"

"Yes."

"*Hija*, we either have a different standard, or we live in different worlds. There are things men could do and still be considered whole." Doña Esperanza took off her pearl necklace and placed it on the table. "Unfortunately, we are born women."

"And we are . . . ?"

"We are delicate. Exquisite but fragile." Without warning, Doña Esperanza crushed a few pearls with her cup, spilling some coffee and pulverizing some pearls. "Once broken, we are rubbish."

A few heads turned their way. Doña Esperanza gathered the remaining strand of pearls and placed them inside her bag. A few loose pieces rolled down the table. "Didn't your mother tell you?"

"Let's not involve my mother in this."

"Of course, she wouldn't want to." Doña Esperanza's eyes narrowed for a split second. "Lest people talk about her."

"My parents' divorce is none of your business or anyone's."

"I'm not talking about your parents' divorce. I can sweep that under the rug. Your father's American. People will understand. So, Aurora probably didn't tell you. Ask her. Ask Mario." Doña Esperanza's voice rose, like she had acquired a new armament. "Better yet, talk to Father Francisco. I wasn't even aware of it—the family secret—until a well-meaning friend came forward to tell."

"There is no family secret."

What else will she uncover that she didn't know? What has Father Francisco got to do with all of this?

"*Hija*, what a shame. You probably didn't know. When you do, then you will understand." Doña Esperanza spoke as if she could read her mind. "I feel sorry for you. I really do. Please don't take this personally. I still like you. Visit us sometime, will you?"

Doña Esperanza gathered her bag, stood up, and walked toward her. Pearl stood up too. She turned her cheek away as Doña Esperanza motioned to peck her. She kept her eyes on the table. She could hear

Doña Esperanza's breathing pick up and then the crisp noise of her silk dress and the tap of her leather soles fading away. She kept her eyes down until she was sure Doña Esperanza was a safe distance from her. Powdered pearl fragments remained on the table. Pearl gazed toward the direction Doña Esperanza had gone.

Her heart skipped. P.J. was at the cafeteria's entrance waiting for his grandmother. He saw her. She was positive. But P.J. chose to ignore her. He walked abreast with his grandmother, talked animatedly with her, and kept pace with the woman's hurried pace without looking back. Pearl's eyes blurred. She waited and hoped P.J. would turn his head, wave at her, and acknowledge her at the last minute. It didn't happen. The two disappeared as they turned down an aisle, leaving Pearl standing up in front of the table, shaken.

Pearl didn't remember riding the elevator, much less leaving the cafeteria. She found herself back in Tatay's hospital suite.

"There you are," Mario said. "We were wondering where you went."

"Pearl, you look pale."

"Pearly, you all right?" Mario rolled his wheelchair closer to Pearl.

"I'm okay."

"You do look pale." Aurora rushed toward her.

"I'm fine. Stop. I just need some time for myself. Alone."

"I'll have the driver pick us up in front of the lobby," Aurora said. "We can go shopping."

"I said I want to be alone. I can go shopping . . . Yes, I can go shopping, alone."

"Sure." Mario interrupted before Aurora could say no. "Auring, hand me my wallet."

Remaining quiet, Aurora obliged. Mario reached for cash.

"Is this enough, Pearly?" He handed some freshly minted cash to Pearl. "Auring, tell the driver to meet Pearly at the lobby."

"*Opo*, Tatay." Aurora dialed the phone.

Aurora tightened her lips. Questioning her father's judgment was disrespect. It was a privilege bestowed upon the elderly.

At the boutique shop where Pearl had been a regular, she made sure she was visible to the owner, a young matron who was a good friend of Techie. Unlike before, the woman ignored Pearl, attending to other customers. There was no fussing about Pearl's presence or asking a sales associate to attend to other customers so she could personally attend to Pearl.

Done shopping, Pearl handed the merchandise to the woman who continued to ignore her. And unlike before, there were no special favors granted. Coldly, the woman rang the register and handed the shopping bag back to Pearl and immediately vanished behind the counter.

Pearl was quick to return. She didn't bother showing off what she had bought. She barely spoke except to voice a need to go home. Tatay insisted Aurora should accompany her, in lieu of a plan for Aurora to stay the night.

"You're quiet," Aurora said, breaking the silence on their ride back to Tatay's place.

"Uh-huh."

"I see you dropped by her shop." Aurora recognized the distinctive paper bag. "How much discount did she give you?"

Pearl did not answer.

"I should talk to Techie. We've been a regular customer and a good one at that. You should get the usual discount."

"Stop, Mother."

"I'll take care of it."

"I said stop."

Aurora and Pearl's eyes locked.

Pearl's gaze pierced. "Tell me, Mother. Why did that woman barely acknowledge my presence in her shop? Why are these people looking strangely at me, like I have a contagious disease? And these are supposed to be people who knew me, people introduced to us by *Tita* Techie or *Tita* Espe. Suddenly, I'm nobody. Insignificant. Before they couldn't seem to get enough of me."

"They're *kuyog*," Aurora blurted to nobody. Disgust and disappointment was written in her voice.

"A bunch of *kuyog*," Aurora repeated.

"Excuse me?" Pearl was confused.

"*Kuyog*! These people are *kuyog*." Aurora's voice trembled. Her eyes watered.

"*Kuyog*?"

"Yes. These are Romualdez and Lopez friends, Techie, your *Tita* Espe, and P.J.'s. Anyone falling out of grace with any of them will also be out of grace with their friends. Any enemy of the Romualdez and Lopez, imagined or real, will also be their friends' enemies."

"Wh . . . what?"

"What happened to you made things worse. Justified their behavior." Pearl clenched her jaw. She wanted to shout. "Pearl, Pearly . . . There's a lot you don't understand." Aurora's voice faltered. She covered her face with her hands. Her shoulders began to shake.

The rest of the ride, the two women were both looking outside their windows. Aurora's soft sobs intermittently broke the silence. Pearl stared blankly into space. It was the wrong time to ask about Father Francisco and hear the "family secret." Anger began to reign. Her eyes stung. She fought and bit her inner lip until it bled. She would not give in. Her eyes remained dry.

Mario was busy watching the early evening news. He was glad he would be discharged the following morning. He couldn't wait. He inhaled the sweet aroma of his cigar, which he had hidden in the pocket of his robe. The temptation to light one was overpowering. His eyes surveyed the then familiar place. The kitchen wall hid his nurse. He could hear water percolating and soon smelled the aroma of freshly brewed coffee. He smiled to himself. What could be better than coffee with your favorite tobacco? He puffed on his freshly lit cigar.

At first, the chest discomfort felt like a jab that came and went. Then it decided to take residence, akin to an elephant sitting on his chest. He began to sweat and feel clammy. *Must be reflux.*

He took a deep breath to ease the pressure. Instead of relief, he felt choked, drowning, and hungry for air. The pressure continued, intense, boring to his back. It spread to his neck and up to his jaw. There was the familiar whoosh of poured coffee followed by the clink of the china and the stirring of the spoon. He called for his nurse but instead made some weak grunt. *Where the hell is the call button?*

He saw it dangling by his bedside. But he had no strength to get up from his wheelchair with his legs shaking under him. With panic taking hold, he didn't think to push his wheelchair toward it. Without warning, pitch darkness enveloped his room. His strength completely deserted him. He slumped forward in a futile attempt to get up, too weak to cushion his fall. There was a fading scream from his nurse.

Then nothing.

CHAPTER 18

TODOS LOS SANTOS
(ALL SOULS' DAY)

Frenzy ushered in the crack of dawn. Everyone seemed bent on beating the traffic. It was only five in the morning, and yet transportation was already out on the street. Jeepney drivers were already flying their routes. Some drank bitter coffee to keep them alert, knowing this would be a very busy day. Buses with their uniformed conductresses were already competing for passengers. Most flower shops had already been armed since the previous night keeping their fresh supply of flowers and wreaths to meet demand. Private cars, vans, and rented transportation were already filled with gas, some even scrubbed clean to transport whole families including extended members who would like to 'visit.' Food that wouldn't spoil easily under the sun had been packed; otherwise, there were ice boxes to salvage perishable ones or huge blocks of ice sprinkled with straw-colored rice chaffs to delay thawing, sitting or covered with jute sacks lying on the floor of vehicles. Ice picks were set aside to chunk off pieces of ice for refreshing cold drinks or to replenish thawed ice in ice boxes. Included were extra umbrellas, blankets to cover grassy parks, collapsible tents, and portable grills for cooking. Soon these cars, jeeps, buses, and trucks would go in similar directions, holding traffic on narrow streets.

An hour later, traffic in Metro Manila was already at a standstill. There was impatient honking of horns, occasional cries of infants and cranky children, a stalled vehicle drawing amused smiles, and an occasional offer to set these useless derelicts on fire. Nationwide, somewhere, someplace, all means of transportation and most of humanity were headed to a cemetery to fulfill this annual obligation.

It was the feast day of the dead, also called All Souls' Day or *Todos Los Santos* to the locals. It is a day reserved for honoring one's departed ancestors, visiting their graves, and remembering them. Cemeteries come alive with mushrooming tents and blooming umbrellas to ward off the searing sun, folding chairs and *bangko* for sitting, ubiquitous fans in half-moon or heart-shaped such as weaved *abanikos*, or perfect circles of fancy Chinese fans. Colorful flowers in wreaths, vases, baskets, or freshly planted or staked around gravesites abounded. Not a few brought pictures of their loved ones who had moved on. Round or tapered votive candles illuminated their likeness in broad daylight. Affluent families were clustered in their own palatial mausoleums with gated entrances, permanent seats of stones, and counters to accommodate a day's supply of food and drinks, some even with their own power to accommodate a ceiling fan and provide light or even a portable TV or refrigerator. Here, the deceased were interred next to each other or tiered on top of each other like in catacombs with marble images of angels, crosses, or the crucifixion guarding them. Even in death, family members preferred to be together. The air was of deference, piety, and camaraderie, though undertones of carnival atmosphere occasionally surfaced with the rousers, the rowdy, the unruly who brought alcoholic beverages, and vandals. Relatives usually shared anecdotes about the deceased, exchanged and updated news among the living, and shared the latest family gossip, such as how much a breadwinner was currently earning and which children got accepted to which prestigious school, mishaps and financial misfortunes, affairs and separations. Occasionally, there would be silence to evade a topic or save one's reputation.

Pictures of Mario and Tinay were propped up at the head of their adjacent tombstones inside the massive Gomez family mausoleum. Aurora, who had her *babang luksa* (end of mourning), again donned a black outfit from head to toe in keeping with tradition. Beside her was Baby in a similar though modest black dress and shoes. Baby wore a black shawl to cover her head. Pearl wore a white sleeveless cotton shirt and jeans. A tiny black ribbon was pinned on her chest, a compromise with tradition. It was a vivid contrast to the familiar ogres, monsters, masks, fictional or historical figures, and characters traipsing from house to house for trick or treat Pearl was accustomed to at this same time of the year. She appeared oblivious to the two women with her headphones on listening to her music.

"Sorry I was late," Aurora said to Baby.

"I thought you forgot to pick me up," Baby said.

"We actually woke up real early. Four o'clock. Had to visit Father Francisco's grave. Brought him some wreaths. By the time we were done, traffic was unbearable."

"You were close to him."

"Yes. Very." Aurora's lips began to quiver. She wiped her eyes of tears. "It's not that long, just over a week. He made it just in time for *Todos Los Santos*. Massive second stroke."

"Funny old man."

"What do you mean?" A sudden flicker of fire lit up Aurora's eyes.

"Forgive me. I didn't mean to offend. I've seen him quite a few times. Whenever you had a party at the big house, I snuck in. I watched him when he got drunk. Sometimes I helped serve food when I knew it was safe. I didn't want to run into you. You really could calm him down. He listened to you. I heard people say you have two fathers. I was jealous."

"You have no reason to be jealous." Aurora saw Pearl remain engrossed listening to music.

"You don't think so? Yes, I have a father . . . and yet I don't have a father."

Aurora continued to gaze at her daughter. She ignored Baby's comment.

This reminded her of Father Francisco's funeral. She had been inconsolable. Her daughter though remained stoic, looking passively at the coffin. She thought it was disrespectful. How could Pearl be so callous? Though Pearl had no idea, this was her flesh and blood inside the coffin. She could at least show some compassion, if not shed a tear. She continued to eye her viciously until Pearl gave her a perplexed, confused look. Cornered, she lowered her gaze. She could feel Pearl's penetrating eyes on her. Realizing her folly, it was her turn to feel uncomfortable. As she raised her head, their eyes met and stayed. Neither of them said a word. *Her daughter knew.* She shut her eyes and pulled her daughter tight against her chest to hide her shame. Her shoulders shook violently, failing to control her emotion. Pearl rubbed her back until she calmed down.

"So, how's your son, Alejandro?" Aurora said, evading confrontation. "Heard he ended up again in the hospital." She looked at Baby.

At her peripheral vision, she observed Pearl take off her earphones. She pretended not to notice.

"He's home now, *Ate. Awa ng Dios* (with God's mercy). Don't know what to do with that child. He's always been sickly," Baby said.

"Have you heard about turtle's meat? It's good for asthma."

"Is that so? Where can I buy some?"

"Somebody I know knows where to get it," Aurora said. "Remind me. I'll give you her name and phone."

"*Ay, salamat,*" Baby blurted. "*Ipagadya mo po kaming makasalanan* (Protect us sinners)." She made the sign of the cross.

"And your two other kids? How old are they now?"

"Consuelo is seventeen."

"*Dalaga na* (a young maiden now). Any admirers yet?"

"A few. She knows better not to be seriously involved with anyone," Baby said. "As the saying goes, she still has milk in her lips."

"Exactly, I'm with you." Aurora repeated, "She still has milk in her lips. I can't believe some are getting married at sixteen or even younger. These are children. And your youngest?"

Baby's face brightened. "Cita's twelve. She's my *sandigan* (support). This early she's doing most of the cooking and household chores. Keeps our house spick-and-span. When I am old and decrepit, she already said I can stay with her."

"Good. At least you have another daughter as a backup, just in case. You never know if Consuelo marries somebody with *masamang ugali* (bad disposition). We all know we are better off staying with our daughter's family than our son's."

"She better learn this early. She better take care of me when the time comes. After all the sacrifices I've done for her. After all the suffering I've endured from their Tatay."

"Now that you've mentioned, how's Renato?" Aurora asked.

"Nothing's changed." Baby's voice turned sullen. "He's married to the bottle. He is home when he wants to. Otherwise, he spends more time with his *kerida*."

"Again, why don't you leave him? Remember Tatay kept telling you to."

Baby lowered her gaze, arranging her veil to shield most of her face. "Easy to say, *Ate*. In spite of all, I love the man. As long as he is sober, he's good to the kids." Baby looked far. "And to me—"

A fresh bruise marred Baby's upper arm. Aurora confronted Baby. "He still beats you." She knew she was lying for him.

"At least the children are not fatherless. You know the stigma of separation. He still comes home to us. Not frequently, but he does. *Paminsan-minsan* (every now and then), he gives me market money."

"Baby, Baby . . ." *How can Baby stay with the man? Lie for him more than once.* "That's the reason Tatay always reminded me to take care of you. Take care of your children. Have you tried separating from him?" Aurora revisited the topic. "For good?"

"*Ilang beses na* (several times). But once he comes knocking at the door with bent knees, I melt, *Ate*. I can't say no to the man."

"Does he have any children with his *kerida*?"

"Two. Eight and ten, a boy and a girl. What hurts, *Ate*, the woman has her own house. The children are all in private schools."

"Where does the *kumag* (jerk) get the money? And his own family . . . Look at you, Baby. He can't even provide for his own family."

"I don't know, *Ate*." Baby appeared resigned to her misfortune. "I guess we all have our own cross to bear. Nanay, how lucky she was with Tatay."

"*Talaga* (You bet). What a gentle man." Aurora reminisced. "Nanay always got her way. Anything she wanted. She managed his money well, though. Invested it well."

"Not with my Renato," Baby whispered, ashamed. "Not my Ato." She repeated, calling him by his pet name. "I wish I handled the purse and managed and budgeted the money, like everyone I know."

"That's one thing I learned from Nanay. Women handle the purse." Aurora thought about the dole Tatay, with Nanay's blessing, had given Baby, a role she had assumed.

What a waste. She opted to keep quiet.

"I had no problem with Red."

"Like a typical Filipino husband," Baby joked. She still considered Aurora and Red as a couple. "Red's his name, right?"

"Yes."

"Any children with this woman . . . he's supposed to be married now?"

"She has two from a prior marriage. She didn't want any children with Red."

"Unbelievable."

"*Sinabi mo* (You said it)."

"That's the purpose of getting married, having children."

"That's a woman's role. Not that she is really married to my Red."

"I don't understand their way of thinking. Forgive me, *Ate*. I didn't mean to be rude. You probably understand better, being married to a white man."

"I don't know if I really do."

"Any regrets?"

Aurora looked at Pearl, who remained uninterested, again listening to her music. "She is a good reason for me not to have any."

"And how is she?" Baby pouted her lips toward Pearl.

"We're surviving," Aurora said. "It's hard."

"If she needs company, Consuelo is available."

"*Salamat.* We might go back to Baguio. She likes the weather. And the peace."

"She still hasn't gained back her weight. Compared to how she looks in her pictures. You could see it in her cheeks."

"I know."

"You haven't either. I could just imagine the trauma to you as well. I would die if it happened to one of my daughters."

"I haven't failed in my devotion to the Sacred Heart to help us overcome this. My knees are calloused from walking on bended knees to the altar."

"I've done some walking on my knees myself asking for intervention for my son's asthma. And for Ato to change his ways."

As the night set in, the cemetery remained alive, with lit candles among the tombstones like fireflies contrasting with the ink-colored sky. Some brought kerosene lamps.

It was dark when the three women decided to leave. The cemetery crowd was mostly gone, the city of the dead back to its solitude except for some flickering candles on their last breath. Occasional gusts of wind chilled the bones. Scattered leaves made crackling dry noise. The smell of food offerings, burnt incense, and paper money for the dead wafted from the adjacent Chinese cemetery. The traffic was lighter. Aurora's driver dropped off Baby at her place.

It was a modest two-story dwelling, hidden from the street with aging acacia trees and narrow winding walk.

"*Daan muna kayo* (Please drop by)," Baby invited.

"*Nakakahiya* (It's embarrassing). Your children must be fast asleep. We hate to disturb them."

"Please don't worry. They probably just came in themselves. They visited their grandparents' gravesite. Ato's parents. I'm sure you're no bother. I should be the one embarrassed. Our house is nothing to brag about. It's not even our house. We rent."

Aurora signaled for Pearl to get off. Their driver, *Mang Tomas*, turned off the engine and stayed behind. Aurora and Pearl followed Baby. The sound of pebbles crushed under their shoes while mosquitoes hovered above their heads, competing with the sound of crickets and other nocturnal insects. Some mosquitoes sucked their blood on their way in. The inside of the house was covered in darkness.

On familiar ground, Baby pulled a tiny metal chain to the center of the room. It made a faint click. The solitary incandescent bulb cast a yellowish glow. There were mismatched chairs and a worn sofa resting against a bare wall.

"We're here. Pardon the appearance. Please take a seat."

Pearl saw a small coffee table with a doily under a ceramic vase holding dust-covered artificial flowers. The opposite wall had a low bookcase littered with magazines, some with missing or torn covers, old newspapers, and a few books. A glossy Chinese calendar with a beautiful Chinese woman in red and gold *cheung sam* dress served as a wall decoration above the bookcase. Chinese and Arabic characters were printed on the calendar. Framed photos of Consuelo, Alejandro, and Cita occupied the top of the bookcase. Two balls of candle drippings—a fist-sized one and a bigger melon-sized one—rested next to each other at the corner. Baby reached for the smaller ball, examining it. Its kaleidoscope of color reflected from the artificial light.

"It's still warm. The children haven't been here long."

"They are good for waxing the floor. Remember?"

"Of course I remember. We would go with our friends to the cemetery to collect candle drippings."

"Or steal candles before they melted," Aurora pointed out. "And compete to see who got the biggest candle ball."

The two women laughed. They stopped, realizing Pearl was listening to them. Embarrassed, Baby placed the candle ball back.

"I see you have already framed all your diplomas."

"Those are the only *kayamanan* (fortune) I can be proud of."

Indeed, the wall leading to the second floor was cramped with framed certificates and diplomas—Alejandro's, Cita's, and Consuelo's elementary-school diplomas; Consuelo's high-school diploma side by side with Baby's own; Baby's diploma from vocational school for hair science and beauty; and her husband's auto mechanic certificate and high-school diploma.

"I am still waiting for Consuelo's college diploma," Baby said. "That's the reserved spot. Please, you two take a seat." Baby repeated and then excused herself to go to the kitchen. "She will be the first college graduate in our family. I couldn't wait."

Aurora threw a glance at Pearl hearing Baby's comment.

Light from the second floor flooded the stairwell.

"Who's there?" It was a gruff, low-pitched male voice.

"It's me," Baby answered. "Did you just come home?"

"A little while ago. The children are tired and already in bed."

"Did you eat yet?"

"I was hungry. I couldn't wait for you." The voice rose. "I ate with the children. What do you expect? Don't forget to clean our mess less stray cats make a feast."

"Auring and her daughter Pearl are here. I invited them to drop by."

"Why didn't you call me?" There was a sudden softening of the voice. "I could have brought home some food."

Aurora shook her head and hands to signal Baby.

"She said not to bother."

Baby came back with a wooden tray and placed it on top of the coffee table, pushing the vase with the artificial flowers on the side. There were a couple of glasses with ice. Baby grabbed a can of pineapple juice resting on it and shook it briskly. She bore holes on opposite sides and poured golden-yellow liquid into the two glasses.

"*Pasensiya na kayo* (My apologies). I wish I had more to serve."

"You really shouldn't have bothered. I'm glad Renato's home tonight."

"He has to be. Otherwise, how can the kids visit the cemetery?"

The sound of dragging slippers on the stairs ushered in a swarthy man in a white undershirt, wearing loosely fitted house pants. Cigarette smoke trailed him.

"*Ano, kumusta na?* (So, how are you?)" He stayed at the foot of the narrow stair.

"*Mabuti. Kumusta na?* (Good. And how are you?) I haven't seen you in a while."

Aurora motioned for Pearl to acknowledge the man. Pearl approached Renato and reached for his right hand to touch her forehead as a sign of respect, bowing slightly.

"Been busy, Auring." He nodded to acknowledge Pearl. "You should be proud of Tatay's roosters, Auring. Two of them won big time. If he were just around." Renato formed perfect rings of smoke. They floated and broke up slowly, vanishing in thin air. "He'd be proud. He'd be glad he left his *alaga* (warden) under my wings. And your daughter, Auring. She's turning out to be a real beauty. No wonder—"

"I know you do, Renato." Aurora cut him short, ignoring his comment. She smiled to hide the disgust on her face. "You're good at it. Tatay expected nothing less."

Satisfied with the comment, Renato excused himself and walked toward the rear of the house. The excited commotion of some roosters was heard as he opened the back door. The ill-fitting metal door made a grating sound.

At Tatay's place, Aurora had already changed to her negligee, exhausted, preparing to sleep. There was a short knock to her door. Pearl barged in, still wearing her white cotton shirt and jeans, minus the tiny black ribbon.

"Can't sleep?"

"I want to go home, Mother."

"You are home, Amber Pearl."

"I mean home."

"You're home, Amber Pearl. Your mother, our house, our friends are here. You're home. Remember, we're leaving for Baguio tomorrow."

"You are home here, Mother."

Aurora grabbed Pearl's shoulders. "You are safe here, Amber Pearl. Look what happened to you in the States. It wouldn't have happened were you here."

"Don't be ridiculous, Mother."

"Don't you want to stay here, at least till you've sorted out everything?"

"I could visit, like now. But not to stay for good. Baguio can wait."

"Everything has been planned. Why?"

"I . . . I've changed my mind."

"Just like that?" Aurora's lips began to quiver. Her eyes glazed. "Your mother's place not good enough for you?"

"Stop it, Mother."

"You are ashamed of your mother, isn't it? I can tell. Your skin may be white, but you were nourished with an Oriental woman's milk. Half the blood in your veins are from me. Don't you forget that."

"You're impossible, Mother." Pearl pivoted toward the door.

"Go ahead," Aurora said, riled up. "Trash me, my culture, my tradition, everything about your mother. Go back to your father where people get robbed every minute, get killed right and left, where the old are dumped in nursing homes, where children are disrespectful, where women are . . . are . . ."

"Say it, Mother. Say it. Rape, that's what you mean. Isn't it? Like it's a dirty word. Like it's a shame to be a person who has been raped. Like it was my fault. For God's sake, don't treat me like a leper. Don't treat me like this is something to be ashamed of. It is not. Hear this. It is not."

Aurora slumped into a lounge chair, talking incongruously between sobs. "Do you realize how hard it was for your mother? If you only knew not for a minute would I hesitate to trade places with you. Spare you the agony. And this is what I get? I will never talk to you ever again. Do you hear me?"

"Yes, Mother."

Pearl disappeared behind the door and closed it with a soft click. Her voice trailed. "If you say so."

The creaking of the wrought iron to the mausoleum broke the solitude of the kneeling woman in black. It was the cemetery's keeper, an old, weathered man.

"I'm sorry to bother you, ma'am, but I am closing the main gate to the cemetery shortly."

The woman gave the old man a quizzical look. "I was just here a week ago today. Nobody told me about the gate." She stood up to wipe the dirt off her knees.

"We just started imposing the rule, ma'am." The old man slightly bowed his head and touched the rim of his woven hat with his fingertips.

"Since when?"

"I thought you'd heard." The keeper removed and rested his hat on his chest. It was frayed at the edges. The top was pale from the sun. "There's been a lot of vandalism lately. Urns missing, and statues vanishing."

"Gosh, Virgin Mary, Mother of God. What else are they planning to steal next?"

"Signs of the times, ma'am."

"I guess." The woman grabbed an expensive-looking leather bag. "It's a good thing I had somebody put a lock here. Give me a few minutes, and I'll be out of here."

"You came by yourself, ma'am?"

"Yes. Why?"

"I wouldn't if I were you, ma'am. A young girl was just found wandering and crying in the cemetery, just recently. Clothes torn. Bleeding. Gang raped. Teenagers."

The woman made the sign of the cross, covered her face with a black veil, and hurriedly locked the gate while the old man started to go about his business, talking to himself.

A dark, tinted car was waiting for the woman under a shady mango tree, barely visible in the growing darkness. The car made two bright holes as she turned on the engine. They illumined the walls of some adjacent mausoleums, their light panning the distant tombstones as the car maneuvered. Their cone of light diminished in size as the car moved away. The sound of gravel and rocks under its wheels broke the silence.

The car vanished in the night.

CHAPTER 19

THE MOURNING AFTER

Red felt the surge of emotion as Pearl tenderly rubbed the stump of his left forearm. It was an acquired habit since Pearl was a toddler.

"How is she?"

Pearl finished the bite of food in her mouth. "You never fail to ask the same question. Every time." Pearl smiled. It was a mix of gladness and sadness. "She does the same."

Like a child caught stealing some cookies, Red bowed his head. He was quiet for some time. "I was married to your mother for quite some time. That's good enough reason."

"Honestly?"

Red's face blushed. A painful sting surged in his ears. He laughed, an awkward one. He raised his index finger to signal the waitress for more coffee.

"How's P.J.? His family?"

"You want to hear about P.J.? You really want to hear about him? His family?"

The blush in Red's face surged like the tide. *What was so upsetting about my question? About P.J.?*

"He's broken off our engagement."

"Oh . . ." Red felt awkward, lost for words. "Well . . ."

"Do you know the reason why, Dad?"

Red shook his head.

"I'm surprised. How much do you know about Mother? You were married for years, as you said. How much do you know about her . . . about her people, her country? Did you even try to know?"

Red's brows knotted. He was unsure what these questions meant. Pearl was raised comfortable with her mixed ethnicity. Indeed, she spoke her mother's native language fluently, to his standard at least. Not like him. He knew a few words, some bad ones, which was not unusual. Aurora's way of life was something he never really immersed himself in. He accepted her for what she was. To the O'Neils, she was an outsider. Just like he was to her family.

"Was she a virgin?"

Red's head sprung back. He was startled at the question and brutish force of Pearl's hands on his stump and tight squeeze on his right hand.

"Was Mother a virgin when you married her?"

"Why are you asking?" Red reciprocated Pearl's tight hold on his right hand. "Why does it matter to you?"

"Because it matters to them." Pearl's eyes begun to well. "It matters to P.J. Romualdez. It matters to Techie Romualdez. It matters to Doña Esperanza Lopez."

"Wait a minute." The blush in Red's face deepened. "You're telling me that P.J. and his family . . . his good-for-nothing family called off your engagement because of that. I'll tell that jerk. If he had the common sense not to open that security door—"

"It didn't matter, Dad. The point is that I am tainted. As that self-righteous woman said." Pearl imagined the smirk on Doña Esperanza's face. "I'm now rubbish. Not good enough for her grandson."

"Is everything okay?" It was the waitress. She poured some coffee in Red's mug.

It was only then that Red noticed that some customers were looking in their direction.

"We're fine. Can I have the check, please?"

Pearl's head was bowed, her shoulders appeared defeated.

"I'm sorry. I am so sorry. I didn't know." Red fumbled in his pants pocket to reach for his handkerchief. It was a habit Aurora taught him. He offered it to Pearl. "So . . . what are your plans?"

He should have said something more substantial, something comforting. He ached for those times he could still scoop his daughter in his arms, embrace and comfort her, and bring the smile back. He felt sorry for his daughter. It must be devastating on her, the rape and the rejection. Is his daughter crying? He can't see her face.

Pearl's eyes were dry when she gazed back at Red. "Dad. It may take a while, but I will survive this. I'll be okay. Remember, I am an O'Neil. Just like what Aunt Millie kept saying."

"That's good." Red swallowed hard. He was not much help.

He paid their check. It was then that they heard a soft knock on the glass window by their seat. It was Mary, his wife. She was all dressed up, signaling with her watch. Pearl smiled icily at the woman. She had never been close to her. Plus, her stepmother never even tried to develop a relationship with her. They remained strange.

"She's waiting for you, Dad."

"She can wait." Red waved his hand dismissively. He didn't bother to look again at Mary. "This is more important. So, you want to meet with me again, Pearl?"

"Sure."

"Say when."

"I'll call, Dad."

"So, you're staying by yourself in the house." The image of the colonial house with green shutters flashed in Red's mind.

"For a short while. Mother needs to take care of some business in Manila."

"Is the grass tall yet?"

Pearl remembered the sound of the mowing machine in the backyard a week ago. It was her dad mowing the lawn.

"I'll come mow this weekend. You can stay in bed and not bother to let me in. I still have the extra key. Ten in the morning should be just fine. I won't be disturbing your sleep by then."

"Dad, I would love to have you drop by for a late breakfast or a brunch."

"Well . . . it's a date then."

There was another series of impatient knocks on the glass window. Red stood up without looking at Mary.

"You stay and finish your food." As he ambled toward the door, he turned once more to Pearl and stage-whispered, "Yes, your mother was."

Red's lopsided smile lingered in Pearl's mind. Sad or happy, he always had that ready smile. Was it sadness or irony he wanted to convey? Her dad, in his own quiet way, was a complicated man. As her mother and grandmother Tinay said, men are different.

*　　*　　*

"G'morning, how can I help you?"

Red shifted his leg. The public library was a place he was not comfortable visiting. He was not even positive he would like anyone to know he visited one. The woman at the counter with the square glasses and red lipstick looked him straight in the eyes

His Adam's apple rose as he swallowed hard. "Yes. I . . . I am looking for a book about the Philippines."

"I'm sure we have some. Sir, did you look? You know they are arranged by author or subject matter." She pointed at a row of tiny shelves against the wall.

When he did not respond, the woman left the counter and motioned Red to follow her.

She was swift. With her pen and paper in hand, she jotted down the information she needed from those tiny shelves with stacks of index cards. She redirected Red to an aisle and pointed to a section where Red could find what he was looking for.

He signed out a couple of books.

At the apartment he shared with Mary, he browsed the books by the bedside that night. It didn't take long before he fell asleep.

"You know you could look at the Internet. It's a lot faster." It was Mary. With her dirty-blonde hair set in huge curlers and her silhouette outlined by the morning sun, she reminded Red of a sitting Buddha.

Her face obscured by the sun, he heard her munching her toast with butter.

"Excuse me?"

"I've never seen you lay your hands on books. If there's something you need to know, look at the Internet."

Red felt the sting in his face. His face must be beet red. He finished his cup of coffee.

"I got to go. I'll be late." He stood up and without bothering to look at Mary brisk towards the front door.

"Fine."

It was several weeks before Red browsed the Internet. He asked one of Mary's sons to show him how to use the Internet. Aurora had quite a few collections of Filipino films. That was where he gravitated first. He then browsed through some popular tourist spots. Then he searched about Filipino customs and festivals. His attention caught an article about Santa Cruzan. He knew his daughter was a *sagala*, whatever it meant. He was not present at the one Pearl was. An article showed a picture of an attractive woman parading as a Reyna Elena. He recognized the woman—Rosario Rosales. He remembered Aurora had sent pictures of her from the Santa Cruzan where Pearl participated. Aurora was boasting to him how their daughter outshone the woman who was an up-and-coming movie actress. That must be the Santa Cruzan Pearl was at. He didn't bother to search for the third Reyna Elena.

He did not see Pearl's picture. She was an unknown while Rosario Rosales was a familiar face. It was a tourist article about the Philippines.

Henceforth Red would occasionally look at the Internet. He would mostly gravitate towards news from Aurora's place. He would run into news about Rosario Rosales and her fast rise to stardom. She was the same age as his daughter, and having shared a spotlight with his Pearl made him read about her.

Then he ran into the news about her suicide at a young age—twenty-eight.

It had been several years since her reign as the Reyna Elena with Pearl. Curious, he searched to find more about her suicide. He learned that a few months before her death she was reported to be missing. It turned out that she was kidnapped by a notorious gang. She was freed walking nearly naked on a deserted street, beaten and bleeding. Recovering after a prolonged hospitalization, she gave a press conference and announced that she was ready for a comeback. She would be the star in a movie chronicling what really happened during her disappearance. It was financed by an independent movie producer who made sure the story would be a carefully guarded 'secret.' Though she would remain quiet about her physical ordeal, she kept denying that she had been sexually abused. The public though knew.

She was halfway through the shooting when she jumped from the balcony of her hotel.

She did not leave any suicide note.

The script was a thinly veiled story of her ordeal where she was subjected to unimaginable physical and sexual abuse. It showed that she was able to apprehend and get her abusers to justice, and she was able to start fresh, get married and even start a family. The truth was, her captors were never brought to justice. The title of the half-finished film was *Heaven Is for Everyone*.

Red smiled and broke into a loud laugh. His ears and cheeks stung. He could feel the rush of blood in his face. He thought about her abusers, the public who under the cloak of pity and charity, silently lusted for blood, parading her like a slave to be devoured by lions, capitalizing on her misfortune. Rosario Rosales was several times a victim.

Pearl's voice was a fresh breath of air. "Yes, Dad?"

"Want to go out with your old man? We could meet at our favorite place."

"Not today, Dad. I'm busy."

"Okay, tell me when."

"How about a rain check?"

"Sure."

"Dad, I got to go."

"Pearly . . ."

"Yes, Dad?"

"I'm here if you need me. Anytime."

Pearly laughed.

He took a deep breath. Pearly is safe.

CHAPTER 20

SINGKIL

It was a ceremonial dance reserved only for a Muslim princess, with a young man, her prince, sporting a sharp, shiny *kris* sword and brass shield, and her lady-in-waiting with an umbrella to protect her from the elements. The ceremony would begin with the princess carried on top of paired crisscrossed bamboo poles by four attendants, her lady-in-waiting surefootedly trailing close with an umbrella poised and ready high up in the air, the prince arriving on foot nearby. Their arrival was accompanied by the beating of musical instrument, which included the gong *kulintang* and the wooden drum *dabakan*.

As the princess alighted down, the attendants would set the two pairs of bamboo poles on the floor, in a figure of a cross, like before. They would guard each end of the bamboo poles, resting them on a short piece of wood. The three principals would then stand at their designated places with necks imperiously craned skyward, unsmiling and unmindful of their audience, and eyes gazing down in apparent disdain. The princess would position the two elaborate fans she held like they were plumage from a peacock. Secure in their position, the kneeling attendants held on to the bamboo poles in complete attention, waiting for a few tappings of one royal foot protected by soft, sequined slippers to signal the start of the *singkil*. The rhythm would be slow at the start, the three principals crisscrossing the bamboo poles with their feet as the bamboo poles would clash synchronously against each other to the beating of the gongs and drum ringing in the air. The rhythm would gradually pick up in pace and sound, the clash of the hollow bamboo poles becoming more frenetic, and the dizzying kaleidoscope of brilliant yellows, reds, blues, greens, and golds, the dazzling sequences, adorning the costumes of the three principals adroitly leaping their feet and avoiding being caught by the bamboo poles.

The alarm clock rang. Pearl got up. She really didn't need its reminder. She had been awake all along, even with her eyes shut. Though she had just taken a shower, she was drenched in sweat. She had time to take another quick shower before putting on light makeup and fixing her hair. She donned her Pan American flight uniform, which was already ironed and neatly hung at the back of a chair. At the Kennedy International Airport, Pearl walked briskly with her handbag on one shoulder while pulling her luggage with tiny wheels, unmindful of people rushing in both directions, passing queues of passengers at the check-in counters, bypassing rows of telephone booths randomly occupied, walking past seats with people of different calling and activities, and hearing yet not hearing the public address system announcing departures, flight changes, and reciting names for various reasons. It was a habit learned, partly a result of regimented training in the flight school. It was also because she was sure of her destination. It also did not allow her mind to linger on her disturbing dreams.

Though less frequent, every night terror remained as vivid as the last, leaving her physically and emotionally drained. Her first flight was between New York and Chicago. It left JFK on time. They were filled to capacity. It was particularly hot that late August summer, making its presence definitely felt. There were quite a few families with young children. Children, unlike adults, were mostly unperturbed by turbulence, common during that time of the year. They enjoyed it as they would a roller-coaster ride. Some adults, in contrast, gripped on their armrests with breathing suspended, eyes shut, and lips sealed. They began to serve breakfast when the captain felt the worst had passed. Everything was routine. It felt reassuring.

The next flight was not much different. Like the first, it was also filled to capacity. Unlike the first, it appeared passengers were mostly college students. They were young, full of life. Some were boisterous.

They were annoying, a nuisance to some elderly and seasoned travelers. She could empathize with them. Before Pearl and the rest of the crew had to warn them, they quieted down. The last flight was a mix—young crowd, families, middle-aged men and women in business attire and suits, and retired, mature passengers. It was a very hectic day with no idle time at her disposal. She had been on her feet for hours. Her feet felt tighter in her shoes. They felt bigger. It would be heaven to soak them in warm, sudsy water with chamomile.

As trained, she still had smiles for the anxious and the haggard. She still carried her frame straight and looked confident. She remained composed while attending to that woman who constantly buzzed the call button, calming and composing her. Aware of the time at their disposal, they began to serve meals. Some passengers declined. Most were eager to eat. It was another routine flight. Before long, it would be another ordinary day until the man in the middle aisle busy with crossword puzzles in the newspaper pivoted his head to respond to her question.

"Sir, fish or chicken?" Pearl asked.

It was him. Though the thin moustache was gone, the upper lip scar was unmistakable. She kept her smile as myriads of thoughts flooded her mind.

"Would you like something to eat, sir?" Pearl repeated.

The man nodded with brows knitted, preoccupied with the puzzle. "Uh-hmm." He barely looked at her. "Chicken."

Pearl put the food tray in front of the man, careful not to make the trembling of her hands noticeable. She remembered her mother's advice. Do not show displeasure. Serve the food with aplomb, like it would be the best he would taste for a while. Ask him later. Was the soy sauce the bitter kind? Were the vegetables overcooked? She avoided meeting his eyes, lest recognition sink in.

She turned her back to him while keeping her posture straight and asked the other passengers at the opposite wing. Just then, an unexpected turbulence happened. With the sudden drop of altitude, it felt like she was sinking. She fought the urge to drop to her knees in fear.

She knew how to take care of herself. With renewed confidence, she finished serving the meal without mishap to the remaining passengers. At the galley kitchen, she poured herself a cup of coffee. She gulped the black coffee. Hot, it singed her lips. She spilled some. She always drank her coffee with cream and sugar. Not this time.

The memory of the assault flashed before her eyes—the ripping of her blouse, the toppled ornate divider, her desperate banging on the piano notes, his constant slap to keep her eyes open to see the smirk on his face, his blue eyes flashing, and his displaying his perfect set of teeth. It was the anniversary of the assault, a year ago to date. *Could this really be happening?*

The curtain opened. Startled, she spilled the rest of her coffee. It was Sue, the most senior flight attendant.

"Are you okay, Pearl?"

Pearl did not answer. With the open curtain, her eyes were focused on the midsection, at the seat where the man was. Color faded from her face. The seat where the man sat was empty. Sue caught her arm as her strength faded.

She whispered to Sue, "The police. Radio the police."

Her assailant was apprehended at the airport. All she remembered was the flashing red and blue lights from the police car, the blaring sirens, and the burst of firecrackers. Those firecrackers turned out to be gunshots.

The man was brought to the hospital. An emergency surgery to remove the lodged bullet in his chest failed to save him. She was asked to positively identify the man at the morgue. His paper-white face stared back at her with half-opened eyes and blue lips, the scar in it less noticeable in death. His wallet carried multiple identities. Nobody else claimed the body.

The following days occupied her nights with disturbing dreams. They were uncannily similar, though variations of her last encounter with the man.

The Pan American flight she was on crashed with two survivors, Pearl and him. Out of nowhere, the man materialized, holding a pair of handcuffs. He locked one on her wrist and then pulled her out of the wreckage, passing corpses—mangled, crushed, and dismembered. A few held on to a thread of life for a few minutes; some begged for succor. She recognized some as her fellow flight attendants. They stepped on some bodies and tripped on others while passing twisted metal and debris. Smoke blinded their path. She had no choice but to run off with the rapist, sprint as fast as he did with her wrist soldered to him. Pearl would wake up with goose bumps on her nape and forearm, gasping for air.

The Pan American domestic flight left JFK in turbulent weather. It crashed in a dense forest. Unscathed, spared bodily harm, she was the only survivor. That was what she thought until she heard a moan in the center aisle. A man with bloodied face was pinned between seats. As she tried to pry the man free, she saw blood had disappeared from his face. Instead, it was the face of her assailant with a sinister grin. He grabbed her wrist. His face was inches from her. She screamed. He opened his mouth to silence her with a kiss, displaying a pronged tongue that slithered down her throat while he bit and ate her lips. She woke up screaming at the top of her voice until she was hoarse and dry.

Another night terror saw her lost in an unfamiliar terrain with towering trees and the plane burning in the distance. A lone man got off from the wreckage. As he loomed bigger and closer, she saw he was her assailant, again with the handcuffs. He locked one of her wrists. As they ran, they could hear search planes above them, the disemboweled sound of the public address system calling for them. He kept running and dragging her along. Her feet started to feel too heavy to lift. Then she saw him gradually disappearing in quicksand. His arms reached out to empty space. He shouted, begging for help while gradually sinking. Realizing his efforts were in vain, he yanked her cuffed wrist to take her with him. She grabbed a sinewy root that suddenly appeared. She held on to her life with her free arm. The man continued to pull her down. The tree root began to break. She woke up sobbing, terrorized.

"*Anak*, wake up. Pearly, wake up." It was Aurora tapping her cheek. "It's just a dream, Pearly. It's only a dream."

The night terrors continued to hound her nights, though they became less frequent and sporadic with passage of time. Still, every dream felt very real, leaving her physically and emotionally drained. She dreaded them so much that Pearl decided to stop flying. Like a miracle, the night terrors vanished. She maintained the habit of leaving the lights on at night, though. She continued to check every closet and every door and close every window.

Aurora continued to live in Manila, frequently staying a few months in their old house in Evanston when she visited. Pearl enrolled in hotel and restaurant management school, moonlighting every once in a while as a waitress to gain more experience. She refused to stay in her mother's place once she had her own place, a condominium she bought with Aurora's help. She overlooked the maintenance of Aurora's place while her mother was gone.

"This one is indigenous to our place," Aurora said as she proudly showed a wood carving to Pearl. She emphasized the word "ours" to Pearl.

Aurora never failed to bring local arts and crafts to decorate her daughter's place when she visited. Pearl remained quiet, giving her mother freedom. Red kept in touch with his daughter, usually to eat out, just the two of them. At times, she would invite him for dinner at her place. She would decorate the dinner table and cook elaborate dishes, mostly Filipino food. Pearl would ask her father to critique her cooking, prodding him to be honest. She only saw her stepmother, Mary, once during these times. Red avoided talking about her when they met.

He never failed to ask about Aurora.

Pearl's eyes roamed the walls of her place. The place was so laden with local arts and pieces from her mother's place that it could pass for a museum. She smiled to herself while she appreciated a painting of young

Muslim maidens in their colorful *malong* costumes balancing *banga* water vessels on their heads. It occupied the foyer of her condominium. A huge *salakot*, a wide-brimmed hat worn by farm hands, hung on the adjacent wall while woven baskets from the Visayan Islands were displayed on a credenza. In the living room, there was a bas relief in *narra* wood of a native maiden crossing a brook in a hammock supported by bamboo poles carried by buff young men in *camisa de chino* shirt and pants. In the background were indigenous banana trees teeming with fruits, some huge ferns, and coconut trees, while a docile water buffalo was grazing nearby. A native parrot and wild orchids perched and hung from sturdy branches of acacia tree. There was a bust of a young woman in butterfly-sleeved *terno* fixing her hair in a bun with *payneta*, a narrow ornate wide-toothed comb resting on top of a pedestal. A gilded oval mirror from Ilocos region hung behind the bust. Reflected in the mirror was a white woman in modern outfit, a contrast to the traditionally clad bust, Pearl.

She draped the bust with a white muslin sheet, leaving only her reflection in the mirror. She removed the *salakot* from the wall. It left a faded circle of paint with a stud of a nail on the wall. She placed the numerous baskets inside a box, knowing she would need more than one. The idea had been percolating in Pearl's mind for a while. She nurtured it, like a nidus of dirt inside a shell that would give birth to a dazzling luminous pearl.

The phone rang. She recognized the person. "I'll buzz you in." She pushed the button to let the moving company inside her building. They were there to remove all of these decorations from her place, nearly everything her mother had brought. She could not wait for the movers to haul all of the stuff to their new place. One of the few pieces that would remain was the three-paneled screen with inlaid mother-of-pearl and other semiprecious stones. It was that gift from P.J.

The frenzy from the bamboo poles clashing was at its pinnacle, the feet adroitly maneuvering themselves in and out without missing a cue. The noise was electrifying; the cadence was dangerous. Yet confidence never left the three principal dancers, their heads cocksure as before, unmindful of the suspended breath of everyone. Indeed, *singkil* is a dance reserved only for a princess and her escort with royal blood flowing in their veins. It was based on a century-old legend about a princess caught in a tumultuous storm in the forest. The clashing bamboo poles symbolized swaying and falling trees. The undulating movements of the fans she carried symbolized winds sweeping all over and beneath her feet. It was created by an evil force that she conquered and won with the help from her prince and her loyal lady-in-waiting. The dance ends with the princess triumphantly stamping her foot one last time and then posing immobile like a tableau with the rest of the participants.

Everyone in the audience held their breath, speechless.

CHAPTER 21

FOOD FOR THE GODS

The chunky pieces of *chicharon* blossomed several times their size in seconds, a minute at the most, while soaked and bathed in scalding honey-brown pork oil. They made crackling noises. At times, splattered oil came close to singeing Pearl. The pieces were harvested into a wooden platter lined with paper towels to absorb excess oil. Pearl rushed them into the main dining room with a saucer of salt and vinegar on the side for dipping, joining the already crowded rectangular banquet table. A forest-green tablecloth covered the table, hiding its feet. On top was a rough textured fishnet in earth brown. A bounty of papaya, fresh coconut, pineapple, and *balimbing* (starfruit) were randomly displayed among serving platters of native ceramics, clay, wood, and woven baskets. A tall pair of sculptured idols from the mountain provinces of Luzon stood guard off center. A woven *banig* sleeping mat was framed into a wall mural while vertical rows of *salakot* hats hung by the foyer, the main dining area, and the entrance to the kitchen, the center of bustling activity. The banquet table boasted a dish of *sugpo* shrimps dipped in beaten eggs seasoned with salt, pepper, and flour deep fried until golden brown, *camaron ribosado*. There were rows of *lumpiang ubod* prepared with banana heart (*ubod*) sliced paper thin and mixed with shrimp and pork, seasoned with salt and sugar, and then wrapped in *lumpia* roll with garnishing of lettuce leaf, all served with piquant sauce.

Galantina, prepared twenty-four hours in advance, was a high note. A dish of steamed chicken cooked on a low flame was stuffed with ground ham, pork, Vienna sausage, eggs, and carrots and seasoned with soy sauce, *calamansi* juice, and pepper, all served cooled.

There were thin pieces of inviting fried *tapa* garnished with red sliced tomatoes. Then there was *pansit molo*, prepared with marinated goat's meat sautéed with garlic, onions, and tomatoes, simmered until the meat was tender, and then mixed with quartered potatoes, red pepper, sweet peas, olives, and liver gravy.

For the brave, there was a steaming pot of blood soup, *dinuguan*, its tender pork seasoned with garlic, onion, vinegar, and a pair of red and green peppers for color.

The fragrant smell of *pandan* leaf placed into the cooked rice percolated in the air.

The atmosphere of the place was controlled chaos. There was constant motion of busy feet coming and going. More food was being prepared or cooked in the kitchen. The ceiling fan made the hanged *parol* paper lanterns dressed with Japanese paper dance with grace, its cascade of streamers fluttering.

"*Ka* Lucia," Aurora called, "the rice? You think we have enough?"

"I can always cook another batch," *Ka* Lucia answered.

"I'll cook some," Fe said, volunteering.

The cling-clang of pots and pans was heard while Fe rummaged for an empty pot to cook extra rice. The rice cooker was already in use. She found one. Fe scooped several *gatang* (measuring cup) of rice from the jute sack, poured it on the empty pot, washed the white grains with cold water, and then measured the right amount of water with her fingertips. She covered the pot and placed it on top of a hot burner to cook.

"There," Fe uttered with pride. "Now we don't have to worry."

Aurora shouted, "The *leche plan*. I can smell it's beginning to burn."

"I'll get them out of the oven," Pearl said. "I need three small flat plates."

Inside the oven were three oval-shaped pans with glazed golden-yellow sweet. They were submerged in a bigger rectangular pan with water. The smell of caramelized sugar sifted in the air.

Ka Lucia didn't waste time looking for flat plates. "Coming."

Impatient rings were heard coming from the front door.

"Somebody," Pearl shouted, "somebody answer the damn door."

Aurora rushed the freshly cooked *pansit luglog* noodles to the main dining room. She squeezed it among the other food at the banquet table. She wiped her hands on her apron while running to answer the door.

"Hi." It was Red, ushered by a bunch of wrapped fresh flowers in his hand. "I got the flowers."

"Good." Aurora smiled awkwardly at Red as their arms bumped each other. She walked toward the kitchen. "Pearl, where do you want the flowers?" Aurora placed the flowers on the sink.

Red, who was close behind, was intercepted by Pearl to reach the top of the cupboard where a vase was. Red placed the vase on the sink beside the flowers. "How much water?"

"Please, be careful . . . the flowers." Aurora avoided Red's eyes. "And don't forget the preservatives."

"I won't." Red tore the small pocket that came with the flowers with his teeth and poured its contents on the vase. He gazed at Aurora, who continued to avoid his eyes. "Is this water enough?"

Aurora nodded without uttering a word. She removed the plastic wrapping and handed the flowers to Red. "Where do you want them?" She repeated to Pearl.

The bouquet found its niche near the main entrance, on a pedestal to greet everyone as they came in. The atmosphere remained fervid. Everyone was aware that the crowd would start pouring in anytime soon. It was the grand opening of Pearl's initial venture, Salakot, a Filipino ethnic restaurant. A Filipino local paper in Chicago carried an article about it. Pearl's former colleagues in the airline industry knew. Red told his coworkers, friends, and family. Aurora spread the news to the local Filipino community. *Ka* Lucia, visiting from Canada with Fe, ended up helping with the food preparation and cooking. All the cooking done, the banquet table was a feast of hot, mouthwatering food. Stacks of plates, bowls, and utensils were waiting for eager, hungry mouths to sample.

"Did you hear the news?" Aurora asked everyone. "P.J.'s in Chicago, visiting."

Pearl smiled, a nondescript one. She swiped a curl of stray hair away from her forehead. She turned her head toward Aurora.

"It's been fifteen or twenty years since we last saw him," Red pointed out. "What's he been up to?"

"I haven't kept in touch with his family," Aurora said. "He's running for congressman the last I've heard. Senator, perhaps. It's closer to twenty years or more," Aurora corrected Red.

"Where is he staying?" Pearl flattened her hair with a hand, exposing an ear toward Aurora.

"Could be the Drake," Aurora said. "That's where his grandma and mother stay when they visit Chicago."

Their conversation was cut short by the door chimes to announce that the initial group of customers had arrived. There was a quick exchange of glances among everyone. It was a group of three, two young Oriental lads with a young white woman. Soon there were more. Everyone—*Ka* Lucia, Fe, Aurora, Red, some hired help, and Pearl—got busy taking orders, manning the kitchen, and answering queries from those unfamiliar with the food. Most tried the buffet tables. The flow of the crowd remained relatively constant for the next hours. Pearl was mostly tied up in the kitchen, replenishing the food. Red ended up assisting the kitchen with her since he was not an authority on answering ethnic questions regarding the food. Aurora joined them washing the dishes. He helped dry them with his right hand.

"You're thinner," Aurora said.

Red smiled. His cheeks turned beet red. "You noticed." There was a moment of silence. "I miss your cooking."

Aurora laughed, a modest, soft one. Her speed in washing the dishes picked up.

"I should try the *kare-kare*. There is something about the way you cook it that Pearl could not approximate yet. Not yet."

"She didn't cook for you?" *You're lying. Mary never cook for you? You even help prepare food. Didn't you help crush the freshly roasted peanuts, wash the* bok choy, *and cube the eggplants? It was a joint effort*, Aurora thought. *Filipino food involves a lot of preparation. Not like American.*

"Not really."

"I'm sorry. I didn't mean to pry." Aurora burst into a nervous laugh.

"You don't have to feel guilty. There really wasn't much love lost between us. Not for a long time." *Stop this false modesty*, Red was also tempted to say.

"What do you mean?" Aurora's speed picked up more.

"I was wrong. I shouldn't have married her." Red cleared his throat, which felt dry. "I should have stayed." He emphasized the last word.

Aurora remained quiet. Her chest was pounding hard.

"I never cared what my parents said about you either. You know that." Red searched for Aurora's eyes.

The gush of water from the faucet drowned the talk between Red and Aurora.

The door chimes' cling-clang reverberated above the din as the crowd continued to swell and ebb. Pearl was replenishing the *lumpiang ubod* when the chime once more sounded.

He strode confident, followed by two young children and a petite Filipina.

"P.J.," Pearl whispered to herself, recognizing him. They had just been talking about him.

P.J. had ballooned. Fe greeted and ushered his group to a vacant table. Shortly, the children and the woman stood up to go to the banquet table. Pearl continued to busy herself.

"Hello. Good afternoon," the woman said with a thick accent.

"Hi!" Pearl said as she was more accustomed to. "Welcome. I'm Pearl. Chef-owner." She greeted them in Tagalog.

"Pardon me, but you made this place beautiful. And those *salakot* . . ." The woman admired a wall covered with them.

"Goes with the name, right?"

"I like your bas relief." The woman pointed at the curved image of a young maiden carried in a hammock by young men crossing a brook. It hung by the wall beside the banquet table. "We are visiting from Manila."

"I'm glad you do. How long will you be in Chicago?"

"A couple of weeks. P.J.'s here to raise some funds," the woman said aloud. She looked toward P.J., who was talking to Fe. "He's a senator from the Philippines."

Pearl handed a plate and a fresh set of utensils in a linen napkin to the woman. "Beautiful children."

"*Naku, hindi naman* (Oh no, not really)," the woman answered, seemingly lost for words.

Pearl hid a smile.

"This is Ting-Ting." The woman pointed to a girl of ten with a pair of pigtails. The girl smiled bashfully. "And this is Adonis." The boy responded by smiling from ear to ear. "He is twelve."

The boy's narrow eyes and Oriental nose reminded Pearl of P.J.

She handed them each a plate and set of utensils. "Well, enjoy the food."

The three huddled close as they began to choose. They soon went back to their table as P.J. walked toward the banquet.

"Hi, *kumusta*?" He offered a handshake like a well-seasoned politician. "I saw the ad in the Filipino paper. I could not resist the urge to see you. It's your grand opening. So, *kumusta*?"

"I'm fine." Pearl noticed some premature grays on P.J.'s temples. He had grown big. His stomach was showing the beginning of a paunch. "So you're a congressman now."

"Yes." P.J. accepted a clean plate and utensils from Pearl. "I am running for reelection. Correction, I'm running for senator."

"Followed your dreams, right?"

"A way of life I am used to," P.J. said. "My family. We're all in politics. It was expected of me." His eyes looked at the choices. "I heard you have a successful culinary TV show. You've written some cookbooks. They're best sellers even at home. But this is your first try opening your own restaurant. It's about time."

"Try this." Pearl pointed at the *tapa*.

"You cooked all of these?" His eyes sparkled.

"With help. The menu choices were mostly mine. Something different from the usual ethnic restaurant."

"They all look tempting." P.J. picked some *tapa*. He placed a bowl on his plate.

"How's everybody?"

"You didn't hear about *Lola* Espe?" P.J. scooped some *pansit molo* with the ladle. He filled his bowl.

Pearl shook her head.

"*Ulyanin*. Alzheimer's. Mother's busy taking care of her." P.J. eyed the wrapped *Lumpiang ubod*. He took some, bathed them with its thick sauce, and then sprinkled crumbled peanuts on top.

"I'm sorry to hear that."

P.J. shrugged his shoulders. "Things happen."

The expression reminded Pearl of his grandmother. He placed some *chicharon* on his plate. "I think she is happy in her current state of mind. It's harder on the caregiver, harder on my mother." He squeezed a tiny saucer on his plate for a dip of tangy vinegar for his *chicharon*.

"I imagine. And how is she, your mum?" Pearl felt uncomfortable addressing Techie as *Tita*.

"She's fine. Doesn't seem to grow old." P.J. burst into a short laugh. He continued to walk around the banquet table. "In spite of everything. So, how are you?"

"I'm fine." Pearl paced her walk with P.J.

P.J. nodded. He seemed deep in his thoughts. He eyed the woman and the two children. They were busy with their food. He spoke when he was sure nobody could hear him.

"I'm sorry about what happened, what I did. I really am."

It caught Pearl off guard. She didn't think it would matter after all these years. She groped for words.

"Things happen," she finally said, still lost for words, recalling Doña Esperanza's words, plagiarizing them. It was also P.J.'s. favorite expression.

"I had no choice . . . obey *Lola*. Listen to my mom."

"Like a dutiful grandson. Like a good son."

"Yes, like a good grandson. Like a good son."

"I understand." Pearl kept the thought to herself. *You were supposed to follow the elderly, show filial loyalty, and obey them, isn't it?* "It was hard on you. Must be difficult."

"I was cruel," P.J. was finally able to say. "Forgive me."

"It's the past."

"It's the bridge to the present and the future."

"You better go back to join them." Pearl eyed the woman and the children while she spoke. "Your food will get cold."

"You're right." P.J. noticed the children. Ting Ting and Adonis were beginning to make noise and couldn't seem to stay put. "I'd better."

The woman stood up to get some more food as soon as P.J. joined them. "These children, *parang hindi pinapakain* (as if they are being starved). They want more of this." The woman took a new plate and filled it with more crunchy *chicharon*.

"They're adorable. P.J. must be proud of them."

"He's a doting uncle to my kids. He spoils them rotten."

"I thought you were his—"

"Wife?" The woman smiled. "P.J.? I'm his cousin. Very picky. He's not married at all. Wouldn't it be nice? He's getting old." The woman cuddled close to Pearl to whisper, "He was seriously in love with this woman. *Lola* Espe orchestrated an arrangement between her family and ours. Somehow it didn't work out. Something happened. I didn't get the chance to meet her."

Pearl blushed.

"I'm sorry to bother you with morbid details. Actually, she was also a mestiza." The woman looked at Pearl. "Like you."

Pearl smiled without saying a word.

The crowd had thinned since it was way past mealtime. Pearl started to feel hungry. She noticed that all the food on the banquet table had been touched. Some platters were empty. Most were nearly empty in fact. They needed to be replenished.

At a quiet corner, Red and Aurora were having a late lunch. They were sharing a hot bowl of *kare-kare* plus some *ukoy* fritters, both Red's favorites. They appeared oblivious to everyone else, a stark contrast to their earlier conduct.

P.J.'s group was the last to leave. The two children were becoming too comfortable and began to be noisy, somewhat unruly. P.J. had asked for the check, which Fe took care of. The children had put on their coats and were eager to leave. The woman waved and smiled at Pearl while putting on hers. She was soon leading her children out the door.

P.J. approached Pearl. "I have a fund-raising dinner among our Filipino friends tomorrow night at the Drake Hotel. Seven p.m. if you are interested . . ."

P.J. let his words drift. He smiled eagerly at Pearl. He waived at *Ka* Lucia, who was gazing his way. *Ka* Lucia waved back. He looked in the direction of Red and Aurora, who continued to be unmindful of everyone else.

"I'll tell my parents." Pearl knew her parents were not interested in anyone else at that moment.

The door chimes sounded as P.J. stepped out. The door closed behind him with a faint thud. Pearl approached and began stacking the dirty plates from their table. The table faced a bay window adorned with potteries from Laguna province. Every spot on both sides of the street facing it were taken by a motor vehicle, guarded by a meter guard.

Starving, she carried a saucer plate with a slice of dessert. P.J. dashed to cross the street. In spite of his weight, he remained agile. *Does he still play* sabong *with his prize-winning cockfighters? Basketball?* He opened the driver side of his red Subaru. *Hmm, my favorite color.*

The silhouette of the woman and busy shadows of the children were visible. He squinted looking back at the restaurant, straining his eyes to figure out who was gazing back at him from the bay window. Recognizing her, he smiled and then waved before disappearing inside the car.

The *bibingka* dessert had never tasted so good as it melted in Pearl's mouth with its lightly salted sliced egg on it. Its crust was slightly burned, the way she preferred. It tasted like heaven.

She continued waving her hand long after the red Subaru had left its spot.

Pearl thought—*P.J. needed eyeglasses.*

EPILOGUE

"You eat like a bird." P.J. smiled and then scooped some seafood alfredo on Pearl's plate. "Here. That's why you're so tiny." He was obviously flattering her.

It worked. Her heart raced. P.J. enjoyed the good life. Pearl could see it in his widening girth, the roundness of his face, and his double chin. His eyes still disappeared when he smiled. Four years since he showed up to the grand opening of her Salakot restaurant, he had put on some extra pounds. More. Stubbles of white hair at the sides of his crew cut were beginning to pepper his once ink-black hair.

"I owe you," P.J. said, never leaving his eyes off her face.

She crinkled her nose. Subconsciously, she lowered her sight.

"I didn't keep up with my promise to keep in touch until now."

We do have a lot of catching up to do, Pearl thought.

For a change, P.J. sounded nervous. She met his gaze head-on and saw the softness in his eyes.

"I'm running for reelection. Another term as a senator. Keeps me—"

"Busy." Pearl finished his sentence. "Politics run in your family. You said that. Both sides of your family."

P.J. nodded. His Adam's apple rose and fell. "It takes a special kind of woman to understand. Keeping long hours. Unpredictable schedule. Not everyone can keep up with that." He roamed his eyes as if anyone could eavesdrop inside the Drake's private function room he reserved. "I didn't want to burden you. But then . . ." He reached for her hand, startling her. "Time is running out . . . for us. I still feel the same. Do you?"

Pearl met his gaze head-on. "Yes."

P.J.'s eyes watered. He grabbed a glass of water and took several gulps. He was nervous, which was out of character for him, a softer, tender side of P.J. that Pearl saw for the first time.

"Then we should get married before I go back to the Philippines . . . I mean, we go back home. We could get married in civil court here. Then, if you want, a grand wedding back home."

Pearl nodded. This was her home. But then, come to think of it, home is where your heart is.

"Should I call your mom and dad? Ask for their permission?" P.J. was back, the old P.J. that Pearl knew.

"Of course. And don't forget *Tita* Techie. Or should I call her . . . Ma?"

"We'll call her last. She's very hard of hearing now. I'll call her in my hotel room later tonight. First, we have to buy your wedding ring."

"Our wedding ring."

"That's right. Do we have Tiffany here in Chicago?"

"I think so."

"Good. Then we'd better eat and finish the food. I paid a fortune for this occasion."

Before Pearl could refuse, he placed several heaping of food on her plate. "Stop. I am not that hungry. I don't want any."

P.J.'s demeanor soured. "You're changing your mind?"

"If you keep doing that, yes."

"Fine. I'll finish your share then."

They looked at each other for a long time. P.J. burst out laughing.

"What?"

"Remember? This is how we met. At the beach house. Déjà vu. That woman was right in her prediction."

"How did you know about that woman?"

The voluptuous woman with Dresden-doll features and surprising agility flashed in Pearl's mind.

"You think my mother would hide anything?"

Pearl ignored his comment. She looked with amusement as P.J. began to eat her share.

"She was wrong big time, though," she said. "That woman."

"About what?"

P.J. took a big piece of lobster.

"With my age, we'll never have three children. Not even one. You realize that, don't you?"

"We'll have each other. We can adopt if you want. Have dogs, three dogs, if you prefer. Cats?"

"I hate cats."

The rest of the day was a whirlwind of activities: making a phone call to Aurora and Red, finding the ring, getting the proper permit for the civil ceremony, Pearl calling some close former flight attendants from Pan Am she worked with, doing some last-minute shopping with Aurora for a suitable dress for the civil wedding, P.J. booking her parents at the Drake, and Pearl getting her own private room for the night at the hotel.

It was late at night when they were finished with the hasty preparations. It was a perspiring P.J. who saw her to her room to say good night.

"Tomorrow is the big day," he said.

"Tomorrow it is."

P.J. grabbed her hand and kissed it. A warm trickle landed on her hand. Embarrassed, P.J. wiped her hand. "You make me so happy."

Pearl cupped P.J.'s face. "I know. You've been a very patient man." She wiped the sweat on his forehead. Her eyes watered.

"Thirty-five years."

"That long?"

"Yes, that long. I've counted."

"We better make up for it then, right?"

"Of course. The election is almost here. After I am sworn in, we could have a late honeymoon. Paris, Rome . . . wherever."

"You're sure you'll win the election?"

"Positive. You're my lucky star."

"Okay then, if you say so . . ."

P.J. stopped her with a kiss. It was a warm, tender, long kiss mingled with saltiness from their tears.

It was never meant to be. The wedding never happened. Late for the afternoon wedding at the city hall, P.J. was discovered dead in his bed, still wearing the street clothes Pearl last saw him in. He was holding tight a blue box to his chest. Inside was the matching wedding ring. The coroner said he died of a massive heart attack.

P.J.'s funeral was huge. The streets leading to the cemetery were lined knee-deep with a crowd—onlookers, sympathizers, politicians, the rich, and the famous. The procession, which inched slowly along Manila's major route took hours. Behind the hearse were several more, teeming with flowers that spilled up to the roof. Pearl saw Techie for the first time in many years. She had aged. Though her posture remained straight, she needed a cane to navigate, her mind remaining sharp.

She was civil toward Pearl but said nothing more. She rode alone in her black Mercedes to accompany P.J. to the family mausoleum, too frail to walk. Her mother, *Tita* Espe, was left at home in the company of her two private nurses. She was too disruptive and confused. It didn't make sense to bring her along, making a spectacle of herself. Techie did not invite Pearl to join her. Pearl rode in a rental car. Several prominent government officials paid their respects as he laid in state. One kept looking at Pearl with knitted brows. Pearl recognized her as P.J.'s *Ninong*. He too had aged, surprisingly losing substantial weight with maturity. Gone was his beer belly. He was then the governor of his province. A corpulent woman accompanied him, standing tall and proud with head high, holding his arm tight. Up close, Pearl recognized her as the slender woman at the barrio fiesta who had proudly showed her a picture of their daughter. Pearl wondered where the wife was. The woman did not recognize her. She looked with disdain at Pearl when she smiled at them. The woman tightened her grip on the politician's arm.

Pearl learned that P.J. was being rumored to possibly run for the president of the country in the near future.

Pearl decided to remain after the funeral. By sheer courage and bravado, she revisited places she had seen with P.J.. To her dismay, some places no longer existed. And some impossible to find. The country, being young, was still in search of its identity. Its loyalty to its heroes was fleeting, fluid if not ruled by political clout. Names of major streets were changed for reasons that seemed flimsy to Pearl. Some were completely obliterated, replaced by buildings or rerouted.

Treated like a princess, she remembered names. She had limited idea how to go to those places. She had limited time to find her bearings and search old names to match with the new. A few restaurants came to her mind. Max, there were many of them, though she could not recall the one they frequented, and the exclusive Madrid, which she heard was no longer in business.

Midway through the week, she received a long-distance call from her mother. Doña Esperanza had passed away. The funeral was private. The news was peppered with long obituaries carried in most major newspapers, her role as the matriarch and wife of a prominent political family, her social life, her charitable works, institutions named after her family, and her being the grandmother of the late P.J. Romualdez.

Pearl still had the Romualdezes' phone number or hoped it was still the right one. Hesitant at first, she finally decided to call. She immediately recognized Techie's voice as it sounded the same.

"Hello?"

"*Tita* Techie, it's Pearl. I heard—"

"Hello, hello. Who is this?"

"It's me, Pearl."

"Please talk louder. Hello?" She hung up.

Pearl remained silent for a long time. *Should I call back?* It would be a rehash, she told herself. In a way, she was relieved Techie couldn't hear well. She probably didn't expect her call. Even if she recognized her, would it make a difference? Techie had ignored her at P.J.'s funeral. That silent treatment was very loud and clear.

Enough is enough.

She again dialed the phone. This time, it was to confirm her reservation back to the States.

Back in Chicago, Pearl immersed herself in her business. She had no time to mourn and did not want to. She had already notified her staff that she planned on cutting her emergency vacation and opening Salakot earlier than planned. She declined Aurora and Red's offer to spend some time with them. She needed time for herself.

In front of her bedside table, she was able to pick up where she had left off in balancing her business account. It was a breeze writing down the restaurant menu that she regularly updated. Otherwise, it was a struggle to write down her thoughts. Everything happened so fast.

She finally did.

I do not know how to start. What to say or how to say it. Probably when I am no longer able to maintain the restaurant, when I am old and decrepit, I'll have the time I need to write everything. I hope my mind remains as sharp as it is now and my hand remains steady. I only learned to love one man. His name was P.J. You know him, I have written about him before. Don't count Brian. He was just a blip in my life.

If things had been different, I could have married P.J when I was younger and had a child with him, three according to that woman. But then, it wasn't meant to be. I wasn't good enough to be his wife. A good son and a grandson, he did what he was told. And when he finally got the courage to ask me, God took him away from me. He died of a massive heart attack. He was only in his late fifties. My mother said it was my kapalaran, *my destiny.*

Where he came from, which also happened to be my mother's birthplace, women are held to a different standard. We are delicate, fragile, and valuable and kept on a pedestal to be admired, guarded, and kept unblemished, immaculate, and untouched except by our rightful owner. I told you I was raped, thus I was no longer fit for a bride. I am then rubbish, soiled, and discarded. Are women properties, fertility vessels, or domestic doyens perhaps? And yet women have as much power as their husbands regarding their children—who they marry and how they live their lives. They run the house as efficiently or chaotic as they choose.

It is a culture of contradiction. Words can have several meanings. What was said does not necessarily mean what was said. Who is an ideal woman? Is it my mother? She remains a good wife to my father, a mother to me, and a daughter to my grandma (even taking care of my grandma when she was dying), and she remained loyal to her husband even when he left her for another woman. Is it that kerida, *bearing this man the daughter he had always wanted, catering to his domestic and carnal need, not questioning her secondary role, and existing solely for the man she loves? Is it Nanay, devoted wife, grandmother, and good Catholic? Is it Tita Espe, the family matriarch, keeping her family united and following her husband's legacy? Or is it that Diamond Queen, catering to a man's fantasy for a price? It definitely wasn't me, with what happened to me and unable to bring children to carry on the family name. How about an ideal man? But men are different. That's what they say. Is it fair? You be the judge.*

Salakot was crowded. One of the cooks failed to show up. Pearl helped with the waitressing, occasionally lending a hand in the kitchen. She hurriedly replenished the banquet table with food—the freshly cooked *rellenong bangus*, the stuffed milkfish adorned with sliced red tomatoes with some fresh cucumbers around it, and the steaming hot *dinuguan,* the blood soup with cubed pieces of pork and few slices of spicy green peppers in a large pot. Resting on its side were gelatinous rice *suman*, the perfect combination. There was still plenty of *pansit palabok*, abundant with sliced boiled eggs and its thick sauce lathering its translucent noodles. Generous pieces of *adobo* chicken were still hot and waiting. Not to be outdone were chunky pieces of *lechon kawali*, crunchy with its thick sauce of minced liver flavored with soy sauce and other seasonings waiting on the side or, if one prefers, dipping them in a tangy clear vinegar with crushed pepper or table salt. It was already past ten when the place finally closed.

The employees put on some fresh table covers and placed some clean plates, glasses, and utensils in preparation for the next day before they left for the night. The floor had already been mopped and dusted, and the garbage had been gathered and emptied at the back lot where there were large plastic bins. Pearl checked the pantry. She wrote down supplies she needed to buy first thing in the morning. Done with her chores, she gave the place a final look before turning off the light. She was always the last person to leave the place. To some extent, she had conquered her acquired fear of the dark if it were for a short time, though she still slept with all the lights in her room turned on. She also never failed to look behind her, making sure nobody was lurking somewhere. A lamppost that shone directly in front of the restaurant kept the place well lit, reassuring her. She reminded herself that she had a TV interview the following day to promote her latest cookbook. Then there was the taping of her show.

She crossed the street where her car was parked. The traffic was light then. Getting into her car, she tuned in to the news and got out of her spot to drive home. She passed by the giant sign of Salakot. It raised her pulse. She imagined a whole new epicurean experience. Not that what she served was pedestrian. She thought of Aurora and Red. Their wedding anniversary would be coming soon. What better way to please them, surrounded by their friends and family, feasting on foods worthy of the gods. Laboring for weeks in her own kitchen, she had tried Bisayan cuisine with indigenous coconut a primary ingredient, the high note to bring out the flavor, the Bicol express and *laing* which represented the spicy and the piquant dishes from Bicol region of southern Luzon, heavenly desserts from the four corners of the islands' seven-thousand-plus islands, more than half of which were uninhabited, unadulterated paradise.

She envied her mother's *kare-kare.* Her dad kept saying she almost got it, except maybe it needed a little more to thicken its sauce, a bit more color, and a dash more seasoning. Or probably it was all her dad's imagination because she had followed her mother's instructions to the letter.

Ahh, what love can do.

P.J. flashed in her mind. Energized, she pushed the pedal and opened the roof, revealing an ink-black sky studded with hundreds and hundreds of stars like diamonds in the sky.

The Philippines, the Pearl of the Orient, is home to gentle yet proud, sensitive, hospitable, fatalistic, fiercely loyal, clannish, resilient, superstitious, and enigmatic people enriched by cultures as varied as its immigrant Malay, Indian, Chinese, and Middle Eastern populace and the influence of its previous colonizers, Spain and the United States. The author, an immigrant to the States, knew firsthand what it was to be torn between two cultures—the one he knew as a child and grew up with and the culture he later adopted and embraced.

This invaluable experience was his inspiration, the nidus of his first fiction, *The Ideal Woman*.

Words with the Tilde Used in the Novel

Doña: a title attached to a rich, privileged woman
Señorita: a young woman, supposedly from a rich background, treated
　　　like a princess; a word to describe a spoiled girl
Niño: a nickname for baby Jesus
Malacañang: the official palace residence of the Philippine president,
　　　the equivalent of the White House

Common Words Used in the Novel

Opo: a respectful way of saying yes while a casual way of saying yes,
　　　Oo, is used to address an equal or acquaintance
Hija: an endearing way of addressing a younger woman
Balae: the in-laws of one's child, thus considered a relation
Boy/Baby: a very common Filipino nickname, Boy could also mean a
　　　male servant
Ate: an older sister, also used to address a woman as a sign of respect
Anak ng pare: a derogatory name of a vanishing breed of woman, an
　　　illegitimate child from a Hispanic priest and a native woman
Mestizo/mestiza: a man/woman of mixed parentage, usually one
　　　parent of white race. While frowned on in other cultures,
　　　being one is considered an asset.
Biyuda sa buhay: a tongue-in-cheek euphemism to refer to a woman
　　　separated though still legally married to her husband
Rondalya: a musical group playing with *bandurya*, a fourteen-string
　　　instrument the shape of a flat oval and plucked in unison
Mukhang pera: literally having the face of money, anyone who values
　　　money above relations. It is considered an insult.
Bakya: equivalent of a redneck